Adam Sarafis was born in 1967 in Auckland, New Zealand. He gained his undergraduate degree at Auckland University before completing his post-graduate studies at the university of Copenhagen. He worked as a reporter for various newspapers in Europe and Australasia, eventually becoming a freelance foreign correspondent for some of the world's largest agencies. Based in Auckland, Adam also spends considerable time in the Greek archipelago and Skagen, Denmark. This is his first novel.

Adam Sarafis is the creation of author Linda Olsson and screenwriter Thomas Sainsbury. He has now taken on a life of his own.

*June - July - August `15*

*Jodie*
*It's been 'awesome' sharing*
*Auckland with you ... come*
*back soon and explore some more.*
*Loads of love bombs*
*Jane, Phil, Olive*
*& Lucille*

# THE MATAKANA SERIES

**Matakana**

**(stative verb)** be wary, watchful, on the lookout

*Kia **matakana** tonu ia. Kia kāeaea ia ki mauī, ki matau /*

He will be continually watchful. He will look rapaciously left and right.

MATAKANA

# SOMETHING IS ROTTEN

## ADAM SARAFIS

echo

# echo

Echo Publishing
12 Northumberland Street, South Melbourne
Victoria 3205 Australia
echopublishing.com.au

First published 2015

Part of the Bonnier Publishing Group
www.bonnierpublishing.com

Edited by Liz Filleul.
Cover design by Anne-Marie Reeves.
Page design and typesetting by Shaun Jury.

Printed in Australia at Griffin Press.
Only wood grown from sustainable regrowth forests is used in
the manufacture of paper found in this book.

National Library of Australia Cataloguing-in-Publication entry
Creator: Sarafis, Adam, author.
Title: Something is rotten / Adam Sarafis.
ISBN: 9781760067762 (paperback)
Series: Sarafis, Adam. Matakana ; 1.
Subjects: Detective and mystery stories.
Dewey Number: A823.4

ISBN 978 1 7600 67762 (pbk)
ISBN 978-1-76006-855-4 (epub)
ISBN 978-1-76006-856-1 (mobi)

Twitter/Instagram: @echo_publishing
facebook.com/echopublishingAU

*In the corrupted currents of this world*
*Offence's gilded hand may shove by justice;*
*And oft 'tis seen the wicked prize itself*
*Buys out the law*

*Hamlet*, Act III, Scene III

Although time and place are real, this story is entirely fictional, and any likeness to real persons or incidents is entirely coincidental.

The epigraphs to each chapter are all from William Shakespeare's *Hamlet*.

# PROLOGUE

11.14 p.m., 2 November 2005, phone call from Auckland to London
'What's your ID?'

'Ovis Aries Six.'

'You are not supposed to make contact.'

'There has been a complication.'

Silence.

'A leak. I need to report a leak. Someone who knows. And might make it public.'

9.12 a.m., 3 November 2005, phone call from London to Wellington
'Good morn–'

'There is a problem.'

Silence.

'We've been alerted to a problem. A leak.'

'So, we have a problem?'

'Nu-uh. *You* have a problem.'

Auckland, November 2005
The stench of stale meat filled his nostrils.

Finally, the time had come.

Brent Taylor loved cheeseburgers. And fish burgers. And chicken burgers. But more than anything, he loved the standard hamburger. He felt his mouth fill with saliva.

He had waited for this moment all evening. Kept the burger

zipped in his tattered backpack, carefully wrapped to disguise any suspicious smells. No food was allowed in the library. But the last student had now left and Brent had locked the glass doors. He had set the lights to night mode. The library was his.

He had bought the hamburger to celebrate.

He was on the cusp of becoming a great man. He could see the vast, wonderful world out there, ready to receive his work and embrace him as its creator. He would be someone looked up to. A bright, shining solitaire.

He turned on the computer. While it booted he couldn't resist taking a quick bite of the hamburger. Then he wiped his hands on his thighs and pulled the manuscript from his backpack. The pile of papers looked worn. He had carried it in his backpack for weeks now, adding pages as they were completed. He patted the front page and his greasy fingers left a set of smeared fingerprints. He felt as though he knew every word. He *did* know every word.

He thought back to that sunny August day. He was sitting at the library counter as usual, working away, when casually he looked up. In front of him stood an extraordinary specimen of manhood, taking his breath away. Clear grey eyes, a perfect nose, perfect white teeth showing between soft lips parted in a confident yet inviting smile. Short dark hair, glistening in the rays of sun that filtered in through the glass above. Wide shoulders, long legs and well-manicured hands holding a small pile of books. Masculine beauty personified.

Brent touched the page as if he were touching the character himself. It had started so well and he still remembered the feelings.

All that was missing was the cover sheet. He opened a new document and typed the required information. Name. Address. Not his home address but the post-office box he had opened in Ponsonby. He had to be careful now. He had to be cautious. He clicked on the print button.

The printer purred. He opened his Yahoo mail account, typed the publisher's email address and a short message. Keep it professional, he thought. Sharp and short. 'Manuscript attached below. Look forward to hearing from you.' Brent's hand trembled and sweat trickled down his spine. He hesitated, then moved the cursor to the Send icon. He clicked. That done, he clicked his way to 'Delete your Yahoo mail account permanently?' He hesitated then clicked 'Yes'. Funny how such a momentous thing could feel so light and easy.

He took a prepaid padded envelope from his backpack and filled in the address field. He slid in the manuscript. The flap ended up slightly askew but it was still safely sealed. He walked to the mail box in the back office. He placed the parcel proudly on top.

*Please send us a hard copy of your manuscript. Feel free to also mail us an electronic copy, only make sure not to send it as an attachment but in the body of the email.*

All done.

Back at his desk he exhaled slowly. At last, time for the celebratory hamburger. His fingers, their nails bitten to the quick, gauged the soggy bread as his eyes focused on the screen. He thought everything through again. Manuscript hard copy mailed. Electronic copy emailed. Yahoo mail account closed. A copy on the CD glued to the lid of the hula-hula box. Who would have thought that that box would one day hold such a precious item? Hiding everything from lollies to joints to Pulitzer Prize-winning novels, it had been with him his whole life. The only person who knew about it was Jade.

Suddenly, he heard footsteps coming down the stairs. He lowered the burger, his brows knitted. A man descended, his heavy workboots making the steps vibrate audibly. The stiff material of his uniform rustled as he approached, his ID card swinging from his neck. Where had he come from? Brent had made sure the aisles were empty before he locked the doors.

'I'm here to check the sprinklers,' the man said. He had a strong accent but Brent didn't recognise it. Brent sighed and looked up with a frown. He noticed a white scar running from the side of the man's mouth and across his cheek. 'There seems to be a problem.' The man crossed his arms. They were muscular, covered in coarse blond hair.

'I don't know anything about any sprinklers.'

'I need to show you. Upstairs.'

Brent sighed and returned the burger to its wrapping. 'I don't know anything about any fucking sprinklers,' he repeated as he followed the man up the stairwell. 'I just work part-time in the evening. You should come back tomorrow.' The man said nothing and Brent's stumpy legs hurried to keep up. He looked at the man's boots. They looked new and expensive. That was something Brent would buy with his first royalty payment. Really nice boots. Not workboots, though. Soft black boots with a stacked heel. A soft leather jacket too. Real leather, not the plastic shit he had now. Tight black pants. A diamond stud for his nose. He smiled.

They headed up three flights of stairs. By now Brent was panting.

It wouldn't have made any difference if he had expected the blow. Not much, anyway. The heavy boot hit him in the solar plexus with tremendous force. He didn't register the pain as his ribs cracked under the impact, but the sound travelled through his body. Air left his lungs with a strange, muted noise. Not a scream, just the sound of air violently expelled from his lungs.

By the time his head hit the linoleum strip on the second step, the message had reached his brain and he lifted his arms, as if to protect his face. His shoulders came to a rest on the edge of the landing, his head on the step. The angle between the parts of his body was too sharp for the neck to sustain and the second and third vertebrae cracked audibly. If Brent had heard that sound, it made no impact. His mouth was open; a heavy sigh was followed by small bubbles of saliva. By the time the man crouched down beside him, Brent's eyes had clouded over.

He never heard the man's toolbox being opened. He never felt the jacket being ripped off his right side, exposing his arm. And he never felt the needle break the skin. By the time his limp body was lifted, he was no longer conscious. As he was heaved over the protective glass barrier and pushed down the shaft between the stairs he did not feel a thing.

As his body dropped to the bottom of the shaft it picked up speed and fell with the accumulated force of his body weight. It landed inside the glass barrier, feet first. The torso slipped into place. But the skull caught on the sharp edge of the reinforced glass wall and the head fell backwards with a loud crack. The neck snapped. The head lolled backwards, still connected by skin and sinew. The dead eyes looked towards the main entrance. In death, Brent Taylor's head was separated from his body as, in a sense, it had been in life, too.

The body sat immobile inside its glass cage, half-kneeling, as if in prayer. Blood trickled down the glass, seeping into the carpet on the floor.

Brent's half-eaten burger sat where it had been placed on the desk. The finger imprints in the bun were lit blue by the computer screen.

The only sound was the heavy steps coming down the stairs, then crossing the reception area. Paper rustled and the padded envelope was retrieved from the mail box. The backpack and computer were examined. Steady steps left the building.

The reception area now reeked of stale hamburger and fresh blood.


London, November 2003

The two distinguished-looking gentlemen sat on either side of the small round table. The cosy dining room had heavy drapery and soft carpets that absorbed the sounds from the surrounding tables. The two men were good friends, the conversation flowing with ease as they sipped their pre-dinner drinks. The guest had thinning grey hair and glasses. The host, though of similar age, looked younger, with a full head of brown hair and lively manners. He studied the wine list briefly and waved for the waiter who approached instantly, smiling and greeting him by name with a measured combination of respect and familiarity. The host introduced his guest then engaged in a brief conversation about the wines before placing his order.

The entrées arrived and the two men began to eat. As they were finishing, the grey-haired man bent forward. His expression was suddenly sombre. 'Howard, I have a big favour to ask you,' he said in English but with a strong French accent. The other man returned the gaze and nodded encouragingly.

'It concerns my Céleste.'

'Céleste? You know I'd do anything for that wonderful daughter of yours,' the other man said, smiling.

But the Frenchman didn't return the smile. 'Well, it isn't exactly about Céleste. Rather, her husband.'

'I see.'

'I really do need your advice. And your help. And there is very little time.'

The old man nervously adjusted his rimless glasses and his brown eyes stayed on his host. 'I wouldn't have bothered you if I had been able to think of another solution...' His voice trailed off.

The other man nodded slowly.

The waiter arrived with the main course. The conversation paused until they were left alone again.

'Give me the full background, Gaston,' the Englishman said.

The Frenchman put his cutlery on the plate, wiped his mouth with the linen napkin and began to talk.

\*\*\*

'Are you still in the office, Brian?'

'Yes, sir.'

'Can you wait for me, please? I have something I would like to discuss. I'm leaving the club now.'

'Yes, sir.'

In spite of the late hour most windows of the Ministry of Defence were still lit up as the Minister arrived in the limousine. As he entered his office suite, he found his brilliant young assistant waiting by his computer.

'Thank you, Brian. Come right in.' The Minister opened the door to his inner office. 'Drink?' he asked as his assistant followed him in.

'Thank you, sir, no.' The tall, pale, red-haired man shook his head and sat in one of the two chairs opposite the sofa in the corner.

The Minister poured himself a generous whisky and sank down into the soft cushions. He turned the glass in his hand, silent for a moment. 'I've just had dinner with my old friend, Gaston Gérard.'

'The French Minister.'

'Gaston and I go way back. Met at the Sorbonne in the late sixties and have stayed in touch ever since. Now, of course, we see each other professionally too. His wife died young and left him to raise their only child, a daughter. She's been like a godchild to me, and when she first came here to study she stayed with us. She's now married to a British officer and lives here in the UK. They have three young children. Lovely family.'

Brian made no comment.

'Gaston has alerted me to an acute problem concerning his daughter and her family. I'd like to see if I can help them.'

Brian nodded, his face expressionless.

'I'll give you the background, and I would appreciate it if you could give the matter some thought overnight. I'd like to stress that it's a very delicate matter. And also very urgent.'

Brian gave another quick nod.

'I have rather a full day tomorrow,' the Minister said, 'but I'm invited to a cocktail function at the New Zealand High Commissioner's residence at five. If you accompany me there we can have a chat in the car. See if we can come up with something.'

'Yes, sir.'

'Now, let me try to explain the situation.'

\*\*\*

The two men left the office together an hour later. As they stepped outside they stood for a moment beside each other in the cool evening air. The Minister looked up into the black sky.

'I am worried, Brian, that all this will blow up in our faces. It feels as if it's encroaching from all directions. And I'm not sure what to do about it. How to protect our clean record.'

He looked at Brian, who said nothing.

'Well, good night then,' the Minister said. 'No need to wait for my driver. You be on your way. See you tomorrow.'

\*\*\*

The next afternoon it rained, and the drive to the New Zealand High Commissioner's residence took well over an hour in dense traffic, allowing the two men time to talk. When they arrived at the Clareville Street address they were quickly ushered inside, escaping the rapidly escalating downpour.

The gathering included a select group of guests, mainly from the diplomatic and government spheres, but also including several senior business representatives. As the Minister entered the room he was greeted by the New Zealand High Commissioner, a senior, bearded man with a jovial air. Beside him was a young man, short and slight, with a moon face. The High Commissioner smiled and shook the Minister's hand. 'Good to see you, Howard. Thank you for making time to attend our small function.' He turned to the young man by his side. 'Ian, let me introduce you to the Foreign Secretary, Mr Howard Bailey. Howard, this is Ian Clarkson, recently appointed special envoy to the EU and presently based here in London. We expect great things from this young man.' The High Commissioner put a hand on Ian's shoulder.

'Thank you, sir. I'll do my best to live up to everybody's expectations,' Clarkson said, unsmiling. 'It's not going to be easy. Particularly with the French attitude to food imports. But New Zealand is a small nation, isolated at the edge of the earth, and we are used to relying on ourselves to resolve things. We're a stubborn lot. And we usually get results. Eventually.' And now he smiled a confident smile.

'So it's the EU food import quota that you're targeting?' the Minister asked.

Ian Clarkson nodded. 'The meat quota, to be precise. Our fine beef and lamb is the best in the world.'

'I'm sure it is,' the Minister said. 'Well, I wish you the very best in your endeavours, Mr Clarkson. Nice to meet you.' The Minister and his assistant moved further into the crowd, leaving the host to welcome new guests.

It was just before seven when they returned to the car.

'What do you think of that man, Ian –?'

'Clarkson, sir.'

'Yes. What do you think?'

'We did have a brief note about his arrival, sir. But I haven't heard anything about him since. I believe he's only been here a short time; six months at the most.'

'I see,' the Minister said. 'Well, it'll be a phenomenally hard task to change the mind of the French. Many have tried, and all have failed.'

'It will be, sir. But thinking about that, I have a suggestion. It may be worthwhile meeting with this Ian Clarkson.'

The Minister frowned. 'Why?'

The car drove into the wet spring evening as the young man began to explain.


### Wellington, November 2003

Gary Spalding, Minister of Foreign Affairs and Trade, stood by the window of his office in the Beehive, New Zealand's parliament building. He had removed his jacket yet still felt the shirt sticking to his back. The office was always either sweltering or icy cold. The air conditioning had been tuned and tested, but never seemed to work properly. He looked at the flowers on the coffee table, an arrangement of flax and proteas in a flax basket. It had strands of flax and feathers suspended over it. Personally, he preferred roses. Old-fashioned ones, with a perfume. He pulled at his tie and returned to his desk.

He wasn't looking forward to the two o'clock meeting with Ian Clarkson. Gary Spalding didn't like making decisions. He liked matters to evolve, to resolve themselves to general acclaim. But this matter required swift and decisive action.

His back hurt. The dislocated disc had a tendency to make itself known when he was under pressure. He decided to take a short break in the Teeter inversion machine that occupied the far end of his office.

Outside, the capital was swimming in intense bright sunshine and a light breeze swept along Lambton Quay as Ian Clarkson made his way towards the Beehive. He walked with light steps and his soft, moist lips were pursed as he whistled 'Jingle Bells'. He had flown in from London that morning, but felt no jetlag. Rather, he felt more alert than ever. Finally, he was part of the real world, where important people did important things. Smack in the centre of power. He crossed the street and carried on towards the main entrance of the Beehive.

Gary Spalding's secretary, Christine Durwell, was a very beautiful woman. A blonde with perfectly symmetrical features and a body with ample curves and long legs, she sat at her desk as Clarkson entered. He had never felt comfortable in the company of beautiful women.

But today was such a good day that he decided to try a personal approach. 'Good afternoon, Christine. You look wonderful on this sunny day,' he said.

Christine looked at him coldly. 'Good afternoon, Mr Clarkson,' she said, her perfect red lips hardly parting. 'Please walk straight in. The Minister is waiting for you.' And Clarkson slunk through the door quietly.

He crossed the threshold but could see no trace of Gary. The chair behind the desk was empty. Then he heard Gary's disembodied voice, a little strained. 'Come on in, Ian.'

As he tentatively moved further inside, Clarkson realised that the voice came from the far corner of the room. He spotted Gary Spalding hanging upside down in a strange steel-and-leather contraption. His bright red tie hung across his face and he pulled it to the side to look at Clarkson. His face looked oddly distorted, as if flesh had shifted upwards from his chest and settled on his cheeks.

'Won't be a minute. My back is killing me and this helps,' he said. 'Make yourself comfortable. Oh, before you do, ask Christine to bring us coffee.'

Clarkson resented being sent out to face the beautiful Christine again. He hesitated for a moment, but did as he was told. When he returned, Gary was extracting himself from the machine and joined him at the table. Christine brought the coffee in on a tray and left.

'Right,' Gary said. 'Shoot.'

'Well, as you know, the proposal is on the table, and we need to respond swiftly. Very, very swiftly. I need to fly back tomorrow.'

Gary stood up, obviously in pain, and walked over to the window. He turned his back to his visitor. 'Sorry, it's easier on my back if I stand,' he said. And saves me from having to look at you, he thought.

'This will resolve all our issues,' Clarkson said. 'Things were looking promising anyway, but this is a unique opportunity to make real headway.'

*Our* issues? Gary thought. We have no common issues, you idiot. This can make or break my political future. And I'll be the one landed with all the risks, he thought. For you there's just an upside. You get the career opportunity of a lifetime delivered on a plate. Don't for a second think I believe this was ever your brilliant idea.

'Well, there are a number of factors to consider,' Gary said without turning around. 'It can work to our advantage, granted, but we have to be very careful. Very, very careful. A substantial increase of the meat export into the EU will certainly be good for the economy. And give the government political points. Things going as planned, we might well see a change in the leadership of the Party after the next election.'

Clarkson knew exactly what Gary meant. He resented his raw political ambition. The man was a user, a vain opportunist. And a lazy coward. 'Sure, and nothing would be more welcome, Gary,' he said. 'That's why we need to manage this with care. We're building something that will serve us well for some time. Something with the potential to deliver considerable political leverage. And with me in London we'll have total control.'

We, we, we. There is no *we* here, Gary thought. And *I'm* the one who'll keep things under control. But there's no such thing as total control. The media picks up the scent, someone slips. The Greens catch on. You can't even control yourself, Gary thought, as was evident at that press conference before I shipped you off to London. He sighed. 'Right, let's go through the proposal,' he said and sat down behind his desk.

And with the bright sunshine glistening on the water in the harbour on the exceptionally calm and warm December day, and with Lambton Quay bustling with Christmas shoppers, Gary Spalding and Ian Clarkson began the process of setting things in motion.

# 1.

*O, help him sweet, you sweet heavens*

It was as if heaven had opened its dams to flood the city. The rain slapped the asphalt and instantly evaporated into grey steam. The storm then abated as abruptly as it had started, leaving behind humidity that penetrated every Auckland home, feeding mould and mildew.

Inside the workshop a heated conversation resumed on talkback. Sam stretched out his arm to switch from radio to the CD. It was good to have noise. Sometimes, listening to the radio seemed like proof there was a world out there where people had the time and the energy to engage in discussions. But music was soothing. It switched off his brain, and he floated weightless in the sea of the sounds. Lately, he'd been listening to the music of John Cage. Hard at first, like a rough sea, but he liked that.

He had a lot of work lined up, which was also good. Wayne, the garage owner, had been taking it easy since his heart scare. He relied on Sam to run the business. This meant Sam worked late most nights, arriving home exhausted and physically drained. At home, reading was the only thing that seemed to keep his thoughts occupied. When deciding on a reading project he had considered the Bible, but then decided on the *Complete Works of William Shakespeare*. He was presently reading *Hamlet*. There was only *Othello* left, then the poems, *Venus and Adonis* and *The Rape of Lucrece*. He wasn't sure he would bother with the sonnets. Sam was looking for distraction, and didn't think the sonnets would do the job.

He wasn't expecting anybody. In fact, he treasured these afternoons with the radio his only company. So at the sound of steps on the concrete floor, he started and frowned as he slid out from beneath the car.

She approached uncertainly, traipsing across the spotted floor in her ridiculously high heels. Her red hair was plastered to her skull and mascara trailed down her cheeks. Somehow the sight made Sam think of a windblown vine that had come loose from its trellis. The denim miniskirt was wet and her green singlet clung to her small breasts. A bright, flimsy scarf was tied around her neck, the ends hanging wet and limp over her shoulder.

'Yes?' he said, as he got to his feet. In the process he accidentally dropped the spanner and it clanged loudly on the concrete.

'Are you Sam Hallberg?' She nervously dug around in her pink plastic shoulderbag and fished out a packet of cigarettes. She looked at him. He shook his head. She put the packet away with a little sigh.

She had green eyes. So green that Sam wondered if they were contacts. It surprised him that he'd noticed.

'Why?' he asked, folding his arms. For the life of him, he couldn't see what she was doing here, asking for him. He was sure he had never seen her before, and it wasn't as though his name was associated with the business.

'Can I talk to you for a moment?' she asked.

'What about?' His instinct told him he didn't want to have this conversation.

She looked over her shoulder towards the entrance and shifted the weight on her feet. 'Can we go somewhere?' When he said nothing, she continued. 'I can wait till you close.' Her voice took on a pleading lilt. She had a sweet little girl's voice and a slight lisp. Again, he was surprised that he'd noticed. Surprised and irritated.

'Can we go for coffee or something? When you're finished?' Again that pleading. 'Won't keep you long, I promise.' She kept shifting her weight nervously and avoided eye contact.

16

And she was biting her lip, as if to prevent it from trembling.

'I'm sorry, I can't,' he said. He turned back to the car, expecting her to leave. He heard her steps on the concrete floor as she tottered away.

Sam looked up at the grimy clock on the wall in the office. It was almost six. He went upstairs to the office, locked the safe and turned off the computer. He had managed to live through another day. If you could call it living. His life had really ended the day Karen died. He hung his overalls on the hook on the door, then grabbed a golf umbrella.

Downstairs, he pulled down the heavy metal door and was just about to open the umbrella when he saw her. She was sitting on the kerb, hunched over, smoking. When she heard the door clang shut she struggled to her feet. She stood in front of him, saying nothing. Sam held out the umbrella, but she didn't seem to notice. To his surprise, Sam heard himself say:

'All right, let's go and have a cup of coffee.'

They walked briskly to McDonald's. The choice of cafés was not the best this end of Great North Road. Sam bought coffee and joined the girl in the corner by the window. She looked even worse in the cold bright light. 'You seem to know who I am. So, can I ask who you are? And how you know my name?'

He offered her a tissue from the small pile on his tray. She absentmindedly took it and wiped her face, smearing the mascara beneath her eyes. 'Jade Amaro,' she said. 'But it doesn't matter. This isn't about me.'

'And why have you come to me?'

'A friend of a friend told me you helped somebody get their child back.'

Sam remembered a woman he had met at the therapy centre a year ago. A case of a father hiding their child. Sam had taken pity on her and agreed to help her find the child. He wondered briefly how these two women were connected but he didn't pursue the matter.

'This is about my friend Brent Taylor. It's been in the paper already. Did you see it?'

She looked at Sam and he got the impression it would have somehow helped if he had. But he shook his head.

'He died falling from the staircase at the library two days ago. At the university. Brent worked there in the evenings. They say he fell – that he was drunk or on something. That he must have done it to himself.' She stared out of the window, unseeing, then turned back to Sam. 'But Brent was clean! He used to be into all kinds of stuff and he almost died last year. But that's when he changed. He got counselling. Turned himself around. He was really happy. For a while, anyway.' She wiped her smudged eyes. The scarf had come loose, and Sam couldn't help noticing that she had a nasty bruise on her neck. It looked recent. She caught his eye and made an ineffectual attempt to tighten the scarf.

'When was the last time you saw him?'

Jade hesitated. 'I saw him the night before he died.' She looked at Sam. 'And then I saw him dead.' The last bit was little more than a whisper.

# 2.

*O, woe is me*
*T'have seen what I have seen, see what I see!*

'It had been such a shitty day and I felt like shit,' Jade began. 'All I was thinking was how much I wanted to be back at Brent's place, just lying there together on his bed, smoking, like usual. I walked through Albert Park; no one was around. It was nearly twelve and I was really tired. But I was early so I stopped by the fountain for a fag. Then I got to Alfred Street and checked the time again. It wasn't quite midnight but I knew Brent would be waiting for me. And he would see me through the glass doors.'

She took a sip of her coffee, holding the cup with both hands. She looked down at the table.

'At first I didn't notice anything unusual. I just stood there, waiting. Thinking that he was busy. Maybe typing away on his computer.'

She went silent and then looked up at Sam. 'But then I saw him. It looked like a doll's head that had come loose. It looked so weird I didn't get it at first. I just stood there, staring.'

'Did you know he was dead?'

Jade nodded. 'His eyes stared at me, but there was nothing. His whole head was upside down.' She rubbed her arms, as if cold. Sam offered his jacket, but she shook her head. 'I stood there forever. Then I looked around. But there was nobody else there, just me. And the only person who I ever went to for help was Brent. I've never had anybody else.'

'What about the police? Or an ambulance?'

Jade uttered a sound that was neither a laugh nor a sob, but something infinitely desolate.

'Definitely not the police. What could they have done? Brent was dead, I knew. And nothing could change that. He was dead. Dead, dead, dead.' She beat the table with her small closed fist. 'That last time I saw him, he made me promise something. And I laughed.'

She looked up and tears welled. 'I laughed,' she whispered. 'I feel sick when I think about it now. But I laughed at him. Then he grabbed my arm real hard and looked me in the eyes and said it again. "Promise. If something happens to me, Jade, promise you'll get the CD." It sounded so ridiculous. I mean, what could happen to Brent? I thought it was just typical Brent stuff. Always making things up.'

She lifted the coffee cup, discovered it was empty and put it back down. Sam looked at her questioningly. She nodded with a weak smile and he re-filled the cup with hot coffee.

'That was the last time I saw him,' Jade continued when Sam returned. 'He wasn't happy any more then. There was something strange in his eyes. But it wasn't drugs, I swear. It was just this weird, wild excitement. Like he was on fire. I'd never seen him like that.'

Sam sat listening, pulled in by the obvious sincerity of her words.

'It started in August but he didn't tell me straightaway. "I've met a guy," he said. "He's so great. You'll like him." We were hanging out at his house as usual. I looked at him to see if he was serious. "Like a *guy* guy?" I asked. Brent went all red. "Nah, just a mate," he said. I could tell it was more than that, though. He told me about this guy called Robert. From England. Brent had met him at the university. An adult student, or whatever. A total babe, according to Brent. Polite, nice clothes, good-looking. It sounded way too good to be true. You have to understand what Brent was like. He was kind, real nice. And smart. Intelligent. But so… well, stupid sometimes. Really gullible, if you see what I mean.'

Sam nodded.

'But he was in love. Obviously. And happy. He looked good. Good for Brent, anyway. He'd been clean for a month by then. I thought a mate was the best thing that could happen to him. And then I got to meet this guy. And sure, he was good-looking. Whenever Brent was in love he would think the guy looked like a Calvin Klein model. But this one really did. Like, totally amazing.'

She shook her head. 'I mean, I loved Brent, but he always looked like he needed a shower. And he was the worst dresser. All those burgers; he was big. But here they were, having a laugh together, looking like a couple. It felt, well, strange. I thought about talking to Brent about it but it never seemed a good time. I just really wanted him to be happy.'

'So, they were going out?' Sam asked.

Jade nodded.

'But they didn't live together?'

Jade shook her head. 'But it lasted for much longer than I had thought it would. So I thought I was being unfair. Maybe Brent had finally found someone who could see the good things inside him.'

'Did you meet them often, the two of them together?'

'No. I guess that's just how it is when you're in love. You forget your friends a bit. I saw Brent sometimes, but not the two of them together. But I could tell when it changed. I knew it would. It was far too good to last. Brent kept *saying* he was happy, but he didn't look it. He was writing like mad and used to stay at the library after it closed. Said he worked better there. He wouldn't tell me what it was he was writing, but I knew he was excited about it. If I hadn't known he was off drugs, I would have thought he was on something. But it was just his writing.'

'And he never showed you what he was working on?'

'Never. Said I would get to know. When it was done.'

'Have you read anything else he'd written?'

She smiled a thin smile. 'I'm not really into reading much. Like I said, Brent was bright, just stupid in other ways. I wouldn't have been able to understand what he was writing anyway.'

Sam made no comment and Jade took a deep breath, as if preparing to leap. 'He came to work and booked me for an hour. I work at –' She looked at Sam and shrugged.

Sam nodded.

'We sat on the bed, talking and smoking. But Brent just couldn't relax. "This is it, Jadie," he said. "All that shit I've tried to write before, forget it. All that crap about the dark Auckland underbelly, forget it. I didn't know fuck." He sat on the bed beside me. "They always say: write what you know. So now I am. People are going to be blown away by this, Jadie." He grabbed my arms and looked me straight in the eye. "Remember what I'm about to tell you."

'I said, "What do you mean?"

'"Listen, Jadie," he said, "there's a CD in that box with the hula-hula dancer on it. It's underneath the frying pan in the kitchen cabinet. If something happens to me, you get that box straightaway and keep it safe." He squeezed my arms. "If something happens, promise me you'll get that CD."

'I laughed at him. It sounded so stupid. I could see that he was pissed off. I said sorry, and promised that, sure, I'd get the CD. But I thought he was just joking. He looked at me real sad and let go of my arms. And that was the last time I saw him.'

She clasped her hands on the tray in front of her. 'But then when I saw him there, inside the glass doors, it all came back to me. All I could think about was what he'd said. So I ran away from the library as fast as I could. I ran up Symonds Street towards Grafton Bridge, over the bridge and on to Glasgow Terrace. It was so quiet that night and I never met anybody. It was really dark when I got there. I walked on the grass up to the door, like I always did when I came late to see Brent. I didn't want Sid to hear me. There's nothing wrong with that guy, he's just, well, weird. I had the key in my hand, but then I noticed that the front door wasn't properly closed. And it just didn't feel right. Brent never locked his room but the front door was always closed at night.

'I stood there not knowing what to do and I got a funny feeling that someone was in there. In Brent's room. So I hid around the side of the house. I stood there for a while, waiting. Then I saw someone come out. It was so dark I couldn't really see what he looked like, but he was wearing some kind of orange overalls. You know, the kind workmen have. He got into a silver car and left. I waited for ages before I went inside. Brent's room was a mess. It was always messy, but this looked different. Not like Brent's mess. It had been turned upside down. I went to the corner where he kept his kitchen things. The cupboard was open. I felt for the hula-hula box inside but it wasn't there. I was on my knees and crept around searching till I spotted it. At first I thought it was empty, but then I noticed some paper was stuck to the lid. The CD was underneath it. I sat down with my back against Brent's bed. That's when I cried. I don't know how long I sat there, but it felt like a long time.'

Sam could tell she was close to tears again, and stretched out his hand and placed it over hers. She didn't acknowledge it.

'I walked all the way home and went to bed with the CD under my pillow. I woke up early. That's when it truly hit me. Brent was dead. And I had the CD. I didn't know what to do with it, but Brent had said to keep it safe, so I stuck it underneath the towels in the heating cupboard. I rang in sick to work and stayed in bed for three days. I didn't know what to do with myself. I didn't know what to do at all. I slept and cried. That's all I did.'

'And that's it?' Sam asked.

Jade shook her head. 'No. Then one day there was knocking on the door. I wasn't going to do anything but it just wouldn't stop, and I was worried that the neighbours would come out. It's a nice place and I paid a big bond on it. So I'm careful. But he wouldn't stop knocking.'

She looked at Sam as if to check that he believed her. He nodded, and she continued.

'He didn't look like a policeman, but he showed me his badge and said he needed to talk to me about Brent. He had this really weird accent but he looked like a nice guy. Tall and blond and smiling. But he wasn't really smiling. It was just a scar on his cheek that made him look like that. I let him in. I thought he would ask about when I last saw Brent. How he had seemed, stuff like that. But he didn't. He started to ask about Brent's book. Did I know what it was about? Did I know where Brent kept the manuscript? I didn't get it. How did he even know Brent was writing a book? I mean, it was just a hobby, Brent's stupid writing. But he went on and on about the manuscript. Asked if I had read it, if Brent had talked to me about it, if there were any copies. I just said I didn't know anything about any manuscript.

'That's when he changed. Like, his face got really white and his eyes really pale and the scar looked like a gash across his face. Suddenly he looked really scary. He pushed me onto the bed, straddled me and put had his hands around my throat. I kept fighting, but he just stared at me with that weird smile and kept choking me. He said, "You tell me everything you know about that manuscript or you'll never see your kid again." I could hardly breathe. And I could see that he'd kill me just like that if he didn't get what he wanted. So I told him where the CD was and he finally let go of my throat. I heard him take the CD from the linen cupboard and then I heard the door close.

'I was shaking, I was so scared. My throat was aching. But more than anything I felt I'd let Brent down so bad.' She paused and wiped her hopelessly smeared eyes. 'But then I thought about Brent and what had happened, and I got really angry. I remembered how excited he had been about the book. I could see him pacing in front of me, talking about it, red in the face, sweaty and excited. I heard him say, "Promise me, Jadie. Promise." And that was when I started thinking about what I could do.'

Her hand was closed hard around the ball of wet paper tissues, the knuckles white. She bent forward, her eyes locking with Sam's. Her words were just a whisper.

'Help me, please.'

# 3.

*Though this be madness, yet there is method in't*

'I'm very sorry you've lost your friend,' Sam said. 'What a terrible thing to happen.'

'Brent is dead. There's nothing I can do about that. But they are lying about him.'

'And you think Brent had no reason to kill himself?'

'No. Definitely not.' Jade shook her head.

'And you know for sure he wasn't on drugs at the time?'

'I'm sure.'

'How long have you known him?'

'Always. We grew up together in Matamata.' She twisted a tissue between her fingers. Sam could see that she was wearing false nails. One had come off and the small nail underneath was gnawed. 'We didn't belong in that shithole. It was us against everyone else, you know?

'We left as soon as we could. Brent started uni and I got a job. Things were looking good then.

'I couldn't have moved here without Brent. I would have got stuck there. There was nothing about Brent that I didn't know. We told each other everything. If he'd gone back on drugs, he'd have told me.'

Jade had stopped crying and her hair was drying, curly wisps of red framing her face. She looked utterly desolate, but returned Sam's gaze with open eyes.

He knew he should have ended it there. Told her to find someone else and wished her good luck. But he didn't. He wasn't entirely sure why. Maybe it was because she looked so pathetic.

'I can't give you much in the way of money,' she said. 'I mean, I can. But I can't give you much right now.'

'I wouldn't do it for money.'

Jade smiled her thin little smile. 'So you *will* help me?'

Sam hesitated. 'I don't think there is much I can do. But I'll give it some thought. And perhaps we can talk tomorrow?'

She nodded, her relief obvious. She stretched across the table and took his hands. Her fingers were icy cold.

Suddenly the sound of a barking dog erupted from her pink handbag. 'Shit,' she sighed, and fished out a pink mobile with a bunch of pendants attached to it. She contemplated the display. 'I should be going. Work, goddamn it.'

And just like that the rain started again, lashing hard against the large windows. 'Where do you work?' Sam asked.

'Epsom.'

'Do you have a car?'

'No. I'll catch a bus.'

'Nonsense, I'll drive you.'

She went to argue but he silenced her with a shake of his head.

They walked back to the garage. He held the umbrella over them both. Sam realised he was no longer tired. The girl's story had stirred something in him. For all he knew, she could have made the whole thing up. Or completely misinterpreted what had happened. But then again, something didn't seem right. And somehow, somewhere deep inside Sam, interest had begun to build. A feeling he hadn't had for a long time.

They reached the garage and got into his car. 'If you give me your number, I'll give you mine,' he said as they drove off. 'We can talk tomorrow. How about you come over during my lunch break? Around noon. And we can talk some more. Like I said, I can't promise that I can help you, but I'll give it some thought.'

She entered his number into her mobile then texted him so he had hers.

They arrived at the address in Epsom where Jade worked. It was a grand old villa. The high wall around the section barely revealed the top floor of what might once have been a generous family home. It now looked stripped of all identity, painted a dark brown. A discreet brass plate on the gate carried the name 'Heaven'. Jade told Sam to push a button on the panel by the entrance. 'What can I do for you, sir?' a smooth female voice said from the intercom.

Jade gave her name. The gates opened soundlessly. Inside, the front yard had been transformed into a small car park. All the windows of the large two-storey building were covered with brown-and-white-striped awnings. The front door had an alcove covering the entrance, allowing visitors to remain invisible from the street while waiting to be let in.

Jade got out of the car, grabbing her things.

'We'll talk tomorrow,' Sam said.

'Great, thanks. Thanks so much. Sorry I have to rush off. But I'm in enough trouble here as it is.' Sam watched her as she ran to the entrance, tripping once on those high heels. He drove out of the section and the heavy gates closed behind him.

It suddenly struck him he had accepted the invitation to his boss's barbecue that night. Now he wished he hadn't. With a sinking stomach he turned west, towards Titirangi. As he got onto the Western Motorway the rain stopped and the low sun penetrated the clouds. He'd brought nothing for the barbecue so would have to stop somewhere and buy something. Salad? Bread, perhaps? Not meat. He knew there would already be plenty of that on offer.

# 4.

*'Tis very strange*

Lynette Church had the best office in the building. It was even better than her boss's, which pleased her more than the room itself. Ever since the hostile takeover of the *New Zealand Tribune*, Roger Evans had been her boss. He was everything Lynette disliked in a boss: weak, vain and ignorant. He was the kind of man who during conversations would throw surreptitious glances at his reflection in the glass walls of his office. He smiled often and widely, but it rarely reached beyond his lips and often seemed to serve to hide a lack of insight. An insecure man's attempt at being accepted at all cost. He carried himself with caution, as if worried about what might happen if he let himself take an unmeasured step. He wore ties in the colours of St David, the patron saint of his home country, Wales: black and yellow.

Lynette shuddered and tried to erase the image of Roger Evans. After all, he mostly left her alone. Her office was on a corner, so had two windows: one facing north, one west. The north one had a harbour view that was totally wasted on the occupant. Lynette rarely looked out of the window. When she did it was not to admire the view, but rather to engage in a moment of intense introspection. Her dark blue eyes, hidden behind distinctive tinted glasses – updated once a year but always of a similar, black-framed style – now rested on the window while her thoughts lay elsewhere.

Today, the disadvantages of the office were obvious. It was sweltering. Bright sunshine forced its way inside through the partially closed blinds. It instantly heated the cool air that feebly wafted from the air-conditioning vent. Lynette perspired. She was prone to perspiration on the best of days. Now, sweat trickled down her spine, collected between her breasts, in her armpits, the hollows of her knees. She could feel her elaborately blow-dried hair sagging. Her cotton shirt was wrinkling by the minute. Her feet were swelling.

She took a deep breath and returned her gaze to the press release on her desk. It wasn't just the heat. There was something that bothered her about this paper, *Report on New Zealand Beef Exports to Europe*. An ordinary title on an extraordinary report. This was quite simply the most remarkable piece of positive trade news ever to come from the office of the Ministry of Foreign Affairs and Trade. Lynette was intrigued.

Her thoughts drifted to a press conference two years earlier, the press conference that had launched Ian Clarkson as the government's special envoy to the EU with the specific task of negotiating an increase in the import quota for New Zealand meat. Only a few months earlier, Clarkson had been appointed director of the new joint venture AME – Aotearoa Meat Export Corporation. Lynette had struggled to understand how such an insignificant little man had been chosen for such a grand position. Then it had been announced that he had been chosen for another prominent task. It seemed a lot of responsibility to be placed on such narrow, sloping shoulders.

The press conference had taken place on another sweltering day. Clarkson made his presentation on stage, behind a podium, smiling at the journalists below. Lynette was in the first row. As Clarkson addressed the audience he focused his pale eyes on Lynette, the only woman in the room. 'Gentlemen,' he began.

It wasn't until Tony Ritchie's nasal voice wormed its way from the back of the room that Clarkson's smug smile had waned. Tony owned the only independent business paper in New Zealand. He was also Lynette's ex-boss and friend. 'What invisible qualities and resources does Mr Clarkson possess that will enable him to succeed where all others have failed?' Tony had asked. 'How on earth is Mr Clarkson proposing to turn the EU, including France, into willing takers of our meat? And not just more of our lamb, but our prime beef! And so quickly! Mr Clarkson, can you walk on water, too? What arsenal do you have at your disposal? Long-legged, big-breasted secret agents to implicate EU officials? Coffers of money for bribes? I'm intrigued, Mr Clarkson. And I can assure you that doesn't happen often. Please enlighten us.'

But Clarkson had offered no explanations and no elaborations about the strategic plans. Just more of the same confident PR talk delivered in his high-pitched voice, which rose to a strained falsetto as Tony continued to interrupt with probing questions. It was like watching a game of tennis, and Lynette knew which player was taking the points. Tony. Long after Clarkson's smug smile had stiffened into a grimace, Gary Spalding, the Minister of Foreign Affairs and Trade, hastily wrapped up the conference.

As everyone was leaving the room, Tony had tapped Lynette on the shoulder. 'A drink? For old time's sake?'

Over drinks – a glass of wine for her, a gin and tonic for Tony – they'd discussed the meeting, the state of the nation's affairs and the upcoming holidays. 'Ever regret leaving me?' Tony asked, his slightly protruding eyes twinkling.

'No way. I do more or less what I want now, in my way, and the pay is better.'

'We could have discussed remuneration, you know.'

'But we never did.' Lynette looked at Tony. Another short man, but a completely different specimen from Clarkson. Tony was raw ambition but paired with considerable intelligence. He feared nobody, was fiercely independent and didn't suffer fools lightly. He did have one weakness, though, carefully hidden. Few were aware of it, but Lynette knew that he craved acknowledgement.

Lynette wondered if he would ever get that ultimate recognition. If he would ever become the equivalent of a Sir Tony. She smiled at him, realising she liked him more now than when she had worked at *BusinessNZ*.

The conversation had turned professional. Lynette asked about the names on the Kiwi Rich List due to be published by *BusinessNZ* in the new year. The list was always eagerly awaited, carefully guarded, and published to much controversy and discussion.

'You'll have to wait, like everybody else, Lynette. But I'll give you one intriguing new name on the list. Eric Salisbury.'

Eric Salisbury was the enigmatic new player in New Zealand, quietly expanding his business interests. Lynette's attempt at finding out more about the man behind the impeccable exterior and discreet confidence had shed little light. There was precious little known about the man.

Born in Yorkshire, public school education, a degree from Oxford in economics, philosophy and politics. No family, no steady partner – just a string of attractive girlfriends. After several unsuccessful attempts at setting up an interview, Lynette had come to the conclusion that Eric Salisbury kept his head down. Few people in business escaped her scrutiny and she found the lack of information about Eric Salisbury frustrating.

In the new year, when the Kiwi Rich List was published, she'd noticed with rising interest how little further information there was. 'Like anybody, I treasure my privacy,' Salisbury had said when asked to comment on his listing as the ninth richest person in the country. 'There is nothing interesting to know about me personally. I prefer to be judged on my business activities.' And, curiously, he seemed to get away with that. Other than the odd photo in the gossip pages of him at some event or other, there had been no information forthcoming.

Now, Lynette took a card from the stack that sat in a holder on her desk:

*Eric Salisbury, Chairman of Demon Holdings, requests the pleasure of the company of Lynette Church to commemorate the successful acquisition of Mahana New Zealand Limited on board the MS Intrepid, departing Westhaven Marina at 12 noon on Thursday 17 November 2005.*

*Dress: Leisurely elegant*
*RSVP to Jeanette Fitzgibbon,*
*jf@demonholdings.co.nz by 10 November, 2005*

Lynnette tapped the card against her palm.

Another major deal, she reflected; this time a step into the energy sector. Soon this man would have a finger in every New Zealand business pie. Mahana was one of those hybrid organisations, part co-operative, part local government, part national government. Now it was a lucrative investment opportunity for a private investor. Her instinct told her there was much to discover behind Mahana NZ Ltd. And behind Eric Salisbury.

She fingered the embossed card. Perhaps finally she would have an opportunity to corner the chairman of Demon Holdings, the elusive Mr Salisbury. On board the ship, the media people would be trapped, but so would the host. She wondered what to wear, wishing she had been more stringent with her diet recently.

She turned her eyes to the report on beef exports. It claimed that what Clarkson had promised at the press conference two years ago, he had delivered. Just like that. Somehow he had achieved an increase in the export of lamb to Europe at two per cent annually for two years.

This was remarkable enough. But then he had also managed

an increase in the export of prime beef to Europe at ten per cent annually. It was an unprecedented trade triumph.

She rang the office of AME and asked to speak to someone who could answer questions about the press release. The secretary promised someone would return the call within the day.

Lynette then made another call, to the office of the Minister of Foreign Affairs and Trade, Gary Spalding. Again, a secretary promised a call back. That done, Lynette grabbed her purse and went to lunch. At a properly air-conditioned restaurant across Queen Street she ordered a sirloin steak, rare, and a tossed green salad. It was time to remount this horse of a diet.

# 5.

*To sleep: perchance to dream: ay, there's the rub*

Sam stared at the wooden door. He held a plastic bag with mixed lettuce leaves and a six-pack of beer. He looked at the pathetic plastic bag and realised it was worse than bringing nothing. He shouldn't have come. He could hear kids squealing in the backyard.

He turned to go, almost making it to the safety of the street when the door opened. It was Wayne. 'Shona thought she'd heard a knock,' he chuckled. 'Come on in! Come on in!' He stepped aside and patted Sam on the back as he entered the warm, homely house that smelt of baking and cooking. Wayne took him through to the backyard where most of his family had congregated. The group contained Wayne and Shona's adult children, their spouses and *their* children. And even though they weren't all genetically connected they sure looked it. They all had a slightly ruddy, smiley, beefy appearance to them. Wayne rattled off their names but Sam didn't take any of them in. They all greeted him with warm smiles.

'Hello, Sammy!' Shona said, pulling him down by his arms so that she could kiss him on the cheeks. Shona was short and plump, with a generous, soft bosom. She took the plastic bag from him. 'Brilliant! Just what we need! Let me add it to the salad.' She opened the bag and tossed the leaves into a gigantic salad bowl, where the addition made no difference whatsoever. 'Perfect timing, Sammy. We're just about to eat.'

'This is my brother, Dylan,' Wayne said.

A near doppelgänger of Wayne's, with slightly ruddier cheeks and hairier white eyebrows, shook Sam's hand vigorously. 'Good to meet you, mate.'

'Dylan's up from Taranaki.'

'Just a bit of a break in the big smoke.'

Sam nodded. 'What do you do down there?' he managed.

'Meat processing,' Dylan replied, tearing two small boys from his legs. Laughing, he took one under each arm and walked over to the trampoline, where, to their utter delight, he released them.

'Things aren't so good for Dylan at the moment,' Wayne said, his eyes on his brother. 'The government's screwing him over. Destroying his business.'

In a truly New Zealand fashion, the men hovered around the barbecue talking about rugby and the housing market while the women set the long table on the deck and talked about children. Sam stayed at the edge of both conversations. He then played cricket with some of the children. He bowled a burly pre-teen girl out, then reminded himself to play a little more kindly.

Dinner was served. Sam sat between two of the daughters-in-law, both attractive blondes. One had a baby on her lap, the other a toddler at her feet. Sam picked at his plateful of steak and sausages. People talked to him, doing their best to pull him into the conversation. Sam had nothing to add on rugby, housing or children and answered in monosyllables. The woman on his left was particularly insistent, asking his opinion on her daughter's potential as a professional model. Sam nodded and smiled. The woman on his right enquired about his background. When had he moved to New Zealand? Where did he come from? What did he do before he worked for Wayne? Half his internal monologue was coming up with excuses to leave, or counting the minutes until it was polite to go. The other half was chastising himself for not being more at ease. It had been over three years now. It was time for him to get back into life, enjoy himself again. Interact with people on a normal level. These were kind, generous people. Why couldn't he just sit back and enjoy the evening? Would he really be better off home alone, reading his Shakespeare?

As all of this was going on, Jade tiptoed around his consciousness. To his surprise he found himself wondering how she was coping.

After the meal, Sam volunteered to do the dishes. He'd begun on the biggest pan when Wayne called him back outside. Sam assumed they were heading to the back deck for a beer and a yarn, but Wayne guided him into the home office. It was a cluttered affair with a plethora of family photos dotted around. 'Have a seat, mate,' Wayne said.

Sam sat. Wayne perched awkwardly on the desk; it strained under his weight. He smiled pityingly at Sam. Sam grimaced. What was this about?

'Have you seen yourself in the mirror lately?' Wayne asked.

Sam shrugged. What did that have to do with anything? He touched his face self-consciously. There was rough stubble.

'I'm giving you two weeks' holiday,' Wayne said.

'Why?'

'Because you haven't had any time off since you started and it really screws over the small business owner when their employees don't take their holidays. The payout when they leave can be crippling. But I don't actually care about that. What I care about is the fact that you need some rest. You're burning yourself into the ground.'

'Ah, Wayne, you know I like to keep busy,' Sam said feebly.

Wayne shook his head. 'You can come in tomorrow and get your things, but for you it's two weeks off from Monday. It'll do you the world of good.'

'Look, Wayne, I really need to keep busy. Give me anything to do. Admin, anything.'

Wayne shook his head. 'I'm sorry, mate. The whole point is to get you away from work.' He smiled awkwardly. 'If you want to talk about anything, you can always talk to Shona. She's a very understanding woman. Or maybe get professional help. A therapist? I don't know much about that sort of thing but I'm sure they're not hard to find.' He was flustered. He sighed. 'Look, I think you're a great bloke, but it's not good to live like you do. Life's too short. I found that out when I got sick. Gave me a bit of perspective on things. You need that, too.'

'Am I that bad?' Sam asked.

Wayne nodded.

Sam felt anxiety building, spreading from his stomach upwards. The idea of time. A chasm of time. Alone. Him alone.

'You could spend time with your son,' Wayne suggested.

Sam managed a short nod.

'Come on, you'll be much better for it. I've got Dylan here to help, so no need to worry about me. You go and smell the flowers for two weeks.' Wayne stood up and the desk gave a little creak of relief. 'Let me return Shona's helper to the kitchen!' He put his arm around Sam's shoulder and led him back to the house.

Sam stood with his hands in the lukewarm, greasy dishwater as family members started to depart. A few hours ago he had counted the minutes until he could leave. Now he was dreading it. Finally, there was just the three of them left. Shona handed Sam a towel and he dried his hands. 'You just enjoy your time off, Sammy,' she said. Suddenly, even the inane conversation in this family kitchen felt infinitely more desirable than his own empty house.

At the door he was chipper, though. 'Thanks for inviting me. You've got a lovely family.'

Shona gave him a warm smile, looking as though she took it as an observation, not a compliment. She pecked him on the cheek. Sam hesitated for a moment, then turned and left. His feet felt heavy as he walked down the steps.

# 6.

*Tis in my memory lock'd,*
*And you yourself shall keep the key of it*

It was dark when Sam got out of the car. The warmth of the day lingered but cool air wafted in from the dark bush behind the house. A light mist was rising. The street was empty. His head was throbbing and he could still taste the charred meat on his tongue. He was on the porch pulling out the door key when he heard a sound. Or rather felt it, like a soft stirring of the air. He stood still for a moment, listening. It seemed to come from the deck at the back. A cat, he thought. Or even a possum. He unlocked the door and entered without turning on the light, tiptoeing through the house to the back door.

She was just a dark shadow, balled up in a foetal position on the deck, her head on her pink purse, absolutely still. He opened the door slowly and stepped outside. She started at the sound of his steps and sat up, eyes wide and red hair tousled.

'Sorry,' he said, 'I didn't mean to scare you.'

She shook her head and made to stand up. 'No, no, it's me, I'm sorry,' she said in that small voice. 'But I didn't want to go home and...' She didn't finish the sentence, but crossed her arms over her chest as if cold. 'So I looked up your address in the White Pages. I'm sorry.'

'Oh. That's fine. I'm glad you did. Come inside,' he said and led the way. He flicked on the light and turned to look at her. She looked worse, much worse. She wore a black dress that looked as if she had borrowed it from someone twice her age. The plunging neckline hung loose over her small breasts and the high split on the side exposed her skinny white thigh.

Sam could tell she had been crying and she shivered visibly. He grabbed a towel from the heating cupboard in the hallway and some clothes from the chest of drawers in the bedroom. 'Here,' he said, offering her the towel. 'Go take a hot shower. And put these on.'

He gave her a folded T-shirt and woollen jumper and pointed towards the bathroom. She said nothing, but took the towel and the clothes, clutching them to her chest as she headed down the hallway.

Sam returned to the deck with a beer from the almost empty fridge and his battered Shakespeare. In the still of the evening he could hear the distant hum of the city. That was all. No specific sounds, just a drone as if from a giant animal, asleep. He lit the candles to read by; the Shakespeare naturally opened to *Hamlet*. He had to go back a page to refresh his memory of the plot.

He heard her soft steps and could smell the shampoo as Jade came and stood in the doorway. She gave a small, apologetic smile and shrugged while pulling at the jersey that reached to her mid-thighs.

'Drink?' he asked and stood up. 'Can't offer a great choice, I'm afraid. Beer or beer?'

She nodded and sat on the bench along the wall on the deck. 'Thank you,' she said to his back as he went inside.

Sam returned with another beer for her and sat down in one of the deckchairs. 'It's been a shit of a day,' he said.

Again, she nodded. In spite of the long shower and the jersey she was still shivering. Sam went inside again, returning with a blanket. He spread it over her shoulders and she pulled it tightly around herself. They sipped beer in silence.

'Anything happen to you after I left?' Sam asked.

'No, it's just… After shitty days I always used to go over to

Brent's. Just to be with him till things felt better. But now, I don't have anybody –' Her voice broke and she started to weep.

Sam said, 'You can stay the night, if you like.' He went inside and returned with a roll of kitchen towels, which he held out to her. She tore off a piece and blew her nose. But she said nothing.

'For a while, well, for rather a long time, I've wanted that. The not having anybody,' Sam said as he sat down again. 'That's why I live here. Why I work at the garage. If you have nobody, you have nothing that can be taken from you.' His eyes looked out over the garden that lay in darkness.

'I have a daughter,' she said. 'She'll be two in February.'

'What's her name?' Sam asked without turning his gaze.

'Lily. Lily Dew.'

Sam could hear her rip off another paper towel. 'I have a son,' he said slowly. 'Jasper. He'll be four next year.'

'He's not living with you?' Jade's question was just a whisper.

'No, he lives with his grandparents. In Matakana.'

'And his mother?'

Sam was silent, and the question hung in the air between them. 'My wife is dead. Jasper was just a baby when she died. He's never known his mother.'

He was grateful for the silence.

'Lily Dew has been in foster care since she was six months old. I had problems...' Her voice trailed off. Then she took a deep breath. 'She's in Hamilton, with good people. I see her twice a month. But she doesn't know me. Not really.'

Sam heard her weep, but he didn't look at her. 'Brent said he was going to help me get her back. Said he was going to find me another job. But God, he couldn't even find himself a proper one! Felt good, though, just talking to him about it. Hearing him tell me I'd get her back. And I *will* get my life sorted. I *will* find another job. I've saved money. One day I'll have her back, I just know I will.'

For the first time since he met her, Sam could hear a touch of confidence in her tone of voice. A touch of life, really. He realised how drained, how utterly without hope, she must have been. 'I'm sure you will,' he said.

'How about you? Will you have Jasper back one day?'

Sam shook his head. 'No, my son is never coming back to me. He's better off where he is.

'You see, it's my fault he lost his mother.' Sam was stunned by his own words. He had never heard them before. But here they were, as clear as if they had been written across the dark sky. 'My wife died because of me.'

He sat down beside Jade on the bench. She sat with her legs up, a little self-contained tent within the blanket. Sam sat with his legs spread, one on either side of the bench. He offered her another beer. She stretched out a hand and pulled the bottle inside the blanket. 'I came because I was scared,' she said suddenly. 'That man, he scared the shit out of me. His eyes. They don't look at you like you're a real person. There is nothing inside them. Freaked me out. It's not what he did to me. It's who he is. I've met bastards before. Real arseholes. But in a way I've always been able to see that they had it in them to be good to *somebody*. Like a child, or a mother. But this man, he can't. It's just not there. I know he would have killed me if he'd wanted to. I'll remember that face forever.' She shuddered inside the blanket. 'Those eyes. And that horrible white scar. Made him look like he was smiling, although he wasn't. At first I thought that was the most frightening thing about him. But it wasn't. It was the eyes.' She blew her nose.

Sam went to sit behind her on the bench. To his utter surprise, he found himself stretching out his arms to hold her. She leaned cautiously back into him, her back painfully bony and narrow. She weighed nothing, and she still smelt of shampoo. Sam let his head rest lightly on her shoulder as he closed his eyes. They sat still and gradually she leaned in closer and he felt her start to relax.

Eventually, he realised she was asleep. Still supporting her, he stood up and hoisted her into his arms. She made no sound as he carried her inside and placed her on his bed. He spread the blanket over her and returned outside.

Sam sat on the deck finishing the last of his beer, then collected the bottles and went inside. He went to the bathroom, undressed and turned on the shower. He stood under the stream of hot water, allowing it to wash over him until it ran cold.

He tiptoed into the bedroom and grabbed a blanket from the foot of the bed. Jade was asleep in the same position, her breaths barely audible. He lay down on the sofa in the living room and pulled the blanket over him. He stared at the ceiling while the past day played before his eyes. It seemed as if the earth beneath his feet had crumbled. As if he was in free fall with nothing to hold on to. The fragile existence that it had taken him such a long time to create had been shattered in the span of just one day. How would he fill his time without his job?

The first streaks of slanted morning light were working their way through the dirty living-room window when at last Sam closed his eyes and fell asleep. He had hoped for a night of emptiness, a dreamless void of nothingness. Relief.

Instead, he entered a world of flesh and blood, a world that occupied all his senses. A world more real than any other world he knew.

# 7.

*This bad begins, and worse remains behind*

It started where it always started. He was walking along the footpath. Everything was blue in the moonlight. The street was quiet apart from the constant droning of innumerable invisible cicadas. Nothing stirred except a few moths flitting around the streetlamp. The sky was clear, covered with stars.

He opened the front door. It wasn't locked. But that was all right. Karen sometimes forgot.

And sometimes when she knew he was on his way she left it unlocked anyway. It was a safe neighbourhood.

He was hoping she would still be awake. He felt a jolt of delicious anticipation at the thought of her warm body in the bed.

Then he heard Jasper crying. Such a strange, tired, miserable whining. Not his usual cry. An exhausted wail, as if he had been crying for so long that he was no longer able to produce more than a thin whimper. He couldn't understand it. Where was Karen?

Abruptly, his anticipation turned to cold dread.

Where was Karen?

Beautiful, beautiful Karen. To him, the most perfect woman on earth. Even the thought of her made him excited. The thought of her face, her smile. Her body. Her skin. It was as though she was lit from within. He couldn't get enough of it. Watching it. Stroking it. Running his lips over it. Although her hair was so black, her skin was milky white. Unblemished, except for that one little flaw. A flaw that completed the perfection. That perfectly round, raised, skin-coloured mole at the ridge of her left hipbone. A jeweller's stamp, he had thought when he first discovered it.

But as he hurried down the hallway towards Jasper's room, he was filled with rapidly escalating dread.

Then he noticed the smell. There was a new smell inside the house. A dreadful, sickly smell.

He was running now, frantic, all the while shouting her name. 'Karen! KAREN! KAAAREN!'

He dashed along the hallway and into the baby's bedroom. He lifted the small body to his chest. The soft hair was plastered to the skull and the sleepsuit was damp with sweat. But he quickly stopped crying as Sam picked him up and held him against his chest. Sam could feel the rapid beating of the baby's heart against his skin while his own heart raced.

Clasping Jasper tightly, he returned to the hallway. The door to the bedroom was open a chink and a pool of strangely slanted light fell through the door. Sam moved towards it slowly, clutching the small body in his arms and filling his nostrils with the sweet smell from the damp hair on the baby's head.

His breaths were short and shallow.

He wanted it to stop at that moment. Before he kicked the door wide open.

A shrill ring jolted Sam awake. He sat bolt upright, disoriented. For a split second he didn't know where he was. On the sofa, in the living room. Was that his alarm? But he didn't even use it any more. Didn't need it. Might never need it again.

It wasn't the alarm. It was his mobile. He tried to clear his parched throat. The dream was slowly fading, withdrawing to the black depth inside his brain where it lived. But the feeling lingered. The foreboding dread. And the accompanying sense of guilt.

He picked up the phone and held it to his ear. 'Hello?'

There was a moment's silence. 'Did I wake you up? I did, didn't I?

Well, it's eight o'clock and I assumed you would be up.' Lynette. Who else?

Lynette was the cord that connected him to the real world. Lynette Church. Funny, fearless, formidable Lynette. Honest, loyal Lynette. She never wasted a word, had no time for pleasantries. Not so now either. 'I think it's time we caught up,' she said. 'It's been a while. How about lunch or dinner soon?' As usual, he couldn't be sure if she genuinely wanted to see him, or if she was worried that if she didn't check up on him he would cut himself loose and drift away for good.

'Sure,' he said. 'Anytime. I have no commitments.' A true statement if ever there was one.

'I'd have liked to see you before I go to London next week, but I'm not sure it'll work. It'd be great to have your feedback on my speech notes for the conference. The topic is ridiculously wide: "Journalism and the new media." I guess they'd like me to be some sort of oracle, telling them what the future will hold.' She added, quickly, as if slightly embarrassed: 'Besides, I'd just like to see you.'

An awkward moment's silence followed. Sam realised he should say something but didn't quite know what.

'Let's see how the week evolves,' Lynette said. 'I'll call you.'

Sam sank back on the hard sofa and closed his eyes. He could sense that the house was empty. Jade must have left without waking him. The usual headache was back and his mouth was dry. Even the slightest move felt overwhelmingly impossible.

He thought about Lynette. Their friendship went back to his early days in New Zealand. A meeting of like-minded brains, he liked to think. Lynette had been the one contacting him, asking if he would be willing to talk with her off the record. She was planning to write a series of articles about terrorism and its effect on international business. Those were the days when terrorism had just become a household word. He'd been surprised because even though they'd met in London, where he and Karen had socialised with the same expat New Zealand set, he didn't know her very well. But at that first meeting in Wellington, there had been instant and mutual appreciation. And then, of course, during those momentous months that followed, he had learned to know her and trust her implicitly.

But it was thanks to her that the friendship had endured. She stayed in touch, called regularly, and always made it seem like she needed his advice. He still liked her as much as ever, and trusted her even more, but he was no longer the same person. He was no longer alive, while she was still out there, in the real world.

He closed his eyes again. Images flashed before him, like photographs. Black-and-white photographs. Only these were blue. Moonlight blue.

Jasper was in his arms. His body still rippled by the odd hiccup and his lips sucking the skin of Sam's throat, as if in search of a nipple. Sam walked towards the bedroom. 'Karen?' he called, for some reason quietly now, almost whispering. 'Karen?'

But there was no reply. The entire house was silent, a kind of dead silence that he had not experienced before.

He stretched out one foot and kicked the bedroom door open.

She lay on the floor, naked, one leg still on the bed and both arms flung out from her body. The bedside lamp lay on the floor, the shade off. Light washed over the carpet, enhancing every detail, casting long shadows. He stood on the threshold with Jasper's warm little body in his arms, staring without understanding.

# 8.

*For murder, though it has no tongue, will speak*


His hair wet from the shower, Sam took his coffee outside and sat in a deckchair. It was a sunny early morning and he watched a shiny bright-blue bird flit back and forth over the lawn. He reflected on how little he knew about this country. Apart from the kiwi, which he had never seen, he couldn't name a single native bird. Here, birdsong left him unmoved. Back home, both in England and in Norway, he knew the birds and recognised their individual songs. There, birdsong was associated with the seasons, evoking strong emotions. Here, it was just background sound.

He took out his mobile and dialled the number he had looked up. He was redirected three times until he heard her voice. 'Saskia Peters.'

He was surprised at his reaction. His heart was pumping hard, his hands felt clammy. 'It's me, Sam. Sam Hallberg,' he said, his voice sounding strangely forced.

There was an extended pause. 'Can I call you back?' she said. Sam gave her his number and hung up.

He felt foolish as he sat holding the mobile. When she hadn't called back after a few minutes, he went inside and started to clear up some of the mess. He pulled off the sheets and collected clothes strewn around the house, put them in the washing machine and turned it on. There was a pile of mail and newspapers that had collected on the kitchen table. He took it outside and sat down to sift through it.

He was throwing the unread copies of the paper on the floor when he came upon the Saturday paper. He flicked through the pages until he found the small notice:

---

**Student killed in accident at Auckland University Library**

Early on Thursday morning two cleaners at the University of Auckland found the body of a man at the bottom of the stairs in the university library. He has been identified as Brent Taylor, 28, a postgraduate student and part-time employee at the library. Police are not looking for anybody else in connection with the death, but are calling for persons with information about the accident to come forward.

---

Sam tore out the page, folded it and put it in his wallet. He finished sorting out the mail and dumped the rubbish in the bin.

Back in the kitchen, his thoughts returned to Saskia. Saskia Peters, his colleague at the Ministry in Wellington. Young and ambitious, and far too good-looking to be left alone with her job and her career. For a long time, though, she seemed to have managed to rise above the gossip and the intrigues, seemingly untouchable.

Then, *that* evening. About two months after Karen had died, when Sam hung suspended between life and death, ready to release his hold on life, Saskia appeared on his doorstep. He let her in. And she stayed the night. The chance that she would be spotted had seemed microscopic, but instantly rumours began to circulate at work. Soon they became common knowledge. Sam didn't think you had to be paranoid to believe that someone was out to get her. Or him. Or both of them. For her, it was damaging. For him, nothing mattered.

It was the beginning and the end. She didn't attend his drab farewell party in Wellington. But from the depth of his grief he noted her absence.

Then, almost a year later, she'd called. Said she was in Auckland for a job interview and asked if she could see him. It was one of those evenings when the struggle to survive seemed particularly daunting. So he agreed. She came to his house, carrying a bottle of wine.

And she stayed the night again. He cried in her arms.

He was awake when he heard her voice, but the room was dark and he knew it was still the early hours of the morning. She spoke softly but clearly. 'I am so sorry, Sam. I shouldn't have come.'

He had been aching to reach out his hands and pull her close, but had remained still, his arms leaden.

'I wasn't honest when I said I only came for your sake. That I was concerned with how you were coping.' She was silent for so long he thought she had finished. He listened to her breathing and waited, expecting her to stir, to get out of bed. But she lay still. 'I came for me, Sam. I came because I didn't think I could live without you. I didn't understand until you left that you had become the reason for my love of my work. For my love of life.'

But he said nothing, made no move. Each breath felt like hard labour; his mouth was dry. The memory of the night before pounded in his head, in his body, mixing with overwhelming grief and shame, paralysing him, binding his hands, silencing his voice.

'I am so very sorry, Sam. I shouldn't have done this.' He knew that something was expected of him, but he couldn't make himself respond.

Now, he knew that there had been choices. That honesty might have changed the course of events. Might have kept Saskia in his life. He could have tried to explain. Could have told her how fragile he was, told her about the struggle to stay alive. And how he did not deserve even the smallest measure of pleasure.

But there, in the darkness of the night, he had been engulfed by shame over the pang of passion of the night before. Over his momentary feelings of joy. Of love. And shame silenced him.

She had left soon after and there had been no contact since. Until now.

Suddenly the phone rang. He picked it up quickly. 'Saskia?'

'No. It's Jan,' the voice boomed. It was his father-in-law, Jan De Haan. 'Thought I should ring to ask when you're coming up. Dottie and I think it would be good if you came up this Christmas, if not before. Good for Jasper.'

Sam felt a surge of guilt, and thought he could hear accusation in Jan's voice. It had been weeks since he last spoke to Jasper. He knew it was selfishness that kept him away. Here, removed from his son, he was able to keep most of his feelings under control, but confronted with Jasper, his serious face with Karen's clear dark eyes, the scabs opened and the pain flooded back. And then, meeting Karen's parents, particularly her mother… Although nothing was ever said, he felt relentlessly pounded, probably reading into every glance, every word, more than there was to see and hear. His visits had become less and less frequent. He missed Jasper, but he felt that perhaps his son was better off with him as a distant figure in his life.

'Jan, hello,' he said, stalling. 'How are you? How's Jasper?'

'Well, if you rang now and then, you would know, wouldn't you?' Jan said. 'We're good. Jasper is good, doing well at kindy. Developing into a fine little fellow.'

Silence fell. Sam was searching for something to say.

'How about next weekend, Sam? Come down Friday afternoon and stay till Sunday afternoon? Won't take much time from your work. Whatever that is.' There it was again.

Those subtle reminders of his inadequacy. As a father. As a human being.

Sam's eyes followed the little blue bird that was still flitting around in the back of the garden. 'I'll see what I can do,' he replied. 'I'll let you know, okay?'

'Okay. Would you like to have a word with your son?' Jan asked, and then, without waiting for a reply, put Jasper on the phone.

'Hi, Daddy.' His son's voice sounded close, as if he were in the next room. 'I have a rabbit, Daddy. His name is Buddy.'

'Great, Jasper. Buddy, that's a great name. How is kindy?'

'I'll be one of the wise men in the play.'

Sam laughed. 'Perfect, Jasper. 'Cause you're a truly wise man.' He rubbed his eyes. 'I'll try and come and see you next weekend. And I'll ring tomorrow. Okay?'

'Okay, Daddy. Then you'll get to see Buddy.'

'Sure, I'll get to see Buddy. And I'll see you. Take care. Love you.'

He ended the call and stood staring at the screen of his phone for a moment.

Then it rang again. 'This is not a good idea,' Saskia said flatly.

'I understand,' Sam said. 'I understand how you feel. I'm sorry to call you like this, out of the blue.'

She didn't respond.

'How are you?' He squirmed at the obvious insincerity. If he had cared to know, he would have been in touch, wouldn't he?

She still didn't respond.

'Saskia, I wouldn't have called you like this if I had thought of another way. But I've become involved in something. Trying to help someone. Someone who really needs some help.' He paused. 'It's not for me.' As if that would make a difference. 'It's about a death at the university library. A guy was found dead there Friday morning.'

'I heard,' she said.

'Well, I was contacted by a friend of his on Monday. She's convinced he was murdered. But apparently the police are treating it as an accident. Or possibly a suicide. The girl says this is impossible. Apparently, her friend was happier than ever.'

He paused, but Saskia said nothing.

'I think she is believable.'

Again she made no comment.

'So I promised her I would make some enquiries. Try to find out why murder is not being considered.'

'I don't think I can help you. It's not my department. I don't have access to any more information than the public.'

'This girl, Jade, says her friend, Brent Taylor, was just finishing writing a book which seems to have vanished into thin air. The CD copy he had asked her to guard was stolen from her a couple of days after the murder. Taken from her by force by someone posing as a policeman. I really do think she deserves some help. But I understand if you're not in a position to do anything. I don't want to put you to any trouble.'

There was a drawn-out silence. Sam felt forced to try to end the awkward conversation.

'Well, I'm sorry I called. You look after yourself, Saskia. Take care.'

'Wait,' she said. 'I'll see if there's anything I can find out. I'll call you back if I find something.'

'Thank you. Thank you so much.' Sam slowly lowered the phone. He felt his cheeks burn. He hadn't felt this stupid for a long time. Nor this alive.

\*\*\*

Sam decided to walk to the garage. He dreaded facing Wayne again. He knew he meant well, but his concern was irritating, his sympathy hard to bear.

When he arrived at the garage, Wayne was in the office with Dylan, who wore the company overalls and a red baseball cap. He looked the part much better than Sam had ever managed to do. They were playing chess and the radio was on talkback. 'Come in, Sam,' Wayne shouted as he heard Sam cross the garage floor. Sam joined the two bulky men in the small upstairs office space and felt there was hardly room for him. Dylan's handshake was hard, his calloused hand like a bear paw.

'Dylan's flying down to Wellington to join a protest march to

Parliament,' Wayne said. 'Then he'll be here and help out until you're back.'

There were no more chairs in the small room and Sam stood, leaning against the wall. He didn't comment.

Dylan pushed back his cap. 'It's a bunch of independent meat-processing companies joining up to hand in a petition to the Minister about this Aotearoa Meat Export Corporation before the holidays begin. Won't hurt to try and make ourselves heard. Things are so bad anyway, can't get much worse. Hopefully there'll be some media coverage. Somebody has to listen. We can't just stand by and watch our business go down the drain. All the hard work that's gone into building our overseas markets.'

Dylan, hands in the large pockets of his overalls, paced the small room. 'All I ever wanted was to leave the boys with a level of security. Never had any grand ideas of expanding or anything. Just to make my business a safe source of modest income for the family. And then to hand over something to the boys. Surely that's not too much to ask, is it?'

Sam didn't know what to say. He knew it didn't matter how modest your wishes were; they could still be crushed.

'And it was going so very well. We did everything right! Specialised, refined our product, found a niche market. All that we were supposed to do. Our small company, Waikato Prime Meat, supplies prime beef cuts, export-quality, export-packaged. Nice design, clever marketing. Mostly beef, a little lamb. And our market focus is on Norway and Canada. The upmarket, delicatessen segment. And it was growing modestly every year.'

Dylan turned his back to the room and looked through the dirty glass partition into the garage space. 'Then, bang. Out of the blue, with no consultation, no information, no explanation, just like that, they impose the ruddy AME on us. We're supposed to cheer and happily accept an export monopoly. A bloody joint venture between the government and some foreign investor. And just like that, they pull the carpet from under our feet. Bloody hell! We're supposed to sit back and accept that our products go straight into the government's big bag. No control over pricing, no say, no alternatives. And the way things are going, no future either. We can only sell our meat to the government at a fixed price. Meanwhile, I can only buy the meat at what the farmers want to sell for. This leaves me with no margin. It's mad.' His despair was so obvious that Sam found it hard to return his gaze.

'You know what's worst, though? It's not the money. It's being treated like dirt. Being stripped of all dignity, all control. Being robbed of your entire life's creation. And nobody says a word. Nobody does anything.' Dylan's voice broke. 'Somebody's making a lot of money, but it's not us meat processors. So I thought a trip to Wellington could stir up some people down there. Let them know that we are out there and still alive. And we damn well will not go down without a fight.'

He finally sat down again and hit the table with his closed fist. The chess pieces jumped.

'I know someone you should talk to,' Sam said. 'A journalist, as clever as they get. Lynette Church. She's a friend of mine. Covers business for the *New Zealand Tribune*. I'd be happy to ring and see if you could get a brief meeting. I think she might be really interested.'

Dylan looked at Sam, but said nothing.

'I'll ring her and ask her to get in touch,' Sam said, and Dylan nodded.

Just then the office phone rang. Wayne answered it and the working day began.

Sam collected his few belongings. He called Lynette and left a message asking her to get in touch with Dylan. Then, with a brief and awkward goodbye, he walked out into the bright sunshine.

# 9.

*Alas poor ghost*

The blue sky was dotted by only the occasional playful white fluff of a cloud. Sam decided to walk from the garage to the university. Karangahape Road was sparsely populated with an atmosphere of a place not quite awake, meeting the day with a hung-over yawn. There was litter on the ground: beer cans, hamburger wrappers and cigarette butts. Forlorn remnants of the night before. The few people he met had a zoned-out look, as if not quite there. A group of young guys lingered drunkenly outside a pub, laughing insanely. Their faces were pasty, their eyes screwed up against the bright light. A stunningly good-looking woman who was not a woman approached with a knock-kneed gait and swaying hips. As she passed Sam her arm brushed against his. But when Sam turned to look at her, her gaze was vacant, and they both carried on their way.

He walked through the glass doors to the university's library, trying to imagine what it would be like to be there alone at night. He walked up the stairs, leaned on the banister and looked down into the main hall. The banister was high. There was no way anybody could accidentally fall over it and land neatly inside the glass shaft. Everything looked clean: he could see no traces of blood, not even a scratch on the walls of the shaft. He walked down the stairs slowly, feeling them vibrate under his weight. The area where the body had landed looked strangely ordinary. It had been thoroughly cleaned. If you knew what to look for, however, the signs were there. A slightly darker patch where the carpet had been cut and a new piece inserted, strips of yellow tape left on the handrail. Students drifted around with arms full of books, seemingly unaware and unconcerned. He wasn't sure what he had expected. Perhaps that it should look more like the scene of a tragedy. A murder.

He walked up to the main counter. He didn't think he would pass for a student or a tutor, and he suspected that his accent still revealed his non-Kiwi background. He gave a smile that he hoped managed to be warm and mournful at the same time. 'Hi,' he said. 'I'm a friend of Brent Taylor.' The young woman started like a rabbit. She stared at Sam but said nothing. 'I've only just arrived from overseas,' Sam continued. 'I left in a hurry when I heard. Just wanted to make sure I got here in time for the funeral.' Sam ran his hand over his cheek and slowly shook his head. 'I still can't believe it.'

'I *know*,' the librarian said, her rabbit-eyes wide open. 'We can't either. It's like Brent was always here. Always sitting there. Smelling like hamburgers. Oops. Sorry. That sounds terrible.' She blushed and put her hand over her mouth.

'You wouldn't have his address, would you?' Sam asked. 'Stupid, I sort of didn't think I would need it. Now I realise I don't know how to get in touch with his family other than by going around to his place.'

'Oh, I'm not sure,' she said, instantly worried again, biting her lower lip. 'He worked here, but I never really knew him. You know, to know where he lived and stuff.' She was silent for a moment. 'Grafton. I think. I don't know why, but I think he lived there.'

'Wouldn't he be in the library database?'

'Of course!' She blushed. 'You're right. Stupid me. Of course.' She quickly tapped on her keyboard. 'Yep, here he is. Sixteen Glasgow Terrace, Grafton. Want his mobile number?' She blushed again. 'Oh. You won't need that. I suppose.'

Sam smiled soothingly. 'Thanks very much for your help.'

He decided to walk to Grafton. By now the sun was high in

the sky, and he felt the shirt sticking to his back as he walked up Symonds Street. But he was walking faster and with more purpose than he had in a long time. Why am I doing this? he thought. What kind of weird satisfaction can this provide? I could be sitting on my deck finishing *Hamlet*.

Glasgow Street lay dormant. Sam walked its full length, then back to number sixteen. Though the houses were modest in size and scope, most looked well kept. It was obvious which ones were rented: clotheslines with a mixed bag of washing all melded into a common pink-purple-greyness and hung to dry in twisted knots; knee-high weeds in the garden; overfull glass recycling bins. Like number sixteen, a pale-blue one-storey wooden villa. It had a front porch that ran the full width of the house. The window to the left was wide open and music blared. John Cage. Sam had thought he was the only person who listened to his music. The window to the right was closed and there was nobody to be seen.

Sam tried the doorbell, which didn't work, then knocked. Several times. He then tried the handle and found the door unlocked. He walked inside. The hallway was dark: the only light came from the far end, where a door to the back garden stood open. There was no sign of life, just the music from the room to the left. Sam knocked on the door but received no reply. He turned and knocked on the door on the other side but had no response there either. He wandered through the hallway into the empty kitchen. A very large ginger cat sat on the floor, staring suspiciously at him but not moving. There was a smell of something slowly decaying, like mouldy bread or rancid milk. But no life other than the cat.

Sam heard a door open behind him and John Cage burst into the hallway. So did the occupant of the room. It was clear that the old man did not often enter the outside world. He stared at Sam with the look of someone watching a hitherto unknown and not very appealing species.

'Hi,' Sam said.

'Are you the police?' He scrutinised Sam's face.

'No. I'm a friend of Brent's.'

'Didn't like the looks of that last guy. And didn't tell him anything.'

The old man shrank visibly, turned and walked back into his room, but left the door open behind him. Sam followed. The dark room was packed with boxes, piles of books and magazines, records, shoes, an old piano. And John Cage, who filled the space with pulsating, constant sound. The old man nodded towards a chair in the corner and Sam sank into the leather, aware of the mould spores that surely must have been expelled. The old man sat down on what might have been a sofa – it was difficult to say with any certainty as it was completely buried beneath clothes, blankets, bags and a few used dinner plates.

'Thank you for inviting me in,' Sam said. 'I'm Sam Hallberg and I'm a friend of Brent's, like I said.'

The old man said nothing, but coughed again and, richly rewarded, chewed on what had been brought forth from the depths of his body. He stared at Sam for a moment, as if evaluating him and considering whether to respond. 'Sid Fielding,' he said.

Sam assumed it was the man's name. 'I'm trying to find out what happened to Brent,' he tried. 'Living in the same house you must have seen quite a bit of him. How was he doing? Was he okay?'

'Listen,' the old man said, holding up one hand. 'Silence.' He leaned backwards on the couch and the bottoms of his jeans rose to reveal his thin, veined ankles and bare feet with yellow toenails. He closed his eyes and seemed to be listening intently. Sam said nothing for a while and the music continued. There was a strange, organic smell in the room and it was very hot. The combination was uncomfortable and Sam took short, shallow breaths. 'You do know that Brent is dead, don't you?' Sam said. The old man opened his surprisingly clear blue eyes and stared at him. 'He had an accident at the library. Last week.'

The old man said nothing, but bent his head and crossed his arms over his chest. He began scratching his arms nervously.

'I'm a friend of Brent's,' Sam repeated. 'I just want to see if I can understand what happened to him.' Sam allowed a little time before his question. 'When did you last see him?'

The old man stopped scratching and just held on to his arms, rocking a little. 'When? I see him all the time. He sort of... comes around.'

'Okay, but when was the last time he came around?'

'He comes around all the time. Sits down, has a smoke. Listens to the silence with me.' Sam tried to think of a way into the murky, meandering tunnels of the old man's memory. But before he could say anything, Sid began to talk. 'It was about his book. This thing he was writing.'

'Book? What book?'

The old man didn't answer, but walked awkwardly to the window, turning his back on Sam. 'He isn't coming back, is he?' It wasn't really a question.

'No, Brent is gone. But I need to understand what happened to him. And I think you do, too.'

'Nah. He's gone. That's it. I don't need to know shit.' Sid looked at Sam. 'Do you have a smoke?'

Sam shook his head. 'No, but I'll get you some. I was wondering if we could have a quick look at Brent's room first. Do you have a key?'

'Never locked.'

The old man walked into the hall and opened the door to Brent's room. Sam stepped inside. It was dark, the brown curtains pulled closed over the large window. It smelled of dirty laundry, mould and stale cigarette smoke. There was little furniture. A futon, a chest of drawers, a bookshelf made from bricks and planks. A makeshift two-burner gas stove was placed on a small cabinet in the far corner. Clothes and shoes were strewn on the floor and on the bed. Sam moved towards an old computer that sat on a trestle table next to the bed. 'Is this where he used to write?' he asked, turning it on.

'Don't know.' The old man looked nervously over his shoulder. 'I don't think you should be doing that. Don't like you to.'

'I'll just have a quick look.' Sam waited while the computer booted. The screen lit up. He was prompted for a password, but clicked 'Open' without filling the box. To his surprise the screen flickered and the hard drive opened. Sam clicked on 'My computer' and it opened too. He clicked on the C-drive icon. This opened too.

There was nothing stored in the computer. There were no 'My documents' or 'My pictures' or 'My novel.' Nothing. Not a single file. 'There's nothing in here,' Sam said.

'There wouldn't be,' the old man said, looking over his shoulder. 'Not after they came here.'

'Who came here?'

'The guy and then the girl, Jade.'

'Did you see the guy?'

'Not really.' The old man shrugged and looked over his shoulder again.

'Did they take anything?'

The old man narrowed his eyes and leaned forward. 'Jade did,' he hissed, expelling a breath of garlic, tobacco and general decay. 'I saw her stick something into her purse.'

'Any idea who the guy was?'

'Never saw him before. Never want to see him again.' The old man shifted his weight from one foot to the other, then back again.

'I'll get you those cigarettes, Sid,' Sam said. 'Just tell me what the guy looked like.'

'Told you I didn't get a look. Just saw him from my window. And it was dark. Drove a silver car. A Toyota. I think. One of those ordinary-looking cars.'

'Good. Great.' Sam said. 'Anything else?'

'He drove off, then came back. Stopped further up the road. Didn't leave till she did.'

He paused, and Sam thought he could see the old man weighing the offer of cigarettes against the effort of digging into his memory. 'Thought he might be a policeman.'

'Why do you think he might have been a policeman?'

'You know, the way he walked.'

Walked? Sam thought. Could you tell a policeman by the way he walked?

'Knew I was right when he came back next day.'

'He came back?'

Sid nodded.

'How did you know it was the same guy?'

'Same car, same walk. Didn't tell him anything, though. Just played the old guy who knew nothing.' Sid smiled and showed a row of decaying teeth. 'Sure know how to do that.'

'Anything else you noticed? Anything at all?'

'Scary-looking guy. He freaked me out. The way he looked at me. Had a scar on his cheek. Made him look like he was smiling. But he sure wasn't. And I could hardly understand what he was saying. Had an accent. Or it might have been the scar.' Sid seemed to shudder.

'You're doing really well,' Sam said. 'Is there anything else you noticed?'

'Nope. How about those cigs?'

He went into the hall. Sam followed. 'Right, I'll get you the cigarettes. Anything else you need from the shop?'

'Just cigs.' The old man shook his head and closed the door to his room.

Sam returned to Brent's room. He sat on the bed, looking over the poorly lit room, trying to picture Brent there. Tried to imagine Brent's dreams of another life as he excitedly worked away at the computer. Who had wiped it? Who had felt it necessary to destroy his work? Possibly murder him? And why?

Sam walked to the corner store and bought a couple of packets of cigarettes, a loaf of sliced bread and a bottle of milk. When he returned and knocked on Sid's door there was no reply, and when he tried the handle the door was locked. He hung the bag on the doorknob and dropped his calling card inside.

Outside, the sky was clouding over. As Sam walked across Grafton Bridge it began to drizzle. He continued down Karangahape Road and soon gave up all attempts at keeping dry. This city devours its houses and its people by slowly soaking them, he thought.

It dissolves concrete and flesh.

# 10.

*Or to take arms against a sea of troubles*

Lynette felt apprehensive. She always did when on board ships. It wasn't that she got seasick, it was the feeling of being trapped. The moment the ship left the harbour she felt distinctly uneasy. There was something sinister about a press conference aboard a yacht, however luxurious. And this one certainly was luxurious. The champagne flowed from the moment guests were on deck. Impeccable service offered dainty delicacies from silver trays; soft music poured forth from invisible sources. The sun oozed down from a clear sky; probably through the widening opening in the ozone layer, Lynette thought, wondering if her 15+ foundation was enough protection. She pushed up her dark prescription sunglasses with the tip of her finger, took a sip of champagne and looked around. Sprinkled in between the usual crowd of dark-suited middle-aged men and motley media were several strikingly beautiful, long-legged and blonde women, all with flawless white smiles, short skirts and generous cleavage. Lynette pulled at her silk jacket. She had bought it for the occasion, but would have been better off with a larger size. Or something entirely different, something cool and loose fitting.

'Ah, Lynette,' said a voice behind her. 'Lynette Church, how wonderful to see you.' Gary Spalding had turned on his considerable charm. The Minister of Foreign Affairs and Trade smiled and opened his arms. For a moment Lynette had a horrible vision of him embracing her. Instead he kept his arms wide open while he inspected her with a small smile. Lynette felt perspiration preparing to break through her pores. It was inevitable. There was nothing she could do to prevent it, and eventually it would seep out and soak her jacket. She shifted her weight and smiled back. 'Ah, Minister, the pleasure is all mine.'

'Sorry I haven't come back to you about that interview. It's been a hectic few days. Always is at this time of the year. As you know, no doubt. I never let a lady down, though, you know that. It's with my secretary. Let's see when we can fit it in.' Half-turned away he scanned the crowd, ensuring there was no lost opportunity anywhere. Spalding's time was of the essence: he never gave away a minute without a good return.

'Let me introduce you to our host,' he said, gently putting his hand on her back and pulling her with him. 'Do you know Eric? Eric Salisbury?' He didn't stop to listen to her reply but turned and moved through the crowd. Effortlessly he made his way across the deck. People stood aside as he approached and Lynette trailed behind, managing to slip through just before the parted sea of guests closed again.

No, she didn't know Eric Salisbury. She knew of him, she knew what he looked like, but no, she didn't know him at all. Now, when she stood face to face with him, she realised he looked like Gary Spalding would have, given youth, an English public-school education and money.

'Lynette Church,' Eric said lifting her hand lightly. As with the Minister, Lynette again feared a moment of uninvited physical intimacy, a kiss on her hand this time, and was relieved to receive it back after just a brief squeeze. 'Welcome on board, Lynette,' he said with a wide smile. Where did they all get these perfect sets of teeth from? Lynette wondered, keeping her own lips firmly closed.

'I have long admired your skills. By far the best business journalism in the country,' he continued. 'You are simply in a league of your own.'

68

'Then it's a mystery to me why you have been so elusive, Mr Salisbury. I've lost count of the number of times I've tried to reach you for a comment or an interview.'

'Eric, please,' he smiled. 'And we really must do something to repair this. I will leave it with my secretary to set up a meeting.'

What was it with these men and their secretaries? Lynette didn't want her matters in the hands of either Gary Spalding's or Eric Salisbury's.

'Time for my speech, I'm afraid,' Eric said. 'But let's catch up later. Enjoy the hospitality.'

He turned and walked over to a small podium at the prow of the yacht and tapped the microphone on his lapel. The sound from the loudspeakers gradually muted the buzz and he began to talk.

'The Honourable Gary Spalding, Minister of Foreign Affairs and Trade. Ladies and gentlemen. Friends. It is my very great pleasure to welcome you to this celebration of the acquisition of Mahana New Zealand Limited by Demon Holdings Incorporated. Mahana is the country's largest supplier and distributor of electricity. Preceding the complex negotiations leading to the successful acquisition that we are here to celebrate today, a thorough restructuring of the energy sector has taken place. The positive effects will soon be obvious. With the concentration of ownership, a strategic partnership with the government and the benefit of the financial resources of Demon Holdings, the energy industry in this country will enter a new era.' He lifted his glass and looked over the crowd. 'To clean, safe, reliable and affordable energy!' The crowd responded enthusiastically. 'Please enjoy this day of celebration. As you can see, even the weather is in a good mood!' He gestured to the clear blue skies above. Glasses tinkled as guests laughed and the buzz rose again.

Another meaningless speech, Lynette thought. A deal of unprecedented implications, yet all they were offered were some clichés. And not a word from that normally keen public speaker, Gary Spalding. She turned and looked for Eric's face in the crowd. She spotted him leaning against the railing, talking into the ear of one of the gorgeous young blondes. Lynette approached. 'You're not giving us much, Eric,' she said.

Eric turned, a smile on his face. Did it stiffen just a touch? Lynette wasn't sure. 'Oh, well, this isn't the occasion for boring lectures on mergers and acquisitions, is it?' With a gesture so discreet she could have been mistaken, Lynette saw him give the blonde a light push on the behind. Apparently a signal for her to withdraw, which she did with a smile and swift wiggle of her taut buttocks.

'This is the largest single acquisition this country has seen,' Lynette said, taking another sip of the now lukewarm champagne. 'Are we supposed to happily sit back and trust a newcomer – a company we know precious little about – to take control of our energy sector? No questions asked?' Again she thought she could see the smile reduce, as if the sparkle was dimming subtly. The eyes grew cold, but the smile lingered on his lips while he remained leaning against the railing with the same casual elegance as before, one hand in the pocket of his white linen trousers, the other holding his glass. Not champagne, Lynette noticed. Water. He didn't respond and she continued. 'Don't you think that we ought to be a little curious? That we have the right to some sort of background on the man and the company that we hand over such a chunk of our infrastructure to?'

Eric took the sunglasses from the breast pocket of his navy jacket and put them on. End of smile. 'Deals of these proportions are not made without due diligence, as you know. I can assure you that the process has complied with rules and regulations. Whatever needed to be explored has been explored, to the satisfaction of the relevant parties. I can see no need for anybody to delve into my personal life. I am insignificant in this matter. As the chairman of Demon Holdings I am responsible to the shareholders, whose trust I have.

Now, if you will excuse me, Miss Church, I must attend to my responsibilities as a host.'

Miss Church. I'll be damned, Lynette thought.

Eric abruptly turned his back on her and pushed his way through the crowd. She felt her cheeks blush, not from the champagne, nor from the sun. It annoyed her that anger had this effect on her. Made her face turn red and blotchy, made the perspiration that had been awaiting its moment burst from every pore of her body. She took a large gulp and finished the glass, and as a waiter passed by she replaced it with a new one. She could see Eric and Gary involved in a conversation across the deck, their heads bowed closely together.

Another waiter offered a tray with miniature hamburgers the size of two-dollar coins. Lynette took one, swallowed it in one bite, and took another before the waiter disappeared into the crowd. The meat was in line with her diet, and the bread was just a tiny sliver. She had her mouth full as Tony Ritchie appeared from behind. He smiled broadly. He had a gin and tonic in his hand; she knew he didn't drink champagne.

'Any luck with the enigmatic Eric Salisbury?' he asked. 'I saw you two talking.'

'Nope,' Lynette said. 'Nothing. He just switched off that bright smile and turned his back.'

Tony laughed. 'Want a tip?'

Lynette didn't respond, just took another sip from her glass. God, she was boiling!

'Come on, it's absolutely free!' Tony raised his glass to her. Though he was smiling, his pale blue eyes glittered and she knew he was very serious.

'Sure,' she said. 'If it's free.'

'No Eric Salisbury graduated from Nuffield College with a degree in economics and political science in 1989. Or the year before. Or the year after.' Tony made a gesture as if offering her a gift. 'There you are.'

Lynette looked at him. There were moments when she wondered if she had made the right move when she left *BusinessNZ* three years earlier. There was less pressure at the *New Zealand Tribune* and the pay was better, but she had no confidante there. As the senior editor of the business section of the country's largest daily paper, the only woman on the floor, she had no friends. And nobody to challenge, or be challenged by. She missed the late nights at *BusinessNZ* and the discussions over innumerable G&Ts in the small board room. She had felt alive. Often angry, upset and challenged. But alive.

'Come on, let's join the crowd,' Tony said and touched her elbow.

And the *Intrepid* purred slowly through the Hauraki Gulf, its passengers increasingly fuelled by food and drink, lulled by soft music, their flesh scorched by the sun.

# 11.

*Each word made true and good*

Sam woke at seven o'clock, the same time as usual. He looked at his watch, then fell back against the pillow. He closed his eyes and tried to go back to sleep. He dozed off and drifted in the restless space between wake and sleep, dreams starting and ending abruptly. He got up an hour later. He sat on the side of the bed, still tired. The night had been filled with dreams, and, although he couldn't remember any of them, they stuck to him like night perspiration. He looked at his running shoes that he had placed by the bed the night before, and stretched out his hand for one.

Today was a new day, and going for a run would mark a change in lifestyle. Exercise was the cure-all. Who was it that said every sickness in life can be cured by salt water – sweat, tears and seawater? He had tried tears.

He ran down the street and into Grey Lynn Park and suddenly felt a stabbing pain in his side. Stitch? He slowed down and considered walking home. Give up the stupid idea, crawl back into bed. The thought was tempting, but something kept him going. He started jogging again, a little more slowly. Just as he completed a first loop around the park, his mobile rang. It surprised him he had even remembered to take it with him. It was Jade.

'Jade. How are you?'

'Yeah. Listen, the police have called me.'

Sam felt a stirring of interest. Maybe there was a lead.

'They want me to collect Brent's belongings. Apparently he put me down as his next of kin.'

So, no lead.

'Can you come with me? It's just that… policemen can be real arseholes to, well, to people like me.'

'Sure. Yes, of course I can.' Sam offered to pick her up and take her to the central police station. He put the mobile back in his pocket and completed another loop of the park.

An hour later he picked Jade up from her place in Newton. She, like him, was fresh from the shower; water dripped everywhere from her hair. She got into the passenger seat and leaned forward. Sam wasn't sure if she expected a hug from him. He put his hand on her back then realised she was trying to find a mirror on the back of the sun visor. She gave him a quick surprised look then checked the mirror.

'How are you today?' he asked, discreetly removing his hand.

'Fine.'

They parked in the Aotea car park. As they walked towards the nondescript grey high-rise building known as Central, Sam glanced at Jade and she caught his gaze. He hoped it was clear he wasn't judging her clothes. By now she had tied back her drying hair. She wore no makeup, and in her grey T-shirt and faded jeans she could have been a student at uni. But as they approached the reception counter he thought the staff still looked at her warily. Maybe they knew her.

'This way, please,' an officious, scrawny, middle-aged receptionist said, looking Jade over. She then smiled almost flirtatiously at Sam. They were led into a plain room with a plain table and plain chairs. A large Polynesian woman in uniform entered with a full tray. 'I'm very sorry for your loss,' she said kindly. 'These are the belongings that we took from the library.'

'As evidence?' Jade asked.

'As protocol,' she said.

'Did they prove anything?'

The woman stopped in her tracks and looked at Jade with a hint of a frown. 'It's a sad case of suicide.'

'But it wasn't,' Jade said quietly. But she was still heard.

The woman gave a distinctly patronising smile. 'Perhaps you should talk to victim support? I know it can be hard to accept that a loved one has taken his life.'

Jade didn't respond. The woman walked over and put a large hand on Jade's bony shoulder. 'Sometimes talking to people can help us accept tragedies like this one. It's a free service. I'd be very happy to contact them for you.'

'I don't need them,' Jade said, shaking her head.

The woman smiled that same professionally kind and patronising smile. 'I'll contact them just in case you change your mind. Take your time now. And if you want to throw anything out there's a rubbish bin just there.' With that, she left them to it.

Sam looked at the cheap plastic rubbish bin in the corner. Jade flicked through the contents of the tray. A small backpack that could have belonged to a rebellious thirteen-year-old boy. By the looks of it, Brent might have owned it since he was one. A laptop and a cable. A series of handwritten cards with inspirational quotes on them. A tattered copy of Stephen King's book *On Writing*, with stickers marking pages. An equally tattered and bestickered copy of *Screenwriting for Hollywood* by Michael Hauge. A sketchpad. A couple of health and fitness magazines. Nothing interesting, and all of it looking somehow soiled.

Jade smelt the backpack. 'Smells like Brent. Smells gross. But like Brent.' Teary-eyed, she flicked open the sketchpad. 'Brent always set his sights too high,' she said as she looked at a drawing of a nude man. From where Sam stood it looked like a decent drawing.

He turned on the laptop.

'The password is Pixie2001,' Jade told him.

'Why?'

'That was his fish's name. He accidentally killed it on New Year's Eve 2001 when he tried cleaning the bowl with detergent.'

Sam entered the password and a desktop with a few applications opened. What struck him straightaway was the lack of files. 'He was a writer, right?'

Jade nodded.

'Had written lots of stuff?'

'Yes,' she said, a little impatiently.

'Then where are all his files?' Sam searched through the computer but couldn't find any files of writing. No files of any kind. No folders, no files. Zip. He checked the recycle bin. There was nothing. 'Is this a new computer?' he asked, looking over the stickers of marijuana leaves scattered over the top.

'He's had that for ages. His mum won it at bingo years ago.'

'Then why are there no files on it?'

He stepped outside the room to look for the Polynesian woman. Then, across the lobby, he spotted Saskia. She was talking to a man with his back to Sam. A tall, blond man. She glanced at Sam and somehow, without making a move of any kind, managed to convey a message for him to go away. The man must somehow have been able to read her, too. He turned his head and for a brief moment his eyes were on Sam.

Sam was jolted. He couldn't understand why the brief glimpse of this man's face filled him with a kind of dread he hadn't felt in years. He turned away quickly and forced himself to be calm.

He walked up to the receptionist behind the counter. 'I need to talk to someone about the belongings that were issued to my friend just now,' he said.

'Sure. Can I ask what this specifically concerns?'

'It concerns the computer.'

'I'll get someone to pop in.'

Sam returned to the room, which by now felt oppressively hot and stale. He sat down at the small table and looked at Jade. 'I think

I just saw the man who came to your house and took the CD.'

Jade stared at him. 'You mean, he, like, he works here?' she said, looking terrified.

'Yes, but I don't think he knows you are here. So let's just stay here and wait for that woman.' He swallowed. 'I can't remember how but I think I recognised him.'

They waited almost an hour before anyone came to talk to them. During that time they went through every page of Brent's books and magazines, looking for a clue. Maybe a scrap of paper. But there was nothing. Sam then consulted the drawn picture of the handsome man.

'Any idea who this could be?' he asked.

'Could be Robert, I guess. Though I don't remember him looking like that. *That* handsome.'

'Tell me about Robert,' Sam said just as the Polynesian woman came into the room again. She apologised for taking so long, but it sounded insincere. There was a new edge to her voice.

Sam asked her about the computer. 'There are no files on it. None at all. And Brent was a prolific writer. In fact, that's why he got the laptop.'

'Well, all I can say is that all his belongings have been returned to you exactly as they were found.' The woman crossed her arms over her chest, clearly dissuading Sam from asking any further questions. 'Might not have wanted to leave anything for you to read. Might have erased them before he took his life.'

***

Sam and Jade sat at Sam's kitchen table. Brent's belongings were spread before them. Sam looked over the sketch of the handsome Robert. Jade sat with Brent's mobile in her hand. 'It's dead,' she said. 'And I doubt anyone in the world would have a charger for it. He's had it forever.'

Sam took the phone. It was a crappy little number with a chip in the screen. He removed the SIM card. He then opened his own mobile, replaced the card with Brent's, and turned it on.

He flicked through Brent's inbox. There were just a few saved messages from the library about his working hours. A few to and from Jade. But nothing of interest. He looked through the call register. Same there; nothing unexpected or interesting. Then he opened the phonebook. There weren't many records but he scrolled down and found what he was looking for. Robert's number. He considered calling it there and then but realised it would come from Brent's number. Instead, he made the call from his landline.

The phone rang seven times and went to answerphone. He hung up without leaving a message and sorted through the loose pages with Jade for a while before trying the number again. This time there was an answer. 'Hello?' He had an English accent. Educated. Measured.

'Is this Robert Black?'

'Who is asking?'

'My name is Sam Hallberg. I believe you were friends with Brent Taylor?'

'I wouldn't say friends exactly, but –'

'I'm sorry but I have some sad news to tell you.'

There was silence on the other end of the line. And then: 'Yes?'

'Unfortunately, Brent was found dead in the university library on Thursday evening.'

A long silence. And then: 'Who are you?'

'I'm a friend of Brent's. A friend of a friend. I believe you know Jade?'

'Ah.' He sounded flustered. 'Yes, well, no, not really. We've met, of course. Sorry. This is all a bit of a shock.'

'I can imagine. I'm sorry to break it to you like this. But Jade and I have some concerns about Brent's death. I was wondering if you would agree to see us and talk to us.'

'Concerns?' He took an audible breath. 'I mean, yes, of course. That's fine. Yes, of course. I'll give you my address. I'm carless, I'm afraid. But we could meet here, if that's okay.' He gave Sam his address and they agreed to meet up the following day.

To his surprise, Sam found that he felt a vague sense of sympathy for the man. At the back of his mind he had considered this elusive British man to be in some way suspicious. But his shock at the news had seemed genuine.

He turned to find Jade standing behind him. 'I'm coming,' she told him.

'I'm not sure that's a good idea.'

'I'm coming.' She was adamant.

# 12.

*How is it that the clouds still hang on you?*

Lynette parked her car in the garage. She had made it home. She really shouldn't have driven.

How many glasses of champagne had she managed to down during that hot and awkward afternoon? Too many, probably. Anywhere else in the world, a city this size would offer trains and buses, she thought. But Auckland required a car to get around. St Heliers was an inner-city suburb, but a taxi from the city centre cost a fortune. So here she was parking her car. It was a good thing she loved driving. Always had. And she was good at it too. Her father had seen to that.

The house was one in a block of six identical, nondescript, two-storey townhouses, connected by garages. She had never thought of it as her home, really. Just a practical place to live while she considered her options. By now, there weren't that many remaining. But she was still here. As she opened the front door a wall of hot, stale air overwhelmed her, and she knew she couldn't face another evening alone in the house. Men could call for an escort woman to keep them company. Were there escort men? If there were, Lynette didn't know where to find them.

She stepped inside and met her own image in the large mirror to the left. She looked how she felt: tired, hot and flustered. She dropped her purse on the table and went upstairs for a shower, tearing off her silk jacket as she climbed. She took a long, cool shower. Still nude, she opened the sliding doors to the balcony. But the air that wafted in was almost as hot as the air inside, and soon she was sweaty again. She searched her wardrobe for something light to wear, and decided on a pair of lime-green linen slacks and a navy singlet.

Downstairs, the kitchen was almost as hot as the bedroom. Lynette opened the fridge and stared at the depressing contents: low-fat yogurt, low-fat milk, low-fat cheese. A bag of spinach that had seen better days, half a grapefruit that had grown a thick skin. She slammed the door closed and returned to the hallway, picked up her purse and left the house.

Ruk Thai in Ponsonby Road was virtually empty when she arrived. It was a little after six and the dinner rush hadn't yet begun. She ordered takeaway spring rolls and satays, stir-fried chicken with cashews and chilli, and king prawns with basil, then sat down at one of the small tables to wait for her food. It had been a bad day, and she had come away from the launch feeling hot and frustrated. Her sense that there was something about Eric Salisbury that she couldn't put her finger on just wouldn't go away. Usually, she would have a plan for how to proceed, but for some reason she felt at a loss. It didn't seem likely that she would get that interview with Gary Spalding any time soon, either. Nor had anybody called her back from AME. The smells from the restaurants in the mall triggered her appetite and she tapped the table impatiently, feeling hungry and thirsty. She was looking forward to venting her problems to Sam. Also, she had a feeling he didn't look after himself. A surprise Thai meal would do him good.

Lynette made a second stop at Glengarry's in Williamson Avenue and bought two bottles of chilled chardonnay. She parked on Sam's quiet street, and was pleased to see that the lights were on in his house. Holding an armful of bags, she pushed the doorbell, smiling expectantly. But when the door opened, a pale red-haired woman peered through the chink, looking distinctly uncomfortable. Scared even, Lynette thought, while her smile died. The two women stared at each other. 'I, ah, I'm looking for Sam,' Lynette said.

'He's gone to the store,' the woman said in a ridiculously childish voice, lisping a little. She made no move to open the door.

Lynette put down the bag containing the wine bottles. 'I'm Lynette Church, an old friend of Sam's.'

The redhead said nothing.

'Do you think you could open the door and let me inside so I can put these down?' Lynette indicated the bags of food. The girl hesitated but eventually let go of the door, allowing Lynette to push it open and step inside. By now, she was perspiring again. On top of the frustration and anger, she now felt stupid. It had been a bad idea to come without calling first. She could have kicked herself. But she walked straight into the kitchen and put the bags on the counter, turned on the cold water and let it wash over her wrists. Her father had taught her to do this when she had been hot and flustered as a child. When the sensitive nerves on the inside of your wrists believe that it's cold, the rest of your body will, too, he had told her. Over the years, Lynette had found that this remedied all sorts of problems. Calmed the mind and cooled the body. After a minute or so, she turned off the tap and wiped her hands. She made a feeble effort to push up her hopelessly sagging hair, straightened her glasses and took a look at the girl. She was tiny; just bones, really. Very pale, with strange green eyes. Coloured lenses, Lynette thought. The faded jeans and the grey T-shirt did nothing for her. She wore no makeup and her red hair was tied back with wisps of loose hair around her face.

Who was she? Family? A neighbour? Surely, this scrawny girl couldn't be a girlfriend? Lynette realised she knew nothing about Sam's private life. Somehow, she had assumed he was lonely, but she could be completely mistaken.

Just then the front door opened and Sam appeared, carrying two supermarket bags. He stopped in his tracks for a moment and looked at the two women. 'Lynette. Hi,' he said, smiling a little. He put his bags on the kitchen table.

'I brought some Thai food,' Lynette said. 'But I didn't know you had company.' She looked at the girl. 'Sorry, I should have called, not just intruded like this.'

'This is Jade,' Sam said. 'And this is Lynette.' The two women looked at each other and nodded.

'Jade's here because she's going through a tough time,' Sam said. 'A friend of hers just died and I'm trying to help her sort out a few things.'

'I'll leave you to it,' Lynette said, and made as if to leave.

'No, no, no,' Sam said. 'Please stay. We have plenty of food now. I bought grilled chicken and bread.' He pulled out a package from one of the bags. 'And some wine. Let's go and sit on the deck and eat. I'm really hungry.'

They carried all the food and drinks outside and sat down around the table. The air was finally beginning to cool, and Lynette took off her shoes and relaxed in her chair.

'Jade and I went to the police today and picked up her friend's things. I don't know if you saw the note in the paper, but he died in an accident at the university library last week.'

'I think I saw that,' Lynette said.

'His name was Brent Taylor. He was working late, and somehow he had a fatal fall from the stairs. But there are some strange circumstances. You tell her, Jade,' he said.

Jade looked bewildered, and took her time. While she was talking, she kept her eyes on the table. 'Brent didn't have an accident,' she ended quietly. 'And he didn't kill himself.'

'This is what intrigues me,' Sam said. 'Nobody would kill himself by throwing himself down those stairs. The whole idea is absurd. Nor would you accidentally fall the way Brent did.

'Yet, officially, this is not a murder. It's been written off, just like that. No investigation. It just doesn't make sense. I know the police are overworked and under-resourced, but they still wouldn't label this an accident just to avoid an investigation.'

'Also, there's something about Brent's book,' Jade added. 'The police took it.'

'Brent was working on a novel,' Sam said. 'Jade thinks he was close to finishing it, and he was very excited. He kept a copy on a CD at home, and just before he died he asked Jade to collect it in case something happened to him. So, for whatever reason, it seems he was afraid for his life. Jade didn't think anything of it at the time. I guess it could have been the product of an overactive creative mind, but now it doesn't seem so. But the CD with the manuscript was taken from Jade. A policeman appeared at her house the day after Brent's death, claiming he just wanted to ask her a few questions. But Jade felt he wasn't really after any information about Brent, just the book. He threatened her and she was forced to hand over the CD that she had promised Brent she'd keep. No receipt, no explanation, no –'

Jade interrupted, 'You see, Brent was happier than ever before in his life. He was in a relationship with a guy, but I'm not sure how it was going. Towards the end he seemed to be more into the book he was writing than the relationship. He was really excited. Said it would change his life.' Her voice broke and she looked up, her gaze wandering between Sam and Lynette. 'Brent was murdered. I don't know why, or who did it. But I know he was.'

They sat in silence for a little while, nibbling at the food and sipping wine. Jade's plate was untouched and she sat with her hands between her knees. 'I think I'll go to bed, if that's okay,' she said quietly. Sam asked her if she needed anything, but she shook her head.

'Well, good night, then,' she said as she stood up.

'Sorry for your loss,' Lynette said. 'I hope the investigation goes well.'

Jade disappeared inside. Lynette made a feeble attempt at

clearing the table, but then topped up her wine instead and sat back in her chair. It was getting dark and Sam lit the candles that sat on a mound of melted wax at the centre of the table.

'Anything you can do to help her?' Lynette asked, looking at Sam over her glasses.

'Not much, I think. I rang Saskia. Remember her?' Lynette nodded. 'She's looking into it,' Sam said.

'Strange story,' Lynette said. 'Very strange. I guess everybody must be keen to see the manuscript. Any chance of there being any more copies somewhere?'

'His computer was wiped, there are no hard copies. And no CD. Not a trace.'

'I have some intriguing matters, too,' Lynette said. 'I went to a launch party today, invited to attend the celebration of the takeover of Mahana Limited. It's the largest provider of energy in the country. For some time, the government has been taking over several of the smaller energy companies and merging them, and now they have sold a majority stake to an investment company called Demon Holdings. The single largest sell-off of state assets since the privatisation of New Zealand Rail and Telecom. Huge. But nobody seems to ask the relevant questions. And nobody seems to know who the man behind it really is. Eric Salisbury. Can't even get a decent interview with the guy.' She took a large gulp of her wine.

'In just a few years he's emerged as one of the most powerful investors in the country. With this deal he controls the bulk of the energy production in the country. But there's very little information about him. English, Oxford graduate, a spell working for an American investment bank. That's about all. But I just heard that there seems to be something wrong with one of those minuscule pieces of information. Apparently, he never graduated from Nuffield College, as he claims. Very odd. Why would he lie about such a thing? Nobody really cares where people got their education. Or even if they had one. If you're seeking employment, sure, but not when you're in business at the level he is. It seems so completely stupid. And out of place. And clearly Eric Salisbury is not a stupid man.'

Lynette took another sip, realised she would have to drive back to St Heliers soon and put the glass down.

'An old friend of mine is a dean at Oxford,' Sam said. 'I could ask him to check it out. An easy thing for him to do.'

'Great! I'm going to ask my old friend Louis in London, too. I'll be staying with him when I get there next week for that blasted conference. I haven't seen him for years, but we were at the London School of Economics together. These days he works for MI5 and his job is so secret I'm not sure even he knows what he's doing. Gay, of course. All intelligent, good-looking single men seem to be.' In spite of herself, Lynette took another gulp from her glass. 'Can't get my speech notes together. "Journalism and the new media".' She snorted. 'What kind of idiotic topic is that? I'm working in the here and now, and struggling just to squeeze a decent laptop out of my mean employer. I'm in no position to speculate what the future of media will hold. In five, ten years' time we may not have any newspapers. We might all read our news on our computers. Those of us who are lucky enough to have one. That'll be a social divide, I think. Or we'll have news beamed to our implanted microchips or whatever.

'There may not be any journalists, for that matter. We seem to be a threatened species already.'

'I'm sure you will deliver a brilliant speech,' Sam said with a smile. 'I'd like to hear it.'

Lynette shook her head, but she realised she felt better already. 'Time for me to go, I guess. I'm not sure there'll be time for a lunch before I leave.'

'I can take you to the airport,' Sam said.

'Oh, thanks, but you don't have to do that,' Lynette could feel that she was blushing.

'I know, I know, but I'd really like to. Can't think of anything I would like more.' The truth, Sam thought. Lynette was life, and he craved her company.

'Ah, Sam. Flattery doesn't suit you.' But she felt even better and was glad the poor light hid her flushed cheeks. 'I'll send you some pictures of the elusive Eric as soon as I get home. Might be useful for your friend in Oxford to know what he looks like.'

They both helped clear the table and carry everything inside. Sam watched Lynette as she stood by the sink rinsing their plates. Here, barefoot and with her hair in disarray, she looked very different from the usual Lynette. Younger and more attractive. He wondered why she hid her natural self inside her black business suits, starched white shirts and shaded glasses.

'Now, tell me, Sam. Who's the girl?' Lynette asked with her back to him.

'I don't know, really. She appeared out of nowhere at the garage. Referred to a friend of a friend that I helped in a custody case last year. I do remember the girl, someone I met through my counselling. One thing led to another. I mean, you know I'm not an investigator or a detective. It was just a friendly gesture, helping that woman find her child. I'm not sure how they're connected. Somehow it didn't seem to matter.'

Lynette removed her glasses and placed them on the counter. Sam felt this was a gesture of intimacy, rarely offered. He wasn't sure how to interpret it.

'The policeman who came to Jade's place,' he continued. 'We saw him today at the police station. He was talking to Saskia. And the weird thing is, I recognised him.'

'What do you mean, you recognised him?'

'It took me a while to remember but I saw him outside the house when I found Karen. He was first on the scene. And then I recognised him at the inquest.' He hesitated. 'When we got back I took out my notes from the inquest.'

Sam took the bottle of wine and offered Lynette a top-up. She put her hand over her glass and shook her head. He filled his own. 'I happened on him in the toilets one day, saw his face flash by in the mirror. It was just a split second, and I didn't make the connection then. But I kept seeing him there at the inquest every day. Always on his own, at the back. I suppose my professional self must have functioned in spite of my private self being numb. I wasn't aware of noticing anything or anybody. But there he was, described in my notes. I suppose there was something about him that seemed out of place. He wasn't media, didn't seem to be part of the police, and he wasn't related to anybody else there. Yet he sat there day after day. My instinct must have told me there was something not right. So I noted it down. But everything was so overwhelming at the time I didn't think any further on it. I am sure now it's the same man.

'And more than any other strange aspect of this case, this guy is what I keep coming back to. And now I know he *is* a policeman after all. It just doesn't seem right. I keep asking myself if there's a connection between all that's happening now, and what happened before. It doesn't make any sense that there should be, but. . .' He didn't finish the sentence.

'Why should there be? It's been a long time, Sam.'

I know, it just feels. . .' He shrugged. 'Anyway, I guess it's getting late.'

'Yes. Time for me to take myself home, I think.' She put her glasses back on. 'I'll send you the pictures tonight. And I'll give some thought to Jade's story.'

'Okay, and I'll send the pictures on to my friend in Oxford and we'll see what he can come up with on this Eric Salisbury.'

'Thank you, Sam.'

'Thank *you* for bringing the food and drink.'

They stood opposite each other in the yellow light in the kitchen. For a moment, Sam got the impression there was something more Lynette wanted to say. She looked straight at him for an extended moment. But in the end she said nothing, just turned and walked out. Sam heard her car start outside as he turned off the light in the kitchen.

Just as Sam was leaving the kitchen his mobile rang. He didn't recognise the number.

'Hello?'

'Are you Samuel?' A woman's voice.

'Sam. Yes.'

'I'm Kim.'

'Yes?'

He waited for her to continue. It took her a few seconds before she said 'I'm Sid's sister.'

It took Sam a moment to remember the frail, strange man who lived with Brent. 'Oh. Yes?'

'Sorry for ringing so late, but I've just come back from Sid's. He told me to ring you. He left something with me. Something for you. I'll take it with me to my store tomorrow; it's Read Me in St Kevin's Arcade. Do you know it? You can collect this any time you like.'

'I can find it. I've got something on in the morning but I can drop in around midday.'

'Whenever is fine. I'm open between ten and five. It's a thick pile of paper. Looks like rubbish.'

It must be the manuscript. For a moment Sam had an urge to wake Jade. But she needed her sleep and it could wait till morning.

He was tired, but not in the least sleepy. He didn't look forward to another night of dreams.

He collected his Shakespeare from his backpack in the hallway and returned to the deck. The candles on the table were still burning, attracting moths. He sat down with the book and it fell open where the bookmark was:

*This bird of dawning singeth all night long.*
*And then, they say, no spirit dare stir abroad;*
*The nights are wholesome; then no planets strike;*
*No fairy takes; nor witch hath power to charm.*
*So hallow'd and so gracious is the time.*

I wish, thought Sam.

# 13.

*How dangerous is it that this man goes loose!*

Robert lived in an apartment in Elliot Place, not far from the university. The architects had attempted a Mediterranean feel but the result looked out of place. Sam pressed the intercom; after a brief moment he and Jade were buzzed in and walked up a stairwell lined with faux terracotta tiles. 'I'll do the talking, if that makes you feel more comfortable,' he said.

'What if it was Robert who killed him?' Jade said quietly.

Sam made a gesture to silence her, pointing to Robert's front door. 'We're just going to chat with him. Find out what he knows,' he whispered. 'Let me do the talking.'

'Do you think the police have already talked to him?'

Sam shook his head.

Robert met them at the door. He was considerably taller than Sam; wide shoulders, narrow hips, with a natural sense of command about him. He was casually dressed in chinos and a sky-blue polo shirt. His smile was suitably subdued, showing off even, white teeth. He had let his stubble grow and a spidery tattoo peeked over his collar. Neither detracted from his good looks. 'Hi, Jade. And you're Sam, I presume?' He stretched out his hand and Sam shook it briefly. 'Come in.' Robert gestured to the end of the hallway. Sam put his arm lightly around Jade's shoulders and guided her into a bright and sunny living room.

'Tea?' Robert asked. 'I'm not your typical Pom, I guess, but I do like my tea.' His smile was truly disarming, yet managed to be slightly sad at the same time. Just right for the occasion. There was a natural ease to him, as if he were comfortable in his body. As Jade had said, he was almost disturbingly handsome. Chiselled features, perfect skin, a straight nose and clear blue eyes under masculine thick eyebrows. A very attractive man indeed. And yet... Sam agreed with Jade: Robert was too perfect. The overall impression was somehow uncomfortable.

'Nice to see you again, Jade,' Robert said and made as if to hug her. She stiffened and took a step backwards. 'I'm so sorry for your loss,' he said softly. 'For our loss, I should say. Such a tragedy.' He shook his head and put his hands in his pockets. Every gesture, every expression, every movement was perfect.

The apartment was sterile. Bright sunshine washed in through the large windows, but there was nothing on the walls and the furniture was generic. A pile of books provided the only personal detail in the whole room. Sam looked over the titles, mostly course literature. Robert brought in the tray of tea and placed it on the low coffee table.

'You're studying classics?' Sam asked.

'And ancient history.'

'A mature student?'

'Obviously.' He smiled again and shrugged.

'Is this something you've always been interested in?'

Robert nodded. 'I've been meaning to get around to studying it for years, but haven't had the opportunity until now. Shall I be mother?'

They sat down, Sam and Jade on the sofa and Robert in the chair. Jade sat with her knees close together and her hands on her lap. Robert poured the tea. 'You from the UK, too?' he asked. 'Can't quite place your accent.'

'I was born in Bergen, Norway. But I lived in London for most of my life.'

'When did you come here?' Robert handed him his cup.

'Seven years ago. For work. How about you?'

'Coming up on ten months. What do you do for work?'

'Oh, first I did boring stuff for a government agency. But I've thrown that in and work as a car mechanic now.' Sam felt that he was losing control of the way the conversation was going.

Robert nodded. 'Yes, there's something very satisfying about good, honest manual labour, isn't there?'

They sipped tea. Sam noticed Jade wince as if she had burnt herself and her cup rattled on the saucer. But she didn't say anything.

'So, Brent's dead,' Robert said.

Sam nodded.

Robert sighed deeply. 'I can hardly say I'm surprised. He wasn't taking his medication.'

'What medication?' Jade asked, instantly alert. Sam tried to calm her with his eyes but she ignored him.

'He was on medication for his depression and what have you. I suggested he go on it. It took them a while to get it right and he went through some wild mood swings.'

'I never heard of any medication,' Jade said, her brows knitted.

Robert gave her a condescending look. 'I suppose you didn't have much to do with him over the last few months, did you?'

She flushed and stared into her cup of tea.

'How long had he not been taking medication for?' Sam asked. He felt stupid. He had never been any good talking to people, reading people's expressions. His field had been strategic analysis. Theories, dry reports. Not face-to-face interviews.

'Hang on,' Robert said. 'Am I right in presuming it was a suicide?'

Jade looked at Sam. Sam nodded. 'Yes, the police are treating it as a suspected suicide.'

Robert stared at him and tears welled up in his eyes. 'Excuse me.' He dabbed at his eyes with a handkerchief. 'I can't help but feel partly responsible.'

'Why?' Sam asked.

'Brent was writing a book. He was obsessed with being a writer. You'd know this, Jade. And to be honest – he just wasn't very good. You probably know that, too, Jade. Years he's been at it, and nothing to show for it. He gave me a few chapters to read.'

'And it was no good?'

'Honestly, it was bad. So bad,' Robert shook his head. 'A weird kind of romantic fantasy story that made no sense whatsoever. So, I told him.'

He offered more tea, but both Sam and Jade shook their heads. 'Look, people here in New Zealand just tiptoe around one another. I was brought up to be straightforward and honest. If I was writing something I'd want honest feedback. So that's what I gave Brent. Now, thinking about it, perhaps it wasn't the best way to deal with him. In his fragile state. He wanted me to tell him it was great, of course. He put everything into that book. Now I blame myself for not putting it to him more gently.'

'So you told him it was no good, and then what happened?'

'He stopped talking to me. Charged off in tears.' Robert shook his head, his face expressing a suitable mix of grief and guilt. 'I don't know if you've read it?' Sam and Jade again shook their heads. 'It appeared to be somewhat autobiographical. I say "somewhat" because the characters were idealised, completely unrealistic. Particularly the narrator who, I suppose, was meant to be Brent's alter ego. And the character that seemed to be based on me is a ridiculously charming fellow.' He chuckled. 'Too perfect. The whole thing was embarrassing, really. Plain rubbish.'

'How well did you know Brent?' Sam asked.

Robert hesitated. He stirred his tea. 'Well, all along I think that Brent's expectation of our friendship was, ah, well, unrealistic. Let's say he wanted more than I could give.'

Jade went to say something but Sam silenced her with a look. Robert looked up from his tea.

'I'm not that way inclined. I just... I arrived in this country not knowing anyone. And Brent was very kind to me. I think he took my gratitude for more than it was.'

'How did you end up in New Zealand?' Sam asked.

'To get away from it all. You know, the rat race. Get a new life. Get away from the polluted and overcrowded Europe. And the UK. I've grown to hate that country and the lifestyle. I guess I had an early midlife crisis, or something like that.'

Sam waited for him to elaborate but he didn't. 'When was the last time you saw Brent?'

'It was here. Last Sunday. I hadn't seen him for a few weeks. He came over to say he didn't care what I thought about his novel. He was going to publish anyway. Claimed that he had interest from a publisher in America. He acted really strangely. Over-excited and all over the place. Cocky and confident one minute, shouting at me, telling me how much he hated me, then throwing himself at me and weeping the next minute. I ended up feeling sorry for him and disgusted at the same time. He was clearly unstable. I was even beginning to fear for my life. I'm afraid it ended really badly.' He shook his head with a mournful expression. 'I threatened to call the police if he didn't leave. And that finally got him out of the house. I tried calling him several times afterwards, just to check how he was, but he never answered any of my calls.'

He stopped talking and poured himself another cup of tea, which by now must have been cold. 'And then, out of the blue, I get this phone call from you saying he's dead. God, what a shock! I tell you.' He considered them both. 'But not a complete surprise, as I said. He was in a terrible state, he really was.'

Jade stared at him, her eyes greener than ever.

'Actually, I've got something of his that I should give you.' He hurried from the room.

'Brent didn't kill himself,' Jade whispered, her face a pale mask.

Sam stood up and stretched his legs. His eyes glanced around the sparsely furnished room and landed on the stack of classical texts again. They sat on a small desk that stood against the wall behind the sofa and Sam stretched out a hand, lifted a few of the books and looked at them. Just as he was putting them back, he spied a passport and wallet beside the books. He picked up the passport. A New Zealand passport with a photo of Robert inside. A newly issued passport.

Robert re-entered, catching him at it. 'Is everything all right?' he asked.

'Just checking your pile of books. Impressive, I must admit I don't recognise any of them.

'Then I saw your passport. So, you're an imported Kiwi, too? Took me a long time to qualify, though,' Sam said. 'It's still hard to get in here, isn't it?'

'Yes, I guess,' said Robert looking straight at him.

'But perhaps your parents are New Zealanders?'

'No. I applied some time ago.'

Sam slowly returned the passport to the desk.

Robert handed Jade a leather jacket. 'Brent lent this to me one day. It was raining and I had a nice shirt on. He was kind that way. Really considerate. But I think you should have it, Jade.'

Jade made no sign of wanting to accept the jacket, keeping her arms folded. 'If he gave it to you, shouldn't you keep it?' she asked quietly.

'Well, it's not real leather. I won't be using it. And I guess I have more than enough memories to keep Brent alive. In my mind.'

Sam thought Robert's smile was finally beginning to look a little strained. He was relieved when he and Jade were finally outside again in the street.

Jade walked very fast, obviously upset. 'I could kill him,' she said under her breath. 'I could kill that disgusting, grinning, plastic fucker of an arse.' There were tears in her eyes. 'My Brent did *not* kill himself.'

# 14.

*What do you read my lord?*
*Words, words, words.*

Kim owned a second-hand bookstore in St Kevin's Arcade off Karangahape Road. A last survivor of a bygone era, it was nestled between trendy vintage-clothing shops and swanky cafes. The small shop was jam-packed with thousands of books, but probably not many anybody would want to read. Outside the front door was a $1 stand containing books on New Zealand cricketing highlights from the 1980s, a book on how to deal with candida using pure oxygen, books on insects and ferns, faded cookbooks and dog-eared Ngaio Marsh crime novels. Sam thought the shop's name, Read Me, sounded desperate. He assumed it was Kim who stood behind the counter, almost like a puppet needing the doorbell to trigger her into life. She looked like a plump and healthier version of Sid, but her blue eyes were clear and intelligent. She had short, frizzy hair, thinning at the top, and she wore a bow tie, a check shirt that strained to contain her bosom, and men's trousers held up with braces. 'Can I help you?' she asked.

'Are you Kim?' When she nodded, Sam introduced himself.

'Ah, Samuel. Please, come inside.' She stepped aside and revealed a curtain that opened up into a small back room.

Sam followed her inside. There were more books: on the floor, on the tables, on the two chairs and obscuring the walls. 'They seem to come in faster than they go out,' she said, removing the piles on the two chairs and placing them on the floor. She sat down on one chair and gestured for Sam to sit on the other. Jade hovered by the door, looking uncomfortable.

'I don't always understand what Sid is going on about. He's not quite right in the head, I think. He's had a, well, a rather rough life. Sad, really, he was such a bright child.' She shrugged her shoulders. 'So I don't always know what to make of it when he calls me or wants me to do things for him. Anyway, he rang yesterday and asked me to come round. He never leaves the house, you know. And then he gave me this.' She turned on the chair and grabbed a package from the shelf behind. 'He told me to keep it safe for you and gave me your calling card. Told me to contact you. Nothing much that Sid wants me to do makes any sense, so I didn't call straightaway. Lord knows what this is. But now it's your problem.' She held the package in her hands and looked at him. 'You don't look like the kind of person that Sid would know.'

Until now, Kim had completely ignored Jade. Now she peered at her suspiciously. 'You're more Sid's type,' she said, and it wasn't a compliment. Jade didn't respond.

Sam said, 'Did you know that Sid's flatmate died last week?'

Kim nodded. 'Sad story. Such a kind little guy. Very supportive of Sid. I guess it won't be long until Sid's evicted now. Brent was the one who held him up, sorted things out for him.'

'Did you know Brent?' Sam asked.

'Not really. I bumped into him a few times. But Sid told me about him.' She shook her head sadly. 'Well, here it is,' she said, holding out the package. 'All yours. Hope it's useful.'

\*\*\*

Sam sorted through Brent's loose pages in his living room. He counted 115 sporadically numbered pages. Some of them double-sided, some with red pen marks struck through them, some with notes written in the margin in sprawling handwriting. Brent's handwriting, presumably. Sam was trying to put together a loose semblance of a story. Man meets man. Man falls desperately in love with man. And then it spirals downwards. It was obvious there were pages missing – several chapters ended mid-sentence.

Jade emerged from the deck, flicking a cigarette away. 'Is it as bad as Robert said?'

'I'm not much of a judge of literary excellence, I'm afraid.'

'But you're reading Shakespeare. I saw it.'

Sam blushed despite himself. 'But this is different. A gay love story, it seems. As far as I can tell, it's not that bad.'

Jade nodded. She bit her bottom lip. 'Look,' she said. 'I know what you're thinking –'

'What am I thinking?'

'You're thinking Brent killed himself, in spite of everything. You're thinking he was depressed and not taking his medication. End of story.' She looked at him. 'Please, don't give up now,' she said very quietly. 'Please don't.' She hesitated. 'If you need to be paid, I can find the money, I know I can.'

'I don't want your money, Jade. It's not about money. I already told you.'

She looked confused. 'But –'

'Let's just say I need something to fill my days. To keep me busy.'

Jade nodded as if she understood. 'So you won't give up just yet?'

'No, Jade, I won't. I'm not sure there's anything more we can do, though. But I'll try and get this manuscript sorted and have a read and decide for myself what I think. Whatever that might be worth.'

Jade shivered. 'Are you cold?' Sam asked.

She nodded.

'Feel free to have a hot shower if you like,' he said. She left the room and Sam attacked the messy pile of papers.

Sebastian prepared tea in the kitchen while Byron showered. Sebastian knew just how to make the tea now. Two sugars and then a wedge of lemon on the side. He had just put the tea on the table on the deck when he heard the sound of loud crying coming from the bathroom. It was a terrible sound. Like someone completely inconsolable, a desperate wailing. He dashed inside and found Byron crumpled in a heap in the shower. His face was turned towards the gushing water overhead, but it was clear he was crying.

'What's wrong, baby?' Sebastian asked as he kneeled down and put his hands on Byron's cheeks. 'Shh,' he whispered as he moved inside the shower and slid his arm behind Byron's body to pull him towards him.

Byron didn't say anything. Just cried and cried. Sebastian held his strong body in his arms, letting his hand gently rub Byron's muscular arm. The shower quickly drenched his shirt, making the material cling to his body. 'Tell me, baby. What's wrong?'

It seemed to take Byron a long time to collect himself enough to be able to speak. He swallowed hard several times, and clung hard to Sebastian.

'I have done some terrible, terrible things,' Byron said. He sobbed loudly. 'Horrible, horrible things.' He choked on his words and Sebastian held him hard, pressing Byron's head against his chest while the water kept washing down over both of them.

And then the chapter ended. The rest of the page was empty whiteness.

***

Jade emerged from the bathroom wearing one of Sam's T-shirts and shorts. 'I found these in the laundry,' she said. 'I hope that's okay.'

'That's fine.'

'Any luck with the book? Making any sense?'

'A complete mess. The pages aren't in order, it seems like some are missing and there are lots of changes and comments that are hardly legible. So far, I've only pieced together one scene. But I don't think it's as bad as Robert was saying. So far.'

'I can help you if you want but I'm not all that good at reading and stuff. Never my thing. I used to like maths at school, but reading was hard.'

'Never mind. I'll work through the whole thing slowly and try to sort the pages in order. I'll get onto it later.' He put the pile of papers aside and stood. 'Are you hungry?'

'I can help make something,' Jade offered.

'There isn't much, I'm afraid,' Sam said as he opened the freezer. 'Sausages – and I think there's a can of beans in the pantry.'

'You go and continue sorting and reading, and I'll cook. I think I can manage sausages and beans.' Jade smiled a weak little smile.

'Okay, thanks.' Sam returned to the lounge and continued going through the pages. Only some were numbered. It seemed Brent had printed them out as he wrote. Perhaps he couldn't afford to reprint. Hence the handwritten changes, too, Sam thought.

He heard Jade banging around in the kitchen for a while, and then the smoke alarm went off. Sam ran in to find Jade fanning a tea towel towards the alarm on the ceiling. He took a frying pan of burning freezer sausages from the element and put them under the tap.

'I'm so sorry!' Jade yelled above the screech. By now Sam was laughing out loud. He climbed up onto the kitchen table to turn off the sound. He stood looking down at the miserable Jade. 'That's the most excitement I've ever had in this house,' he said as he climbed down.

And at last Jade smiled. She looked at Sam and she started laughing. They both bent over double and staggered around the kitchen until they stood still in front of each other. They were both breathing hard. Sam lifted his hand and pulled away a strand of hair away from Jade's face. 'I guess we'll just have beans,' he said. 'And there might be some bread in the freezer.' They turned at the same moment and their bodies touched.

'I'm pretty sure I can manage toast and beans.' She stepped forward and touched his face. It was just a quick little brush, but he felt himself blush.

He cleared his throat but didn't move.

She breathed slowly. 'We can if you want to.'

He stared at her flecked, very green irises. Suddenly she looked beautiful. He pulled her close and held her for a moment. She felt tiny, like a bird. He held her hand and looked at her and shook his head. 'You are very beautiful, Jade,' he said slowly.

'But...'

Something seemed to switch off behind those strange green eyes of hers.

'It's not a big deal,' she said quietly, opening the pantry.

Sam tried to pull her towards him again, but she tore herself free. 'It's okay,' she said.

'Sorry.' And they left it at that.

Jade started making the toast, and Sam returned briefly to the papers.

They ate beans on toast on the deck, with mosquitoes swarming around them. Jade didn't seem to care but Sam kept waving them away from both himself and her naked legs.

'I do have a friend I can stay with tonight,' Jade said. 'But –'

'You can stay here if you want.'

Her eyes were on the long shadows in the garden beyond the deck. She shook her head.

'I mean it, Jade. I like having the company.'

'Thank you. I just can't face going home. It will get better. It's just so hard right now. Everything is just –'

'It's fine, I promise.'

They sat in relaxed silence for a while, listening to the sounds of the approaching night. Insects, the odd bird. Distant cars and a dog barking. Sam's mind wandered to Robert and their exchange that afternoon. Once upon a time he had believed himself to be a good judge of people. But he wasn't sure what to make of Robert. A new New Zealand passport. How had he managed to get that so quickly? Surely you needed to be a resident for at least three years first. Or was it five? And Robert hadn't even been here a year. It seemed odd. But perhaps there were special cases, special reasons. And for all his willingness to talk to them, his hospitality and his friendly smiles, there had been something about Robert that Sam couldn't quite put his finger on. A vague sense of something false, a façade. Robert was well presented, seemed educated and he was certainly very good-looking. Yet there was something disconcerting about him.

He looked up to find Jade eyeing him. 'If Brent had been on medication it would have been in his things from the police. Or I'd have seen it at his flat,' she said.

'You might have missed them.'

'I can spot drugs a mile away. And Brent would have no reason to hide them from me.' She lit her cigarette.

Sam returned to Brent's loose pages. He reread the same passage:

```
Byron didn't say anything. Just cried and cried.
Sebastian held his strong body in his arms,
```

letting his hand gently rub Byron's muscular arm. The shower quickly drenched his shirt, making the material cling to his body. 'Tell me, baby. What's wrong?'

It seemed to take Byron a long time to collect himself enough to be able to speak. He swallowed hard several times, and clung hard to Sebastian.

'I have done some terrible, terrible things,' Byron said. He sobbed loudly. 'Horrible, horrible things.'

# 15.

*Nay, answer me. Stand and unfold yourself.*

**From:** Sam Hallberg [mailto:iamsam@gmail.com]
**Sent:** Monday, November 21 2005 7:38 a.m.
**To:** Lynette Church
**Subject:** Re: Re: Eric Salisbury

Hi Lynette,
Just had this from my friend at Oxford. I think you will find it very interesting. Talk soon. Sam

---

**From:** James Harvey [mailto:j.harvey@nuffield.
oc.ac.uk]
**Sent:** Monday, November 21 2005 6:27 a.m.
**To:** Sam Hallberg
**Subject:** Re: Eric Salisbury

Hi Sam,
Great to hear from you. I hope you are doing okay. Would be great to hear more about your life these days. I understand you are still in New Zealand. We are pretty much the same, too, except Mary is finally pregnant, due in April. I don't know if you noticed, but I was appointed Warden

last year. Plodding on with my research. Nothing
exciting to report.
I have looked into the matter, and I think
you'll find the results intriguing to say the
least. Have a look at the attached pictures.
As you can see, your Eric seems to have been
Christopher, aka Chris, Wakenshaw in an earlier
life. He graduated from Nuffield in 1989 with a
respectable degree in Economics. Although he is
a member of the Nuffield Alumni Society, nobody
here that I have talked to seems to have had any
contact with him after he graduated. Are you sure
we are talking about the same man?
I'll let you know if I find anything more.
As I said, great to hear from you. Stay in
touch!

James
PS Any chance of seeing you here any day soon?
Baby due soon, so no travel for us. Taking it
very easy. Fingers crossed this time.

Lynette clicked on the first of the two attachments and the face of a
youthful Eric Salisbury covered the computer screen. He smiled at
the camera with confidence. It looked as if the image had been cut
out of a group portrait. She clicked on the next attachment and this
time she got the entire picture. Eric was the third on the left in the
front line of a soccer team, all wearing Nuffield College shirts. She
read the names below the picture but there was no Eric Salisbury
among them. The name referring to the third person from the
left was Christopher Wakenshaw, not Eric Salisbury. Lynette lifted
her eyes to the window and the view, as she always did when her
mind went to work. The glittering water of Waitemata Harbour was

dotted with cheerful sailing boats. Her eyes returned to the screen as she lifted the receiver to make a call.

\*\*\*

Lynette stood waiting for the lights to change at the intersection of Queen Street and Victoria Street. The gigantic Santa loomed above the Whitcoulls bookstore, his disproportionately large, crooked index finger moving obscenely and one enormous flesh-coloured eyelid blinking luridly. This Santa would scare any normal child for life, she thought. The lights turned to green; she crossed the street and carried on down towards the harbour. She smiled a little as she thought about the morning's phone conversation.

'Hello, this is Lynette Church from the *New Zealand Tribune*. Can I talk to Mr Salisbury?'

The professional voice at the other end apologised and asked Lynette to hold. Lynette tapped her fingers on the desk as she waited. She didn't like to be put on hold.

'I'm sorry, Miss Church, but Mr Salisbury isn't in the office at the moment. May I take your details and come back to you and let you know when he will be available? He's a very busy man.'

My arse, Lynette thought. Not in the office! So why make me hold the line? I'm too busy for this. I should be preparing my speech notes. Or at home, finishing my packing.

'Considering the number of times I've called, I'm sure you have my details. I would be grateful if you could let Mr Salisbury know that I have just received some very interesting information concerning his time at Oxford. Tell him I would value his comments. Oh, and can you let Mr Salisbury know that I'll write an article on him, with or without his co-operation. It's long overdue.'

There was a slight pause, and Lynette was again asked to hold. Not in the office, ha!

'Miss Church, I have just been able to reach Mr Salisbury.

If it's convenient, he could see you here at the office at eleven. He's going overseas this afternoon.'

'That will be just fine,' Lynette said and took down the address.

Lynette had time to consider her reflection in the polished steel walls while taking the elevator to the eighteenth floor. It was not encouraging, and she lifted her eyes to the ceiling only to discover that it was a mirror. She closed her eyes and focused her thoughts on the meeting ahead. The doors opened with a soft sigh and she was buzzed into the reception through the sliding glass doors. She took in the room: a coffee table with expensive glossy magazines on golf and sailing fanned neatly beside a white orchid in an oriental pot; a beige suede sofa and two leather chairs; a large Bokhara rug on the floor, and black and white framed Chinese calligraphy on the wall. For all its discreet elegance, it didn't inspire confidence, as must have been the intention, but looked fleeting and temporary, as if hired for the occasion. Like a movie set. The receptionist looked like a movie star, too. Tall and blonde, of course, with a professional, measured smile and dressed in a suit that managed to look sexy and businesslike at the same time. Lynette introduced herself.

The blonde stood and indicated for Lynette to follow. 'Mr Salisbury is waiting for you in the board room,' she said as she walked ahead and opened a door at the far end of the corridor. 'Can I get you something to drink, Miss Church?' Lynette declined and the blonde left.

Eric Salisbury stood by the window. Today he looked completely professional in a perfectly cut dark-grey suit, white shirt and impeccably tied purple silk tie. He didn't smile or offer his hand; merely nodded and gestured for Lynette to take a chair at the spotless, empty elliptical glass table. 'So, Miss Church,' he said as he sat down opposite Lynette, his hands folded on the table, 'what gives me this unexpected pleasure?'

Miss Church again, Lynette thought, as she pulled at the hem of her skirt. She detested transparent glass tables. 'Considering the many requests for an interview that I have made, it can't be that unexpected, Mr Salisbury.' And not that much of a pleasure, she thought. 'There's so much I'd have liked to talk to you about, Mr Salisbury. Your background, your career. Your interests. Not least your strategic vision when it comes to your investments here in New Zealand. My readers are interested in the business leaders of the country, they demand background and information, and it's my job to satisfy them. But this is a hastily arranged meeting, and we are both very busy people, so let's skip all that for now and cut to the chase.'

Salisbury made no comment.

'This morning I received an interesting message from England,' Lynette said, opening her briefcase and pulling out printouts of the two soccer pictures. 'And I think you'll find this interesting, too, Mr Salisbury. Or whatever you prefer I call you. Mr Wakenshaw, perhaps?' She cocked her head and looked at him steadily as she pushed the prints across the glass surface. Salisbury lowered his eyes but didn't pick up the offered papers. Instead, he leaned back against the uncomfortable backrest of the chair, as if recoiling in disgust. Or did she detect a flicker of fright?

In the silence that followed, Lynette cast a quick glance around the room, landing eventually on the man opposite her. Fake, she thought as her eyes swept over the spotless surface of the table, the pale walls, the discreet drapes. Nothing here is genuine. And you're a fake, too, Mr Salisbury.

'Why are you showing me these? What do you expect me to say?'

'Well,' Lynette started, 'a simple explanation would do very well. Your real name, for example.' She put her hands on the table in front of her. 'Who are you?'

'Miss Church, you are a highly regarded journalist. One of the best. Surely you are able to distinguish between matters of general interest and private affairs. I value my privacy. In fact, there is nothing I value more.' He paused. 'As I am sure you value yours,

Miss Church.' His eyes focused on Lynette's face. 'Just because there is a public facet to our lives, it doesn't follow that we have an obligation to publish our private lives. We have the right to protect our families, our loved ones. Don't you agree, Miss Church?'

Lynette looked him over. That must be such an uncomfortable position he's in, she thought. One arm over that high metal back rest, slouching a little, staring me down. I guess he thinks it looks casual and confident.

She said nothing.

'We all have things in our lives we'd rather keep private. I'm sure, if I wanted to, I could find things in your past that you would rather not have exposed to the public.'

Lynette stared at the man across the table. Suddenly, his suave charm was all gone. He slowly lowered his arm and placed both hands on the table again. His nails were well manicured, but his fingers were short, with dark hair growing down to the first knuckles.

'My private life is not the issue here,' she said.

'Exactly. That's my point. We all have private lives that we wish to keep private.'

'It's a little different, don't you think?' Lynette said. 'I have no interest in your family. Or your personal matters at all. And I don't expect you to be interested in mine. I just want to know who you are and why you're here. They are legitimate questions and they relate to your professional life here in New Zealand. Your private life is of no concern to me.'

The room went silent. After a long pause Salisbury said, 'All relevant information about me and my business interests in the country is readily available from Shaun McGrath, the CIO of Demon Holdings. I'm sure he'd be very happy to talk to you, Miss Church.'

Lynette adjusted her weight on the uncomfortable chair.

'And before you leave, let me tell you this,' Salisbury continued as he walked to the window. He remained there with his back to

Lynette for a moment, one hand clasping the other behind his back, before turning to face her. 'My privacy is not just about me. I can assure you, Miss Church, that you'll discover this quickly should you decide to persist in your enquiries against my advice. Sometimes it's wise to drop matters before they taint you.'

'Are you threatening me, Mr Salisbury? If that's your name. I don't respond well to threats.'

Salisbury looked down at her. Standing, he seemed to have gained a slight advantage, and Lynette scrambled to rise.

'Oh, no, Miss Church, nothing of the sort. Let's say that I am just clarifying the situation.'

'I would say that you are constantly doing the opposite.' Lynette tried to stay calm and keep her voice under control. 'As you said before, I am one of the most highly regarded journalists in the country. Yet in spite of numerous attempts at getting an interview with you, this is the first time I get to meet you properly. And you're not giving me one iota of real information! I find this extraordinary, considering the impact you and your companies have on this country's economy, which I am covering for the country's largest newspaper.' She took a deep breath. Calm, she thought, stay calm. Speak slowly and clearly. 'I will write an article on you, with or without your co-operation.'

'Before you do that, Miss Church, I really think you should consider the consequences.' He walked over to the door and opened it. 'May I accompany you out?' He made an exaggerated gesture with his arm, as if scooping her up and throwing her out.

If he says Miss Church once more I will slap his smug face, Lynette thought. She stood for a moment fixing him in a long gaze, then turned and took her briefcase from the table and straightened her jacket. 'As I said, Mr Salisbury, I don't respond well to threats.' She walked towards the door, avoiding his outstretched arm, and carried on briskly through reception and out through the glass doors to the elevator. Inside the elevator, she sighed and stared at her blurred image on the wall. And to her utter annoyance, she felt tears brimming.

\*\*\*

As the reception doors closed behind Lynette, Salisbury appeared behind the secretary's desk. 'I'll be in the office, Susan. Hold all calls for now.'

Back in his spacious office, he dialled the direct line to Gary Spalding, Minister of Foreign Affairs and Trade. The call was brief, with little said on either end. Salisbury ended the call with: 'This woman journalist – get her off my back ASAP. Before she does some serious damage.'

# 16.

*I must to England. You know that?*

Sam drove his old Subaru along Manukau Road towards the airport. Lynette sat in the passenger seat with her hand luggage perched on her lap. 'Thank you for this. I really appreciate it.'

Sam just nodded. The traffic was infuriatingly slow. 'What are all these vans doing on the way to the airport at this time of day?' he asked, nodding towards the row of white rental vans ahead of them, all with Tongan flags flapping in the wind.

'I saw something about the Tongan rugby team arriving today. All these people must be on their way to greet them. God, they're everywhere! Glad I'm not in a hurry. And glad I'm flying business class. Makes my life a little easier.'

'Finished your speech notes?'

Lynette shook her head. 'Hope to get my head around them on the flight. Again, it's good to be in business class and get some peace and quiet. It must be at least six months since I was asked to give this lecture, and I've only just got onto it. Not like me at all.'

She waved to a passing van with people hanging out of the window.

'I really don't like the topic much, though I think I might have come up with it initially. "Journalism and the new media." God, what a stupid topic! It'll be me trying to look into the future like some kind of frigging oracle.'

'So, what's your take on it?'

'Newspapers will be a thing of the past by 2009.'

'The internet is our future?'

'The internet is our future. Makes for a very short speech, doesn't it?' she said with a little laugh. 'And all this is going to take a week out of my life, while there's so much happening here.'

She looked at Sam. 'That meeting with Eric Salisbury really shook me. If there's a simple explanation for him changing his name, why doesn't he just come clean about it? What's so secret about it? And why those thinly veiled threats? God, he must be desperate! I just don't get it. Doesn't he understand that this will only make me more curious, more suspicious? And more persistent.'

They finally made it onto the motorway and the traffic flowed a little better. 'How's Jade?' Lynette asked.

'I think she's all right. Coping.'

'Any developments with it all?'

'We've talked to this friend of Brent's. Robert Black. Lover, friend, fellow student, acquaintance – it's all a little unclear. A British guy that Brent met at the university. Jade thinks they had a relationship of some sort, but it was more or less over when Brent died. To me they seem like such unlikely friends. And even more unlikely lovers.'

'Another British guy? What's with you Brits? You seem to be everywhere.'

'He hasn't been here for long; less than a year. He doesn't seem to have a job, but he seems to have money. Smartly dressed, expensive shoes, expensive watch, well groomed, all of that. He's all that Brent wasn't, according to Jade. Apparently he met Brent when he signed up to do some classics papers. Seems Brent offered a bit of tutoring and then it went on from there.'

Sam overtook a particularly slow van, and then returned to the left lane. 'What intrigues me is he has a New Zealand passport. I don't know, but from memory I thought you need three years of permanent residency before you can apply for citizenship.'

'Changed last year to five years, I think,' Lynette said.

'Salisbury hasn't been here much longer than Robert. Just over two years or so. And he too is now a citizen.'

'Any family?'

'Robert? No, I don't think so. Single. Possibly gay. Doesn't seem to have any connections here, really. How the hell does a student of ancient history and classics, with no connections and no friends and no employer, jump the immigration queue? Salisbury I can understand: an important businessman with heaps of money. But this guy? I don't get it.' Sam shook his head and stopped at the traffic lights. As they waited he told Lynette about the visit to Robert's apartment, about his apparent concern for Brent and his conviction that he had been on medication and killed himself.

As they reached the airport car park Sam said, 'Oh, we also got hold of the book. At least some of it. The one Brent was writing.'

'What's it like?'

'Not sure. Not sure I'm the best person to tell, really. But the writing seems okay to me. Not the most exciting story in the world, perhaps, but surprisingly well written. Some of it's quite raunchy. You know.' Sam cast a quick look at Lynette and she smiled back. 'I spent all evening trying to sort out the pages, and I'll go through it all again when I get back home and see if I can make any sense of it.'

'You think it might hold a clue?'

'Who knows?' Sam shrugged and found a park.

Lynette checked her watch. 'I've got plenty of time. Feel like a coffee or a drink?' Sam nodded and Lynette tried to protest when he grabbed her suitcase from the boot, but he just smiled and held on to it. He thought he saw her blush as she quickly turned and led the way towards the terminal.

Lynette's check-in was swift, and they went upstairs for a drink. White wine for her, a beer for him. 'I'll see if James at Oxford has more to tell about Salisbury. If so I'll let you know straightaway,' Sam said.

Lynette nodded. 'My friend Louis has arranged for us to have lunch with another friend of ours from the old days when I get to London. John Miller. He works in Brussels these days, covers EU news for the BBC. I hope to get a little background on this meat import quota thing.' She took a sip of her wine. 'After that I'll see my "friend" Ian Clarkson. Not sure what that'll yield, but still.'

'I'll have a couple of days of reading, I guess,' Sam said and saluted her. 'Might go and see Jasper.'

She cocked her head and looked at him. 'It's been a while, hasn't it?'

When Sam didn't respond she let it go.

'Have a great flight,' Sam said when it was time for Lynette to go through immigration and security. 'Let me know how it all goes. Speech and meetings. I'm sure you'll be the star of the conference.'

Before Lynette had quite understood what was happening, she found herself in Sam's arms.

He hugged her with warmth before he let go. She smiled a little foolishly and adjusted her hair. 'Well, you look after yourself, Sam,' she said. She turned quickly and disappeared around the corner.

# 17.

*And in this harsh world draw thy breath in pain,*
*To tell my story.*

The street was quiet when Sam parked outside his house. He took the key out of the ignition, but remained where he was, closing his eyes. He felt tired. The enthusiasm he had felt when talking to Lynette was gone, replaced by a dull sense of the futility of it all. What could be achieved? A naive young man murdered over a manuscript? He thought about Jade and was overcome by sadness. He could feel the familiar headache coming on.

The air inside the house was stagnant and he opened the doors to the deck and went outside. He took deep breaths of the cool evening air and stood for a while looking up at the sky before returning indoors. The manuscript pages covered the entire kitchen table. He sat down and started reading, flicking through the pages, trying to put them into chronological order. There were passages missing, passages crossed out and illegible scribbling in the margins and on the backs of pages. There were whole chapters missing and some ending abruptly mid-sentence. But eventually he came across a chapter that seemed intact. He took the pages into the living room, lay down on the sofa and began to read:

It had been Byron's suggestion that they meet at the Occidental, a posh beer bar in Vulcan Lane. Sebastian felt uncomfortable. Something felt wrong. It wasn't their kind of place at all. And why out, and not at Byron's place? He couldn't understand it.

He was early and sat at a table with a good view of the entrance. He wore a new pale green T-shirt with 'U R why I am gay' printed across the chest in pink. He hoped Byron would like it, but he wasn't sure. It wasn't easy to know what Byron liked, or didn't like. Lately, he had seemed more difficult to please than ever. Sebastian caught himself chewing his nails and clasped his hands around the cold beer in front of him.

There he was! Sebastian's heart started, as always, at the sight of Byron. He still couldn't take his eyes off him. Byron hadn't spotted him yet, so Sebastian had an uninterrupted view of him as he stopped just inside the entrance and slowly removed his sunglasses. He wore a white shirt under a navy blazer, grey trousers so well pressed you could cut yourself on the creases. Sebastian felt his manhood stir and was glad he was sitting down. Just then Byron caught his eye and walked over to the table. He sat down. Just like that. No peck on the cheek. Not even a word. Nothing. The waiter came over and Byron ordered a fancy Belgian beer. Sebastian wondered if he would have to pick up the tab again and tried to calculate how much money he had in his account. Surely, it would be enough. He liked to be the one paying, liked feeling in charge.

'How are you, Byron?' he asked nervously.

'Okay,' Byron said. No 'And how are you, Sebastian?' or 'How was your day, Sebastian?' Just 'Okay.'

He stretched out his hand to stroke Byron's beautiful tanned hand resting beside his glass. But just then Byron lifted the glass. 'Sebastian,' he said, frowning.

God, he was attractive when he looked serious and worried! Sebastian looked at him expectantly.

'This is hard for me to say.'

Sebastian withdrew his hand. His heart pumped hard, but no longer to fill his manhood with warm blood. No, now he felt as if all the blood was draining from his body. His felt pins and needles in his fingertips.

'You know I'm fond of you.' Sebastian couldn't catch Byron's eyes, but they seemed to be focused on something behind Sebastian. What did he mean? Fucking 'fond of'?

'But there comes a time when it's no longer working. A time to end it. While the memories are good. You know...'

Sebastian was speechless. He could hardly breathe and the room seemed to shrink until it contained just the two of them.

'We've had a good time, Sebastian. Hell, there's no easy way to say this.' Byron finally looked him in the eye. 'Sebastian, it's over. I'm sorry. But I hope we can still be friends.'

Sebastian was gulping for air. There was no way he could speak. He stared at Byron.

'I was hoping you would understand. See it the same way I do. It was good while it lasted, but the time has come to break up, carry on. I was hoping you'd agree.'

Sebastian opened his mouth to respond, but all that came through his lips was a heart-breaking sob. He was stunned, frozen, and his lips refused to obey.

Just then a man passed their table on the way to the bar. Byron seemed to double-take as he noticed the man. Sebastian knew Byron well enough to pick up even the smallest reaction. Sometimes, he felt like he knew Byron better than Byron knew himself.

Byron stood up. 'Excuse me a moment, Sebastian. I just saw someone I think I know from way back. Be right back.'

Sebastian watched Byron walk up to the man at the bar and saw them talk, their heads close together. Byron had his hand on the man's shoulder. Were they old lovers? But somehow the other man's body language didn't look right. Then Byron nodded towards Sebastian and made his way back. The other man slowly followed and they both sat down.

'This is Sebastian,' Byron said with a gesture. He didn't introduce the other man, but the man slowly stretched out his hand and took Sebastian's. 'Philip North,' he said.

Sebastian nodded. He was still unable to speak, and struggled to keep his composure.

'Philip and I go way back,' Byron said with a wide smile. 'From our Army days.'

Robert looked steadily at Philip with a wide smile. Philip stared back, but said nothing. How could Robert suddenly smile like that when just a moment ago he had said what he had said? Sebastian stared at him. 'But it's been a long time, hasn't it, Philip?' Philip said nothing; he just looked at Byron. No, not lovers, thought Sebastian. Never. Not very friendly either. At least not Philip. Actually, he seemed quite uncomfortable. Hostile, even. But Byron kept smiling.

'So, what's brought you to New Zealand?' Byron asked.

Philip gave Byron a cold look. 'Work,' he said.

'Oh, and what kind of work are you up to these days?'

'I'm teaching Arabic Studies at the University,' Philip said, adjusting his rimless glasses. He wasn't unattractive, Sebastian thought, just looked a little academic, a little lacklustre. Cropped fair hair, grey eyes. A navy polo shirt and tan chinos.

Sensible sports sandals. Not Byron's type at all. In spite of the situation, Sebastian felt a little surge of relief. Perhaps he had misunderstood. They hadn't finished the conversation, after all. When this Philip guy disappeared they might be able to sort things out.

'I should be on my way,' Philip said, as if he had read Sebastian's mind, and stood up. 'Nice meeting you,' he said, nodding to Sebastian.

'Great meeting you again, Philip,' Byron said. 'We must catch up soon.'

'Sure,' Philip said without looking at him. He nodded again, and was gone.

'God, there goes a nasty piece of shit,' Byron said. 'You wouldn't know it, would you? Those friggin' academic's glasses. And sandals.' Byron shook his head in disgust.

'What do you mean?' Sebastian managed.

Byron looked at him for an extended moment, as if judging how much to tell. In the end, he just said: 'That was the man. That was the officer.'

Sebastian gasped. 'What do you mean? Why would he be here? Will you be okay now he knows you're here?' He started crying despite himself, overwhelmed with the familiar urge to comfort Byron. He reached to take Byron's hands but Byron casually slid them under the table.

'I'm not sure. All I can say is, you stay out of the way of that man. He's dangerous.'

Byron stretched across the table and wiped away a tear that trickled down Sebastian's cheek. Sebastian surreptitiously tried to find Philip within the crowds. But he had disappeared.

'You're such a sensitive soul, Sebastian. Let's have another beer. And give us a smile!'

He lifted his glass in a salute.

***

Sam put down the last page. He was sure now that this was somehow autobiographical. Or at least that the two main characters were based on Brent and Robert. So Robert had been right. Idealised, sure, but still… However, it was hard to tell if the story itself was fictional or true.

Sam went to his desk and started his computer. He searched for 'Auckland University' and 'Arabic Studies'. The one professor in the department was called Peter West. The biography said he had recently arrived from Britain. And his picture matched the description from Brent's writing. Glasses. Cropped fair hair. Sam jotted down the phone number and decided to call this Peter West first thing in the morning.

# 18.

*'Tis well. I'll have thee speak out the rest of this soon.*

Sam walked around the campus of Auckland University for the second time. He passed all the great lecture halls and 1970s science labs and found a small bungalow perched tightly between a parking building and a student theatre. There was a plaque outside: Centre for Arabic Studies. He opened the unlocked door and peered inside. It appeared empty. He called out 'Hello?' and after a moment a man stuck his head out from one of the many doors off the hallway. He wore glasses and had closely cropped blond hair and a serious expression.

'Sam?' he asked.

'That's me.'

'Come on in. I was just boiling water for some tea. Would you care for some?'

'Thanks.'

Sam entered a small office. It was cluttered and had piles of papers everywhere. 'Please excuse the mess. I'm usually quite organised,' Peter said. 'But we've just had exams and I've got all this marking to do. Have a seat.'

Sam moved a collection of folders from a chair and placed them on the floor for lack of any clear surfaces. Peter made tea. 'Sugar? It's rather strong, I'm afraid. With cardamom. I hope that's okay.'

'I'm sure it is. One sugar, please.'

Peter dropped in a heaped teaspoon.

'So you're a professor?' Sam asked.

'Yes. Just finishing my first semester of lecturing.'

'How long have you been in New Zealand?'

'About ten months now.'

Ten months? 'Like it?'

'Nice enough. I guess it takes a while to settle in.'

Sam looked around the room. The shelves held mostly books in Arabic. The desk was filled with papers and books. An expensive-looking oriental rug hung on the wall. 'What made you decide to come here?' he asked. 'I mean, it's such a small country, and the Arabic Department must be very small.'

Peter smiled. 'Yes, very small. Basically it's just me. But I thought it sounded interesting. A bit of a challenge, compared to working at a larger university with a larger department.'

'New Zealand can't be cutting-edge when it comes to Arabic Studies.'

'No, that's true, but this position gives me quite a bit of time for my own research. And more teaching experience.' He stood holding the two mugs of tea. 'I also liked the idea of a change of scene.' Peter's eyes narrowed slightly. He gave Sam one of the mugs. 'Sorry I don't have any teacups. That's next on my to-do list.'

He sat down at his desk and made a little space for his mug. Sam considered him. Another British man fresh to the country. He seemed more skittish than Robert. More reserved, but also somehow more genuine. If Sam hadn't known he had been a military man, he would never have guessed. He looked more like the academic he was. Slim build, pale skin and glasses.

'So what brings you here?' Peter asked, meeting Sam's gaze briefly for the first time.

'I've been investigating a recent death here at the university library.'

'Oh yes. That was very sad.' Peter avoided eye contact again.

'A friend of the deceased asked me to look into it and your name has been mentioned.'

Sam thought he detected a flicker in Peter's eyes. He didn't move or change his position, yet his body tensed and his face became even paler. He said nothing.

'Did you know him? Brent Taylor?'

Peter shook his head. 'I mean, I knew of him. He worked at the library.' He stood up and reached over to open the window. 'I knew he'd died, of course. It's been all over the campus. Terrible, just terrible. I understand he killed himself. Very sad.' He shook his head again. 'Very sad.'

'So you think he committed suicide?'

'Of course. I mean, it's common knowledge.' He frowned and looked at Sam. 'Where are you going with this? Are you a policeman?'

'No. Brent's friend who approached me doesn't think he committed suicide. She thinks the police have it all wrong. So I promised her I would ask around a little. See if there's something the police might have missed. Just to comfort her a bit. She's very upset.'

'Well, as I said, I didn't really know Brent at all –'

Sam cocked his head and looked at Peter. 'Did you know he was writing a book?'

'No,' he replied, licking his lips. Sam thought he looked distinctly uncomfortable.

'Seems Brent was writing something that he was very excited about. Vaguely autobiographical, I think. Are you sure you never heard him talk about it?'

'No. Of course not. I never talked about anything personal with him. He was just one of the many staff in the library.' Peter's face seemed even paler and his skin had a sheen, as though he was perspiring.

'Apparently you feature in the book.'

'Me?' Peter's voice was shrill. Then he tried a little laughter, but it came out more like a snort.

'Yes, it seems you and Brent have a friend in common here in Auckland. Robert Black. And I somehow got the impression that you and Robert might have known each other.'

Another snort. 'Whatever gave you that impression? I don't know anyone called Robert Black.'

Sam shrugged. 'Oh. Maybe I've got my wires crossed.'

'Tell me, this book of Brent's – has anybody read it?' Peter asked.

Sam shook his head. 'I understand it's with the police. According to Robert it's crap.'

They both sipped their tea. 'As I said before,' Peter said, 'I never really knew Brent. But from what I saw, he seemed a little, you know, a little unstable. Dirty and scruffy. I got the impression that he had a history of mental issues. Drugs. That sort of thing. But I really don't know. May just be rumours.' He glanced at his watch. 'Sorry, I have to get going. I'm meeting somebody at Britomart in half an hour. And I don't have a car.'

'I'm heading that way too. Perhaps we can walk there together? It'll give us a little more time to talk.'

Peter hesitated, as if searching for a way out. Was that fear in his eyes? Or anger? Anxiety? Whatever it was, it was clear that he was not happy. 'Sure,' he said. 'Just give me a couple of minutes. I have to collect a few things from upstairs and then I'll be right back.'

Sam waited. His eyes fell on a beautiful copy of what he assumed was the Koran. It sat at the far corner of the desk and on top of it lay a beautiful ivory string of prayer beads. Sam picked it up and weighed it in his hands. The beads were exquisitely carved and tied together with a red silk tassel that held a red stone that, if it was a real gem, must be quite valuable. Sam put it down and took up the book. This, too, looked valuable. The green leather cover was soft and embossed with gold script. Sam opened it carefully. The paper was thin and the wide margins on each page were beautifully decorated in black and red. He was just about to close it when it opened on the last page. Sam realised that this might really be the first page. He had a vague notion that Arabic was read from back to front. On the fly page there was a short inscription in Arabic. But it was the name above this that caught Sam's eye: Kenneth Beaumont. And a date: 21 April 1994. So, not Peter's name? Kenneth Beaumont? Why would Peter have such an expensive item on his desk if it wasn't his? Sam returned the book to its place on the desk and put the beads back on top.

Just as he sat down again, Peter returned. 'I just checked my diary and my meeting isn't actually till tomorrow. But I'll use the time to do some work in the library.'

Sam stood up. 'Couldn't help but admire that beautiful book of yours. It's the Koran, isn't it?'

Peter nodded. 'Yes. My father gave it to me when I graduated.'

'Oh, I see. I thought it might not be yours at all. I noticed it is inscribed to a Kenneth Beaumont.'

Peter kept his eyes on the book. He was silent for so long that Sam began to wonder if he had heard him. But then he looked up and inhaled audibly. 'Yes, it is. Kenneth Beaumont was a friend of my father's and the book used to belong to him. He died just before I graduated.' He drew another deep breath. 'Shall we go?'

They walked together to the library, talking about New Zealand. The change in topic seemed to make Peter far more at ease. Sam asked how long he planned to stay; Peter said he didn't know. The conversation turned to what they both did before they came here. 'I worked as an interpreter for the last six years,' Peter said.

'In the UK?'

'And in the Middle East.'

'How interesting. Which countries?'

'Dubai, Saudi – wherever my skills were in demand.'

'I understand the Army had a need for interpreters during the Iraqi conflict?'

Peter looked towards the library and pointed to the entrance. 'Excuse me, I just saw one of my students go inside. I really need to talk to him.' He stretched out his hand. 'Sorry to have to run. Nice meeting you. All the best with your enquiry. I hope your friend accepts the truth eventually. Oh, what was your last name again, Sam?'

'Hallberg. Sam Hallberg.'

'Sam Hallberg,' Peter said, almost to himself.

'Kenneth Beaumont,' Sam said to himself as he watched Peter run up the stairs to the library.

# 19.

*Am I a coward?*
*Who calls me villain?*


He stood inside the library doors and watched the other man disappear down the road. Then he slipped outside and made it back to his office. He picked up the phone and dialled the scribbled number in his diary. A UK number. A few rings went through, then there was a short silence, a sound as if the call was put on hold, then, finally, a voice:

'What's your ID?'

'Ovis Aries Nine.'

'You're not supposed to make contact.'

'Someone was here. Asking questions.'

'About what?'

'Brent Taylor.'

'Name?'

'Hallberg. Sam Hallberg.'

# 20.

*Before my God, I might not this believe*
*Without the sensible and true avouch*
*Of mine own eyes*

Sam sat in front of his computer. The outside heat and moisture was seeping through the open back doors. A mynah stood on the railing of his deck, its round eyes fixed on the setting sun. The fan turned lazily from the ceiling. The internet connected lethargically, as if it too could feel the heat. Sam waited impatiently. He needed to replace this damn dial-up. Not that he used it much normally.

As he waited, he considered Peter West. His sweating forehead. The startled eyes that refused to return Sam's gaze. His cluttered office. His English accent. His pouring of tea.

The first thing he typed into the search engine was Peter West and then Pete West. Of course, there were hundreds of Pete and Peter Wests from all over the world. He refined his search by adding 'Arabic' then 'University'. A couple of pages featuring Peter West at the University of Auckland appeared. He flicked through them. Nothing of interest. He searched the Pete and Peter Wests in Britain, adding 'Arabic' to the search words. Again, there was nothing of note; Peter West was such a generic name. The search turned up hundreds of pictures of west-pointing signs, or West Berlin, or westerly winds. There was even a series of pictures of an American housewife catching and cooking squirrels. Her last name was Peters and she lived in West Virginia.

Sam rested his fingers on the computer keys. He thought of Peter

West's Koran and the name scribbled on the first page. He typed 'Kenneth Beaumont'. There were plenty of Kenneth Beaumonts out there. He scrolled through the pictures. Gummy-looking faces. A teenager with acne. A picture of a tsunami. And then he saw him. Although he had been searching for it, the reality gave him a jolt. Peter West's face, and the name Kenneth Beaumont. He stared at Sam from the screen. He wore a military uniform and looked straight into the camera.

Sam opened the page. Along the left-hand side of the screen was a long column of photos, each one of a soldier. Male, female, black, white, Asian, young, old – but mostly young British soldiers who had been killed in the conflict in the Middle East. Beside each photo was their rank, a brief biography and a short description of how they died. In combat. On landmines. In vehicle accidents. Helicopter accidents. Explosions. Snipered. He found Kenneth's profile. His rank was corporal, he had worked as a translator for some years before the war and he'd died when the truck he was in drove over a landmine in southern Iraq. And that was it.

Sam found he had been holding his breath. He exhaled. Holy shit!

He searched through the rest of the information. There wasn't much, other than a note that Kenneth Beaumont had graduated from Oxford University with a degree in Arabic Studies. He also found an obituary for a Lady Margaret Beaumont whose son Kenneth had been tragically killed in the Iraq conflict. According to the obituary she had never got over the death of her only son.

What did this mean? Kenneth Beaumont was dead and Peter West was now living in New Zealand. And not even his mother seemed to have known.

Why? And how had it happened?

Sam dialled Lynette's number without even thinking. It went straight to answerphone and he remembered she'd be in the air somewhere. He considered calling Jade but decided against it. He wanted to get his head around this before he involved her.

Could it be that Brent had somehow stumbled upon this information? Or even just a part of it? And if Peter had died in Iraq, could it be that Robert wasn't really Robert either? How much might Brent have found out?

What was Sam to do with this information?

He went back to the page of fallen war heroes. He stared at Peter's photo. Had he faked his own death? Had he chickened out? Deserted? Gone AWOL? Was he forced out of the military because of a scandal? Had he become sick? Had a nervous breakdown? Needed to get away from it all? Did the military know he was here? Or was it a secret? If so, why?

Sam scrolled through the rest of the website. Some faces were fresh and smiling. Some looked very serious; movingly so. Most of them looked young. And there were so many of them. Page after page. And then, out of the blue, there was another face Sam recognised. His hands dropped from the keyboard. He bent forward, not quite trusting his eyes. But there could be no mistake. Those too-beautiful features. That confident smile. It was Robert.

Bloody hell!

But the name underneath wasn't Robert Black. It was Sergeant Jonathan Golding.

Again, a tragic death involving a landmine. Again in southern Iraq. And when Sam checked the dates, they matched, too. As did the platoon.

Could it be the same incident as Peter's? It seemed very likely. Although landmines seemed to be a common cause of death, two such incidents on the same day in the same platoon seemed improbable. Heart beating fast, Sam began to type an email for Lynette. He opened his inbox and found another email from James, who said he had dug a little deeper into Eric Salisbury's past and found something quite intriguing. Sam began to read. At the same time, a silver car quietly came to a stop outside his house.

# 21.

*You shortly shall hear more*

Lynette spotted Louis the moment she came through the doors with her luggage trolley. A head taller than everybody else, and absolutely black, he stood out. He waved like mad, grinning. As Lynette pulled up her trolley beside him, he took her in his arms and lifted her off the ground. She could smell his perfume, still Chanel Antaeus. 'Ah, Cricket, great to see you,' he whispered into her ear. He put her down and looked at her. 'And as pretty as always.'

Lynette blushed, but couldn't help herself smiling. 'You, too, Louis. As pretty as always!' He laughed, that laugh she had always loved so much. It poured forth like dark honey and soothed all and everything.

They walked outside into the grey November London morning and found Louis's car. 'I'll take you back to my place and you can get yourself settled and have a little rest. I've booked lunch at an Italian restaurant close to the office at one. John is absolutely thrilled to be seeing you again.'

Louis lived in Knightsbridge, in a top-floor apartment with a roof terrace. Lynette knew nothing about his current life, either professional or private. As she stepped inside, she couldn't see any immediate traces of a live-in partner. But everything was so tidy it was hard to see traces of anybody living here at all. It was very stylish, though, and very Louis. All black leather, glass and steel. Bold modern art on the walls – several large male nudes – and a gigantic flat TV on the wall. Through the doors to the bedroom,

Lynette caught a glimpse of a huge bed with burgundy sheets. Louis smiled when he saw Lynette eyeing it. 'Well, I'm prepared, just in case the opportunity should come my way. At the moment it's just me in there, though. Now, let me show you your room.'

The guest room was thoughtfully furnished and equipped. The bathroom had a shower as well as a tub, a range of soaps and shampoos that looked expensive, a pile of luxurious towels, a hairdryer, a white terry-cloth dressing gown. 'Love it, Louis,' she said. 'I might move in for good.'

'That's all right,' he called from the hallway, 'you know I love having you around. Take your time, I'm off now. See you at one.'

Louis left and Lynette took a long bath. She had missed a good soak. There were only showers everywhere these days, even in her own home. A good bath healed anything from a sore back to a broken heart. No shower in the world could do that.

She unpacked and did her hair, a time-consuming process. It was a luxury to have time to do it properly for once. When she was ready she called a minicab and went off to have lunch with Louis and their friend John Miller.

Louis had chosen an intimate Italian restaurant. It was warm and cosy, a nice contrast to the bleak chilly day outside. Louis and John were waiting for her when she was escorted to their table. John gave her a bear hug and stood back, holding on to her hands. 'Just the same, Lynette,' he smiled. 'You look just the same.'

'I do nothing of the sort,' Lynette said, but couldn't help smiling. 'And nor do you, John. But I like what I see. You're looking good. It's only Louis that has that Peter Pan gene. Forever a little boy.' Louis grinned and they picked up the menus and placed their orders.

'This is just like old times,' John said, putting his elbows on the table and resting his chin on his clasped hands. He had gained weight, Lynette thought. But so had she. He had lost some of his thick red hair, but his eyebrows were bushier than ever. His grey eyes were the same, though, inquisitive and sparkling. She felt good being with these two men. 'How are you, John? Anybody special in your life?'

John's smile faded. 'No, not since Jill. I guess I haven't made much of an effort.'

'Me neither. Somehow I thought it would happen by itself, that it was a generic part of life. But here we are, all of us single, having turned the corner already.'

'Speak for yourself!' Louis said.

Their drinks arrived and they toasted. 'To friendship,' John said, and the other two chimed in. 'To friendship.'

'So, what about work?' Lynette asked.

'I live in Brussels these days,' John said. 'But I've kept my old flat in Hampstead. Brussels feels suffocating from time to time, and I come back here to recover. Everybody knows everybody in Brussels. It's like a miniature world, I guess. Interesting, but it can get a little overpowering, for lack of a better word.'

'What exactly do you do?'

'Good question.' John smiled. 'I sometimes wonder. I guess you could say that I keep my ear to the ground. I work for the BBC, covering the EU from an economic and financial point of view. I travel a lot. I like what I do. Gives me a good overview of this part of the world.'

The starters arrived and they attacked the stuffed courgette flowers. Louis asked the young Italian waiter how they were able to source courgette flowers in November. Blushing profusely, he admitted they were imported from Australia.

'Ah, hence the price, I suppose,' Louis laughed, which made the waiter blush even more. 'Delicious regardless,' Louis said. The waiter responded with a relieved smile. Who wouldn't have returned Louis's smile, Lynette thought, and watched the young man wander off, glancing at Louis over his shoulder.

They finished the main course of grilled veal cutlets and green beans, and ordered coffee. Lynette and John declined dessert, but Louis ordered a slice of chocolate cake which Lynette and John both looked at enviously.

'John, can I ask you something?' Lynette said.

'Sure.'

'A couple of years ago, I went to a press conference in Auckland. The Ministry of Foreign Affairs and Trade had appointed a special envoy to be based at the High Commission here in London. His name was Ian Clarkson, and his task was to negotiate an increase of the EU meat import quota for New Zealand beef and lamb. Six months earlier, the same Ian Clarkson had been appointed one of the directors of a newly formed joint venture between the government and a privately owned investment company. The joint venture was to be the exclusive exporter of all quality meat from New Zealand. It is not dissimilar to how the dairy industry manages exports, only the farmers have no direct ownership interest in this one – Aotearoa Meat Export, or AME for short – and no say on pricing. This has caused a lot of grief among meat processors, but that's another matter. Off to Europe he went, Mr Clarkson. And lo and behold, now I get a press release and it seems he has achieved what he set out to do. There seems to have been a remarkable change in the EU's stance towards New Zealand and our meat. And it intrigues me how this happened. So quickly, and to such an extent. The increases are substantial. Does this make any sense to you?'

John nodded. 'Yes, it does. There were rumours circulating in Brussels at the time. Some raised eyebrows. From what I understand it was the French Foreign Minister, Gaston Gérard, who was instrumental in convincing their government to agree to increase the import quota. Considering the French attitude to meat imports it was rather remarkable. But Monsieur Gérard was a very senior minister with the ear of his government. And the British were very supportive, too, not surprisingly considering the ties with New Zealand. I guess anything is possible in politics. And who knows what was going on in the background? But, yes, it did raise eyebrows at the time.' John shrugged. 'Gérard retired shortly afterwards, though. For personal reasons, I think. Something to do with his daughter. A tragedy of some kind. That's all I can remember. If you like, I can ask around a bit when I get back.'

They finished lunch and parted. Lynette went straight back to Louis's flat and put her feet up. She wasn't sleepy, but she felt a little dazed. After a rest and another coffee, she opened her laptop and clicked on her inbox. There were several messages, but the one she opened first was from Sam.

**From:** Sam Hallberg [mailto:iamsam@gmail.com]
**Sent:** Tuesday, November 22 2005 11:55 p.m.
**To:** Lynette Church
**Subject:** news

Hi,
Hope your flight was ok and that you arrived safely. I've been busy sorting and reading the manuscript ever since you left. Found one chapter that made sense, sort of. At least it was a complete chapter. I think the book is autobiographical, at least to some extent. The two (idealised) main characters, who seem to be based on Brent Taylor and Robert Black, meet with a third person in a bar here in Auckland. It's an awkward meeting and it transpires that Robert and the third guy, Philip North, know each other from way back, in the UK.
According to Brent's manuscript, Philip teaches Arabic Studies at the university. So I checked this, and found that a Peter West was the only

member of the Arabic Department. But he fitted
the description of Philip North in Brent's book.
Today, I rang this Peter West and asked if he would
see me, which he agreed to do. It was a strange
meeting, though. He seems like a decent person, but
very defensive. Comes across as almost paranoid.
Didn't really want to talk about anything. Claimed
he didn't know Robert. While he left the office
briefly, my eye caught a very elaborate copy of the
Koran that sat on his desk and I couldn't resist
the urge to open it. All in Arabic, of course.
But on the fly-leaf there was an inscription in
English. But not to Peter West, as you would
have expected, but to a Kenneth Beaumont. When I
commented on this, I seemed to scare the shit out
of him (excuse my language). He claimed Kenneth
Beaumont had been a friend of his father, and
had died a short time before he had received the
book. He looked very uncomfortable, and he ended
the meeting there and then. When I got home I
googled the name, Kenneth Beaumont. And I landed
here: www.ourheroesofiraq.co.uk. As you can see,
it lists soldiers killed in Iraq, with obituaries.
And Corporal Kenneth Beaumont is one among those
killed. Only he looks exactly like Peter West!!!
Mourned by his mother, Lady Sarah. If you read the
whole obituary you will see that Kenneth Beaumont,
just like Peter West, was into Arabic language
and Islamic studies. He was a corporal in the
army, deployed to Iraq as an Army interpreter. His
father, Sir Ralph Beaumont, was a diplomat and
Kenneth was born in Cairo, hence the interest in
anything Arabic, I assume.

As if this is not strange enough, here is something
else! I sat there scrolling all those faces of dead
soldiers, and suddenly I recognised another one.
Robert Black. Only his name wasn't Robert Black
at all, but Sergeant Jonathan Golding. And when
I read HIS obituary, I realised he served in the
same platoon as Kenneth Beaumont. And died on the
same day, in the same place! So, I presume that
Robert aka Jonathan was the head of the platoon,
and Kenneth aka Peter served under him as an
interpreter. So much for not knowing each other!
And then I received an interesting email from
my friend at Oxford. But I will forward this
separately. This should put your normally active
grey cells into overdrive.
Cheers.
S

Lynette looked up from the screen. I'll be damned, she thought.
Curiouser and curiouser on all fronts. Then she clicked to open the
second email.

**From:** Sam Hallberg [mailto:iamsam@gmail.com]
**Sent:** Tuesday, November 22 2005 11:59 p.m.
To: Lynette Church
**Subject:** news

Hi Lynette
Here is another message from my friend at Oxford. I
think you will find it very interesting, too. Talk
soon. S

**From:** James Harvey [mailto:j.harvey@nuffield.
oc.ac.uk]
**Sent:** Tuesday, November 22 2005 6:27 a.m.
**To:** Sam Hallberg
**Subject:** Re: Eric Salisbury

Hi Sam,
Some more news. According to a note in the
Nuffield Alumni Newsletter, Christopher Wakenshaw
was killed while on some kind of government
mission in Iraq. It's rather a strange one in
some ways. I attach it here, and you can try to
draw your own conclusions. Seems he died not
in combat, yet he was given the George Medal
posthumously. What kind of mission, I don't
know. It's all very vague. I haven't been able
to establish when he left his career as an
investment banker and joined the army. If that's
what he did. Looks odd to me. The note mentions
a younger brother, Stephen Wakenshaw, living in
London as the only relative. The only contact
details are those of a law firm in London,
Lloyd, Evans & Partridge. I assume they were the
executors of the estate.
Now, I am really intrigued. Keep me posted!
All for now,
James

Lynette removed her glasses and rubbed her eyes. She really was
quite tired. But it wasn't even five yet and Louis wasn't home.
She had decided to try to stay awake until the evening and get
a full night's sleep, and then, hopefully, be on British time. So

she had to stay awake, and in order to do that, she needed to keep busy.

She decided to try to find Stephen Wakenshaw and looked up the London phone book on the internet. There were only two S. Wakenshaws in London, and she ruled out the one who lived in Brixton. She dialled the second number. She was about to hang up, when someone finally answered. Lynette introduced herself and asked to talk to Stephen Wakenshaw.

'Speaking.' The voice was gentle and cultivated, the tone a little cautious.

'I'm a journalist from New Zealand,' Lynette began. She explained that she was in London for a conference. Which was true. That she was interested in UK loss of life in Iraq. Sort of true. And particularly the loss of UK civilian lives. Sort of true, too.

'I understand that your brother was one of those civilians tragically killed while on business in Iraq.'

Stephen Wakenshaw confirmed that this was correct.

'Would you consider giving me a little of your time, Mr Wakenshaw? I would be very grateful for an opportunity to hear you talk about your brother and his tragic death.'

'Well, I don't go out much –'

'I would be very happy to come to you, Mr Wakenshaw, if that would make it easier,' Lynette said. 'But I'll only be in London for a couple of days more.'

'Well, I could see you on Thursday, but it would have to be in the early morning.' He still sounded a little reserved. 'If you would take the trouble of coming here. I live in Belgravia. Would nine-thirty be convenient?'

When Lynette put the phone down she felt pleased with herself. She went to the kitchen and opened the fridge. She wasn't hungry, but felt like a glass of wine. She smiled when she saw that Louis had put a bottle of her favourite Chablis in the door with a note on it: 'Help yourself, don't wait for me!'

Lynette poured herself a glass and returned to the computer. What was the French Foreign Minister's name again? She checked her notebook. Gaston Gérard. She googled him. There were lots of links, mostly in French. She clicked on 'Images' instead. The first few pictures were portraits of a distinguished-looking older gentleman. Impeccably dressed, with rimless glasses and grey hair. But in the second row there was another picture. Lynette clicked on it. It opened in a new window. It was an image of a small group of people – a young woman with three children who looked to be aged between three and eight, Lynette thought. Not that she was an expert. But they were young. The woman held the hand of the smallest child, and beside her to the left was an older man with his arm around the woman's shoulders. He held the hand of the little girl in his other hand, and the oldest child, a boy, held the other hand of the girl. They were all looking to the left, where a casket draped in the British flag rested on a raised platform. It seemed to have been unloaded from a plane, but only a small portion of this was visible. It was a touching image.

Lynette clicked on the photo to go to the website. This took her to the newspaper article, all in French. Lynette's French was minimal, but she managed to decipher most of the article. The people in the photo were Céleste Valentine and her three children Frederic, Isabelle and Marielle. The man was her father, Gaston Gérard, and the occasion was the return of the body of Major Lawrence Valentine, her husband and father of the three children. Major Valentine had tragically been killed in a failed raid on a hostile village just outside Basra. He was thirty-eight years old. Lynette was just about to close the window when her eye caught the name 'Nouvelle-Zélande'. New Zealand. Lynette sat up straight and read on: 'The recently resigned Foreign Minister, Gaston Gérard, who has been appointed Ambassador to New Zealand, will take his daughter and her young family with him as he travels to New Zealand to take up his post next month.'

I'll be damned, said Lynette to herself. This is too much of the same thing. British soldiers dying in Iraq, and new lives started in New Zealand.

She checked her watch. It was now almost six-thirty. She decided she could call Sam; he would be awake. He should be. Either way, he would be in a moment. She took out her mobile and dialled his number.

# 22.

*'Seems', madame? Nay, it is.*

Sam crawled under his desk and looked over the modem with its flashing green lights. He turned the power on and off and wiggled the cord and connection leading into the telephone's wall socket. He tried connecting to the internet again and was successful. Lynette's instructions had been clear. Locate Céleste Valentine and try to find a way of talking to her.

Sam wondered if they might be getting carried away; making connections where none existed. He had to admit there was an intriguing number of coincidences: the French Foreign Minister happening to have a son-in-law who died in Iraq, the Minister retiring soon after helping secure the votes required for the New Zealand export quotas to be raised, *and* being appointed Ambassador to New Zealand, *and* bringing his daughter and grandchildren to New Zealand. Each circumstance on its own might seem plausible. But taken together they were intriguing.

It seemed a giant leap to suspect that the French woman's husband had also somehow survived his own death. They had no reason to believe that his death was not genuine. But *if* – and it was a huge if – he was still alive, they were on to something extraordinary. They had the 'what' but lacked the 'why'. Why were these men in New Zealand? And how was Brent's death connected?

He searched the online White Pages for Céleste Valentine. There were none but he found three C. Valentines. Two lived in the South Island and one in Auckland. He considered their names on the screen then picked up his phone. Without much thought he dialled the Auckland number, deciding to introduce himself as a time-share marketer. The phone was answered by a gruff older-sounding man.

'Hello, may I speak to Céleste Valentine please?'

'Who?'

'Céleste Valentine.'

'You've got the wrong number.'

Before Sam could apologise the man hung up.

He called the two South Island numbers. One was a young dog groomer called Chloe Valentine and the other number was answered by a distraught widow of a recently deceased professor called Christopher Valentine. So there was no listed phone for Céleste Valentine. Now what?

Sam decided to try her first name only. Céleste was a fairly uncommon name after all. There were fifteen Célestes listed, scattered over the country. Three of them also gave professional details: One a dentist; one a nail technician; one a naturopath. No real leads.

He decided to give Google a try. Her name produced hundreds of results. He browsed through them, without finding anything of interest until he found a webpage listing UK naturopaths. He opened it and scrolled down to find Céleste Valentine's details. He clicked on the link to her website, which was no longer functional.

He returned to the New Zealand White Pages and the Céleste who was a naturopath. Her full name was Céleste Marshall and her naturopathy clinic was in West Auckland, in Titirangi. There was a picture of a blonde woman smiling confidently above a list of her credentials – naturopathy, homeopathy, kinesiology. Sam compared the photo with the one of the mourning wife Lynette had sent him. He couldn't be entirely certain they were the same person. The mourning wife's face was partly turned away from the camera in the grainy black-and-white picture. But her name was Céleste and she was a naturopath just like the one he had found in the UK and who didn't seem to practise there any more. It was enough reason to investigate. Sam rang the clinic. It rang twice before being answered. 'Hello, and welcome to Luna Health and Wellbeing, you are speaking with Céleste. What can I do for you?' Céleste! It didn't sound like a French accent, though; it was British, as far as Sam could tell.

'Hello, my name is Sam Hallberg.' Sam had no idea how to continue the conversation.

'Would you like to make an appointment?' When Sam didn't respond immediately, she continued, 'Do you have a particular treatment in mind, or would you like me to run through them?' She sounded pleasant.

Sam made an appointment for a one-hour kinesiology treatment at four that afternoon. She asked him to think about the issues that were on his mind. Preferably write them down. Also, if he liked, she would be happy to do a quick homeopathic check-up. For that, he should bring a list of what he'd eaten during the last three days. Sam hung up and considered what he actually *had* eaten during the last three days. It hadn't been much.

Before he left he searched the internet for images of Lawrence Valentine, UK Army. A photo of a proud-looking man appeared. Full military regalia and a jaw that looked rock-hard. The name Lawrence Valentine also resulted in an article about a raid that had apparently gone 'tragically' wrong, and a subsequent investigation putting no blame on the UK command.

\*\*\*

Sam drove to the clinic in Titirangi. He felt a little giddy. He had prepared a sandwich before he left but had forgotten to eat it. The clinic was on the bottom floor of a two-storey house. It was after school and he could hear kids running and squealing upstairs. When she opened the door, the blonde woman took one look at him and cocked her head, smiling comfortingly.

'Welcome,' she said with what sounded like genuine warmth. 'I'm Céleste. Come this way.'

She was attractive. Slim. Glowing skin. What people would call a picture of health, Sam thought.

'Please, sit down.' She indicated a chair in her office and closed the door behind them. Along the far wall were what looked like certificates of her degrees and posters of human anatomy and herbs. The room was bright and airy and smelled faintly of incense. 'How are you, Sam?' she asked with that same comforting smile, looking at him with an expression of concern.

'Oh, not too bad,' Sam said. 'Headaches, sometimes. And I don't sleep that well. Nothing too bad. I just thought I should give this a try. Never done anything like this before in my life.'

He tried a little smile.

'Come over here and lie down.' She pointed to a table covered with a white blanket.

Sam had a momentary vision of a table in a morgue, but he complied and lay down. Céleste busied herself behind the table, out of Sam's vision.

'Impressive number of degrees,' he commented for lack of anything else to say. 'Are they all from New Zealand?'

'No, mostly from France,' she said.

'Oh, so you're French?'

'I am.'

'I couldn't tell.'

She came around and stood by the side of the table. 'I had my education in England. Boarding school, then university. But I consider myself French at heart.' She smiled.

'When did you move here?'

'A couple of years ago. And you? I can hear you're not a Kiwi either,' she said.

'Seven years ago. For work. What brought you here?'

'A fresh start, I guess.'

'With your family?' Sam made a gesture towards the ceiling. The children playing upstairs were still clearly audible. For a split second the image of his own son flashed in his mind. He couldn't remember the last time he'd heard Jasper playing.

She nodded and smiled. 'They are noisy, aren't they? Maybe I'll just pop upstairs and tell the au pair to take them outside. Won't be a moment.'

Alone in the room, Sam took the opportunity to check out the mounted degrees. They were all awarded to a Céleste Gérard.

He'd found her.

'Now, let's talk about you and I will make some notes,' Céleste said when she returned to the room. 'I need to stress that the kind of treatments that I give should not be seen as one-offs. In order for you to get the full benefit you'll need to run through at least one full series of six treatments.' She held a clipboard. 'I've got some questions that I need to ask you before we begin.'

'Okay,' Sam said, returning to the table.

'It helps me get a full understanding of my clients so that I can help them in the best possible way.' She looked at him thoughtfully. 'And I can see I've got to you in the nick of time.'

'Really?'

She smiled, but he wasn't sure how to interpret her expression. Compassionate? Sympathetic? Or was she making fun of him? No, not that. She looked very professional.

She looked at her clipboard. 'How old are you, Sam?'

'Forty-one.'

She scribbled it down. What followed was a series of questions, mostly health-related, but some more personal. Do you often feel anxious? Do you/did you have a good relationship with your mother/father? With your children? All the time, Sam was trying to find a way to turn the conversation back to Céleste.

'I feel you're holding onto something emotionally, Sam,' she said. 'But this only means we have things to work on.'

He shrugged, then nodded.

'You don't have to tell me anything you don't feel comfortable with. We'll take it as slowly as you like.'

Sam nodded again. This was not how he had planned for things to go. He hadn't found out anything about her.

'Do you know how kinesiology works?' she asked. 'That's what you booked for. Let me give you a little introduction.'

He looked away and tried to work out a natural way of changing the topic. But he couldn't think of anything.

'Kinesiology works with resistance,' she said. 'What I practise here is applied kinesiology. According to the theory of kinesiology, every organ dysfunction is accompanied by a weakness in a specific corresponding muscle. And by testing your muscles, their ability to resist force, I will be able to assess the state of your organs. Later on, we might also try nutrient testing, where I'll explore your senses' reactions to various chemicals. But that comes much later.'

'Sounds like there is a lot to learn,' Sam said. 'Perhaps we could get more into it next time?'

'Oh, but we have a whole hour today.' She looked at him with a slight frown. 'Perhaps kinesiology isn't quite the right thing for you. At least not at this early stage. Perhaps a more general assessment would be better today. What do you think, Sam?'

Sam nodded enthusiastically.

Céleste bent down over him and looked straight into his eyes. Hers were large, clear and grey with streaks of green. 'I'll just do a quick check of your iris.' Sam stared into her eyes trying not to blink. 'Beetroot,' she said after a time.

'Excuse me?'

'Do you like beetroot?'

'It's all right.'

'I can see your liver isn't working at its best capacity. And you don't drink enough water. Your liver might just be sluggish.

Beetroot will sort that out. It's quite nice grated over salads. Or juiced. Do you have a juicer, Sam? It's a good investment if you are really committing to making a change to your lifestyle.'

'I'll think about it.'

Sam looked at his watch self-consciously. He felt like an amateur actor in a community play.

'I'm so sorry. I didn't realise this would take so long. I actually have to get going.'

'But you did book for an hour.'

'I guess I wasn't listening properly. I just assumed it was half an hour. But I'm happy to pay for the full hour, of course. I just need to get going.'

'It's such a shame. We haven't really achieved anything.'

'Oh, but we'll get onto it next time, won't we?' Sam said, squirming at how the words came out. Surely she must hear that he was lying.

She looked at him closely then nodded. 'Shall I book you in for another session, then?'

'Perhaps I can call you when I've checked my diary? It sounds good – I'm keen to give it a good try.' Oh, God, it's just getting worse, he thought. Céleste nodded, but Sam couldn't read her expression. Did she suspect he had an ulterior motive? Hopefully she just thought he was a typical middle-aged bloke who had booked a session at a weak moment, and then chickened out at the reality of it all. Someone who couldn't cope with anything touchy-feely.

He paid her cash. She gave him her card and held on to both his hands for a moment. She looked straight at him with a concerned frown. 'I really encourage you to persist, Sam. You will find that the benefits will flow once you get over the initial resistance. When you allow yourself to open up.'

Sam assured her he would get back to her once he had checked his itinerary. 'It feels like… I think this will be just right for me,' he said. 'Sorry about the mistake with the time. And thanks again.'

He pulled open the front door with excessive force in his effort to escape as fast as possible, and walked straight into the large bulk of a man. 'Sorry,' Sam managed, smiling apologetically, taking in the man's chiselled jawline. He knew that face even though it was now hidden behind a rugged beard and a dark tan.

Jesus Christ! Here it was! The information he had been after was standing right in front of him. Lawrence Valentine. *The* Lawrence Valentine. Another dead soldier living in New Zealand.

'This is my husband,' Céleste said behind him. 'Mark.' She snuggled up to the big man and he put his arm around her shoulders. 'And Mark, this is Sam... Sorry, I don't remember your surname.'

'Sam Hallberg,' Sam said, taking Mark's strong hand.

'Mark Marshall. Pleased to meet you,' Mark said, shaking Sam's hand vigorously. 'How did your session go? Isn't she great?' His English accent was refined.

'Better than her patient deserved, I think,' Sam said smiling weakly. 'Are you another Brit in the Kiwi diaspora?'

Mark smiled and shook his head. 'No, no, I'm a real Kiwi. Just had my education in the old country, hence my posh accent. Not always an advantage here.'

'Mark was one of my first clients,' Céleste said, putting her arm around his waist. 'He was reluctant at first. But I cleared up his eczema just like that.' She clicked her fingers.

'Wow. Okay. Great.'

The three smiled at each other for an awkward beat too long. Sam said he'd call as soon as he had checked his diary, and he hurried to his car. He sat for a moment staring straight ahead.

Another British soldier with a new life. What was going on?

# 23.

*Is there not rain enough in the sweet heavens*
*To wash it white as snow?*

Lynette and Louis sat at the little glass table in the kitchen, Lynette
in the white bathrobe, Louis in his burgundy silk dressing gown.
He had made perfect coffee using the impressive-looking espresso
machine that stood like a miniature factory on the kitchen bench,
and he offered freshly baked croissants.

'What time did you get up to manage to make these?' Lynette
said with her mouth full.

Louis grinned. 'I have them delivered. One of my small luxuries.'

Lynette, shook her head. 'Oh, Louis, Louis.' Then she told him
about the information she had received the evening before. Louis
listened, but made no comment. 'It's so strange,' Lynette said. 'Not
one, not two, but three people seem to have died in Iraq and been
resurrected in New Zealand. I just don't understand it.'

Louis was standing with his back to Lynette, making more
coffee. She looked at his taut bum under the smooth silk. What
a shame. 'Are you sure you should be digging into this?' he said.

'What do you mean? Of course I should! I haven't come across
anything this interesting in a very long time.'

'I'm just concerned that this might be much bigger than you
can ever imagine. And potentially dangerous.'

Lynette looked at him, her head cocked. 'Do you know
something I don't know, Louis?'

'No, no, no. But I hear what you are saying and it sounds...

well, it sounds like it could be part of something bigger. Something dangerous. That's all.'

'Oh, Louis, you've read too many thrillers. There's a perfectly understandable explanation, I just haven't found it yet. And I'll keep searching until I do.'

They cleared the breakfast table and as they were leaving the kitchen Lynette turned to Louis.

'Can I ask you something? How do I find the list of members of the platoon where Robert and Peter served? Is it public information?'

Louis looked at her for a moment. 'Just give me the details and I'll see what I can do when I get to the office. Shouldn't be too hard to find.'

'Ideally someone who lives in the London area,' Lynette said. Louis nodded and they went to get themselves ready for the day.

*** 

The sky was leaden and the air chilly when Lynette stepped out of the minicab outside Clement House. She stopped and looked at the façade. Her years at the London School of Economics had been the best years of her life. These were the blocks where she had moved, the streets she had walked. And it was here that she had met Louis and John. And Sam. Not that Sam had become a friend, really. He had held a guest lecture on global security. She had asked questions, and they'd ended up having coffee afterwards. And because his girlfriend, Karen, happened to be a New Zealander, their paths had continued to cross. She had meant to stay in London, live there permanently, become a brilliant, world-renowned journalist. But then her father died. The realities had weighed down upon her, and she had returned to New Zealand to help her mother. As she stood there, reminiscing, she felt a hand on her shoulder and turned around to find John beside her. 'Thinking about old times, are you?'

Lynette nodded. 'They were good times, weren't they?'

John bent forward and gave her a peck on the cheek. 'Lovely lunch yesterday,' he said.

'Yes, great to catch up. Doesn't happen often enough.'

'Ready for your speech?'

'Oh, as ready as I ever will be, I guess. I just want to get it over and done with. I'm fully occupied with the here and now. Can't really be bothered with what journalism will look like in ten or twenty years' time. Or even five. I guess I'm old enough to have learnt to appreciate the present.'

John smiled. 'Oh, I don't know. I think we are creating the future with every action we take. Or don't take. We are the creators of the world that our children will live in.' He looked at her. 'Well, not yours and mine, perhaps. But the children of the world.'

'Ever the idealist, John.' She reached up and kissed him on the cheek. 'By the way, can I ask a favour?'

'Sure.'

'Would you know anyone who was in Baghdad in January 2002? Someone who would have covered the comings and goings of foreign business people?'

John looked a little taken aback.

'I'll explain,' she said. 'I've been trying to look into the background of one of New Zealand's most influential investors, a certain Eric Salisbury. British. In spite of his rapid ascension to the very top business echelon, precious little is known about him. I tried to get an interview with him for ages, and when it finally happened, it yielded nothing more than a lingering suspicion that he's hiding something. Now I've found some very intriguing information about him, which indicates that he died in Iraq.'

'What do you mean died? Didn't you just say that you interviewed him the other day?'

'Yes, that's the mystery. He seems to have died while on some unspecified business in Baghdad in early 2002, then been resurrected in New Zealand shortly afterwards.'

'Doesn't make sense to me.'

'No, it makes no sense whatsoever. Which is why I'd like to talk to someone who was there. Someone who might have met him in Baghdad. Even known what kind of business he was doing. How he died. Well, anything, really.'

'I know just the person you're looking for. Charles Omura. I've known him for many years. He's one of the most experienced war photographers there are. He's won so many awards I've lost track. Totally dedicated to his job. An unusual war photographer. He still has that passion for his job. And morals, I guess you could call it. Highly ethical. He really wants to show the ugliness of war. The terror. The corruption. The consequences for the ordinary people in war-torn places. I've got a feeling he's in the country now. If I'm right, you're really lucky – he's away more than he's here. Let me see if I can get hold of him.' John took out his mobile.

'Great, thanks,' Lynette said. 'I have to go. Can we talk again after my lecture?' She blew him a kiss and ran inside.

***

Lynette's speech was warmly received and she had a line of people waiting as she got off the stage. Some just wanted to give their compliments, some had questions, others wanted to exchange business cards and discuss future projects or collaborations. Lynette was flattered, but she kept looking for John among the crowd. When she spotted him, she excused herself and wandered over.

'Talked to Charlie,' John said, 'and he's keen to meet up. He wondered if we could come to him, though. He lives in Camden. Straight after the last lecture, at five.'

'Wonderful! Thanks, John. I'll see you here then. I think I'll skip the next couple of sessions and take a little walk.'

'Is that another term for shopping?'

Lynette smiled and waved goodbye.

\*\*\*

Charlie Omura lived in a two-storey brick building in Greenland Street. As there was only one door, and only one letterbox, Lynette assumed he owned or rented the entire building. John rang the doorbell and the door opened almost instantly.

On the way there John had explained that Charlie's mother was Scottish and his father Japanese. They had split up when Charlie was little, and he'd grown up on a remote island off the Scottish coast with his mother. John had often wondered what it would have been like being half-Japanese in such a place. John had met him when he was working for BBC Scotland in Glasgow; Charlie was an up-and-coming news photographer and John an ambitious news journalist. They had quickly become friends and the friendship had grown over the years in spite of long periods when they didn't see each other.

Charlie looked nothing like Lynette had expected. Not that she was sure what she had expected. He was very tall, and his dark hair was wildly curly, standing straight out from his head in all directions. He had vaguely Asian features, but when he opened his mouth he spoke with a thick Scottish accent. The combined result was very attractive, Lynette thought. He smiled and invited them in.

Charles Omura's world was white. The floors were painted white; what little furniture there was, was white. He wore white jeans and a white T-shirt. Lynette was worried that her shoes would leave marks on the floor. As if he had heard her thoughts, Charlie pointed to a row of slippers in various sizes just inside the front door. 'I guess I am Japanese in some ways,' he said. 'I don't wear outdoor shoes in here. I am a Scot in my heart, but I am Japanese when it comes to hygiene.'

'Good combination, Charlie,' said John.

Lynette and John took off their shoes and put on slippers. Charlie led them into the bright, unadorned open space. The only decorations were large black-and-white photographs on the walls.

165

Lynette stopped in her tracks. On the brick wall at the end of the large space was a picture of three young children huddled together. They were naked and dirty, and sat in a pool of dark water. They had their arms around each other and only one of them looked into the camera. The face of the child was ageless. Ancient and new-born at the same time. It expressed such fundamental despair that Lynette felt her heart contract and skip a beat.

'Moving, isn't it?' John said. Lynette could only nod.

'Come and sit here at the counter,' Charlie said and pointed to the high chairs at the kitchen counter. 'I'll make us some snacks to go with the drinks.'

They sat down and Charlie turned on some soft guitar music. 'It's Omar Bashir playing the Iraqi lute. I thought it would suit the occasion.' He smiled and turned his back to them and started preparing the snacks. 'You go ahead, Lynette. I'll listen while I prepare this. And help yourselves to a drink.' He nodded towards a bottle of chilled white wine and a couple of Asahi beers on the counter.

John looked questioningly at Lynette. 'Wine, please,' she said and he opened the bottle and poured her a glass.

'How about you, Charlie?'

'Beer, please.'

John opened two beers and gave one to Charlie. 'Cheers, and thanks for this, Charlie,' John said and sat down again.

'So, Lynette, what's the story?' Charlie said, keeping his eyes on what he was doing.

'Well,' Lynette began, 'I don't know how much John told you over the phone.'

'I just told him that you are one of the world's most brilliant journalists,' John said.

Lynette felt herself blush. 'Well, okay,' she said. 'I'm in London because of this conference, but just before I left New Zealand a couple of things happened that in a convoluted way seem to have British connections. For some time now I've been trying to research the background of a British man living in New Zealand. Eric Salisbury, his name is. In about three years he has emerged as one of the country's most influential investors. And one of richest. Just before I left I had some very strange information from Oxford concerning his education. Armed with this information, I was finally granted an interview on the day I left Auckland. It didn't go particularly well and it didn't yield anything much, other than that I got the distinct feeling I managed to upset him.'

Charlie turned around and placed a glass plate with exquisitely made sashimi in front of Lynette and John. He sat down opposite them.

'Now, this will sound absurd, but here we go. One of the few pieces of information about Eric Salisbury that I've managed to find is that he graduated from Nuffield College in Oxford with a degree in economics in 1989. I have just had it checked. And he did. Only his name wasn't Eric Salisbury then. It was Christopher Wakenshaw.'

'Neither rings a bell,' Charlie said.

'According to the Alumni Association he went into investment banking after he graduated, first in the UK and then in the US. He seems to have done well for himself, and apparently it was a surprise when he resigned and moved back to the UK in 1999. Anyway, yesterday I received another message.' Lynette swirled the wine around in her glass. 'It transpires that Christopher Wakenshaw died in January 2002 while on business in Baghdad.'

'But you think he is alive and well in New Zealand?' Charlie asked.

Lynette nodded. 'A complete mystery. It is definitely the same man.' She took a sip of wine.

'I understand you were in Iraq towards the end of 2001 and beginning of 2002?' Lynette continued.

'Yes, I was. Mostly in Basra, but also quite a bit in Baghdad.'

'Would you have known or at least recognised the other international people who were in Baghdad around that time?'

'Not sure. I stayed in the Rixos al Rasheed every now and then when I was back in Baghdad. But I kept to myself, and I came and went. Some business people seemed to stay for extended periods, and I guess many got to know each other. I wasn't one of those.'

Lynette opened her purse and pulled out a folded piece of paper. 'Here are some pictures of Eric Salisbury. Or whatever his name is.' She gave Charlie the paper.

He looked at it for a moment. 'I recognise him,' he said. 'But I never knew his name. He was one of the people that seemed to spend longer periods in the hotel. But like me, he didn't belong to a group. I only ever saw him on his own. He used to have his own reserved table in the dining room. I remember talking about him to a journalist after the news of the OFF scandal broke.'

'OFF?' Lynette asked.

'Oil for Food. The UN-managed scheme to allow Iraq to sell oil for essential foods and medical supplies, in spite of the oil embargo.'

'Yes, I remember,' Lynette said. 'I just wasn't familiar with the acronym. It didn't work so well, did it?' Charlie shook his head. 'I seem to remember that the abuse of the scheme allowed Saddam Hussein to sell oil to buy weapons and build bunkers and palaces. And it implicated UN staff, all the way to the very top, didn't it?'

'Yes, it was a complete disaster,' said Charlie. 'But personally, I think the UN were only puppets and the money that staff skimmed, however large the amounts may seem, was peanuts compared to the serious abuse of the scheme. The whole thing was politically driven, I think. And it did its job. Destroyed a country that had only just managed to pull itself out of misery. From complete economic ruin in 1996, Iraq had managed to build itself up and by 2002, on the eve of the invasion, Baghdad was a city booming with business. The streets were safe, the restaurants full. Sure, it was a dictatorship that executed gross tyranny. But compare that to Baghdad of today – the devastation. A whole country in ruins. It is a human tragedy on a colossal scale.'

They were silent and the lute music filled the room. Lynette felt a little dizzy and put her glass back on the table. Must be the jetlag, she thought.

'Anyway, shortly after the news broke, I was having dinner with Leila Eghian, a friend who had covered Iraq since the Gulf War. We started talking about the people staying at the Rixos al Rasheed. Somehow, people you meet in places like that seem to have some common traits, whether they are diplomats, journalists or business people. Or even photographers.' Charlie smiled a little. 'We're a bit like junkies, seeking ever-higher highs, ever more excitement. And we flock to places like Baghdad. We sit in hotels like the Rixos al Rasheed. We take in the luxurious dining room with its heavy drapes and crystal chandeliers. But that's not what excites us. It's the fact that we can hear the distant sounds of the war, feel the ground shake, hear the clinking of the chandeliers above us. We like it more than we would like a similar dining room in a normal environment. We love it; we're addicted to the rush of adrenaline that it causes.

'Anyway, that evening we were back at the Rixos, Leila and I. We talked about the news, of course, and started talking about old times. Wondering if we should have been more alert. Understood better what was going on. Somehow the conversation turned to people we had met in Baghdad, and Leila mentioned that man we both recognised but didn't know. I remembered that we had jokingly referred to him as Mr Bond. I suspected that Leila might have noticed him for reasons different from mine. He was a good-looking guy, I guess, and always immaculately dressed. Unlike most of the others in Baghdad. I think he did arouse a bit of mild curiosity, but that was all. I don't think people were that interested. And people kept coming and going, few staying long enough to really care about anybody else. However, that evening, when Leila and I were sitting there in Baghdad, she nodded at the table where he used to sit and said, "I wonder if that guy had something to do with it. He always seemed... Well, I don't know how to explain it. As if he was somehow in another league. Not like the contractors who were chasing new business, or the business people who were chasing their money. Or the diplomats. He stood out, in a discreet way, if you see what I mean. It would make sense to me if he had something to do with it."

'I have the utmost respect for Leila's experience and intuition. After all, they have kept her alive while she's gathered information in some of the world's most dangerous war zones.'

'Interesting,' Lynette said. 'Very interesting.'

'I think it's still unclear to what extent the British abused the scheme. It's estimated that the value of the flow of oil under the scheme was worth fifteen billion US dollars a year. More money than it is possible to envisage. At least for me. More than five times the UN's annual budget. Just stop and consider that. The temptation to get their hands on even just a tiny portion was irresistible to even the most noble UN staff, politicians and business people. Everybody was in there, trying to grab a morsel of the cake. But it seems like the British mostly stuck to the political use of the scheme, not so much financial. At least that's the official story. Which, as we all know, doesn't mean there wasn't something going on. The French did it, the Russians, the Chinese.' Charlie shrugged. 'You wouldn't need to arrange many successful under-the-table oil deals with Saddam to make enough commission to live comfortably forever after.'

'Are you saying that you think that it could be possible that Eric was in Iraq to negotiate the illegal trade of oil for the UK government?'

'I have no idea, but, yes, I guess it could very well be true. Stranger things have happened.'

'And his sudden "death" would be a way of taking him out before the scandal broke?'

'It's possible, isn't it?' John said. 'Fascinating theory. Imagine that little fairytale country of yours providing a haven for a fugitive from international corruption of the worst kind.'

'Fairytales are often grim, John,' Lynette said. 'Very grim.'

*** 

Lynette let herself in as quietly as she could. She wasn't sure what hours Louis kept, and it wasn't very late. But it *felt* late. So much had happened and she was tired. But when she opened the front door she could hear the TV going in the living room. Or a film. Possibly something she shouldn't see, so she made a point of making herself heard. 'Hi, Louis, I'm home!' she called out.

'Welcome home, Cricket,' he called back.

Lynette hung up her coat and took off her shoes. She thought about what Charlie had said about shoes and hygiene, and decided she should adopt the rule when she went home. No outdoor shoes indoors. She walked into the living room and sank down on the sofa beside Louis. 'What are you watching?'

'Not sure, I just turned it on. Some crappy American crime series, I think.' He took the remote and turned it off. And with another remote he turned on some music and Abba's 'Dancing Queen' filled the room. 'Still the same music?' Lynette asked, laughing.

Louis grinned. 'Till they make something better.' He turned down the volume. 'How was your day? Did the speech turn out all right?'

'It did, actually. And then I had an interesting meeting with a friend of John's, Charles Omura, a war photographer. John took me to his house and we had drinks and talked about Iraq.'

'Charming,' Louis said. Lynette threw a cushion at him.

'Be serious for a minute, Louis.'

'Yes, Cricket,' he said and sat up primly with his knees tight together.

'Charlie was in Baghdad at the time Eric Salisbury was. He didn't know him, but he recognised him. And he had some interesting theories to do with the OFF scheme.'

Louis abruptly stood up. 'A drink?' Lynette shook her head and he poured himself a whisky. A large one. 'I said this morning that perhaps you are on to something that's too big for you,' he said.

'What do you mean?'

'Something that could potentially be really dangerous. Something you had better stay out of.'

'Can I change my mind about that drink? White wine, please.'

She sipped the Chablis and thought for a moment. Did Louis know more than he was able to convey? She knew his work was very secret and she had never tried to pry. It was an unspoken rule of their friendship.

'Did you manage to find any members of that platoon?' she asked instead.

'Yes,' Louis said. 'I'll get the list.' He disappeared into his study and came back with a piece of paper. 'Only five live in the greater London area. Two more have died, one in Iraq, one in a traffic accident, and the others are scattered around the country.' He gave her the paper.

'Thanks, Louis, I really appreciate it.'

Louis returned to the sofa and they sat in silence, listening to the music and sipping their drinks until Lynette excused herself and went to bed. When she eventually fell asleep she dreamt that she was running across a desert with sand lifting around her, obscuring everything.

# 24.

*You shortly shall hear more*

Sam stood in the shower letting the hot water run over his body. His skin was blotched red and white. It clung to the muscle and bones and sagged in places. His mind was elsewhere, though. He was going through what had happened.

Brent had been killed. There was no doubt in Sam's mind any more.

Brent had written a homoerotic novel about a Brit whom he had named Byron. This man now seemed to be Robert and, along with at least three other men, he was now living in New Zealand under a false identity.

Robert/Byron could have found out what Brent was writing. He could have felt threatened by the content. But if it was biographical, surely Robert must have provided his back story? So, what could be in it that concerned him so much that he would kill Brent? Or have him killed? It sounded completely unbelievable, but it *was* possible. Or could it be Peter? Perhaps *he* was worried about the contents of the book? *If* the story was biographical. But how could a love story, even if it was a homosexual one, pose such a threat? Especially when written by someone who had never managed to have anything published? Sam just couldn't make sense of it. Had any of them even read the book? Had *anybody* read it? By the look of the crumpled papers, it had been sitting in Brent's backpack for a long time. Robert claimed to have seen just enough to deem it rubbish, and Peter claimed not to have known Brent, much less read his book. Sure, there seemed to be bits missing, but for all Sam knew those bits might never have been written. There were chapters that ended in mid-sentence, which indicated that there were pages missing, pages Brent might have written but never printed. Or perhaps he had discarded them, planning to replace them? He might have run out of ink or paper when printing. It was hard to know. Most of all, it was hard to know how this seemingly innocent love story could have been the reason for a brutal murder.

Sam got out of the shower and towelled himself vigorously. Who had made it possible for Robert and Peter to arrive in New Zealand with new identities and new passports? And were they even connected? They might not have anything to do with each other. People had perfectly legitimate reasons for changing their names, didn't they? Though it did seem that they had had some connection in the past, although Peter denied it.

And why here, why New Zealand?

A towel slung around his waist, he called up the second-hand bookstore in St Kevin's Arcade. Kim answered after one ring.

'Hello, it's Sam.'

'Sam who?'

'Sam Hallberg. Friends with Sid. You gave me those documents, remember?'

'Oh, yes, of course, Samuel. What was it?'

'It's a manuscript. Or part of a manuscript. For a novel. Sid's flatmate Brent was working on it when he died.'

'Oh, how interesting. Any good?'

'It is. In its own way. Listen, there seem to be a lot of pages missing. I wondered if you might still have some. If Sid might have given you more than this lot.'

'No, that was how he gave it to me. In that bag. I never even opened it. Sorry, no, there is nothing more. At least not here.'

'Do you think Sid could still have some? Or could he have given the rest to someone else?'

'Why would he do that? But anything is possible. He's not quite with it any more. As you know. Your best bet would still be to ask him.'

'I suppose I could. He doesn't have a phone, does he?'

'Actually, he does. Not that it will do you any good. He doesn't use it. Never answers. Says he thinks it's tapped. He believes somebody, Big Brother or God knows who, is listening in. You'll have to contact him the old-fashioned way. Face to face. Actually, it would be good if you could pop in. I haven't heard from him for a couple of days.'

Sam thanked Kim for her time then called Jade. It had been days since he'd talked to her. The phone went straight to answerphone. He asked how she was, said he felt they should talk, that he had some news for her.

He got dressed and drove to Grafton to see Sid. No one answered the door when he knocked. He hesitated for a moment then let himself in. It was bright outside and so dark inside.

'Hello,' he called out. There was silence apart from a buzzing fly hovering over some dark mound in the corner. 'Sid?'

'Hello.'

Sam jerked back. He was about to cry out but controlled himself. Sid was standing before him, less than a metre away, in the shadows. 'Sorry, mate. You gave me a fright.'

Sid didn't say anything.

'Are you all right?'

No response. Sam could barely make out Sid's features in the darkness. 'Do you remember me? I'm Sam, Brent's friend. I was here the other day, remember? Bought you cigarettes.'

There was still no reply, but Sid turned, walked down the hall and disappeared into his room. Sam followed. The room stank worse than last time.

'How are you doing?' No reply. 'Is anybody helping you now

that Brent isn't around any more?' Sam asked, trying to breathe through his mouth.

Sid said something that came out as 'Mmmshowsh.'

'Sorry?'

'Meals on Wheels.'

'Oh, good,' Sam said.

Sid sat on his bed and stared at Sam. He looked much worse than last time. His clothes were stained and the smell was overwhelming. 'Perhaps I should call Kim?' Sam said.

Sid just kept staring at him, his pale rheumy eyes unblinking. 'They're listening.'

'Who's listening?'

'On the phones. They listen. So I don't answer the phone.'

'Who's listening, Sid?'

Sid held a finger to his mouth to silence Sam. He scanned the room. 'There might be microphones in here,' he whispered. 'I've searched through everything but couldn't find them. They came knocking.'

'Who came knocking?'

'I didn't answer the door that time.'

Sam picked up some rubbish. A magazine, its pages screwed up into tiny balls. He found a plastic bag and put them into it. 'What are you doing?' Sid asked.

'Just cleaning up a little.' He looked through a pile of community newspapers and real-estate flyers. Words had been circled with red pen. He binned it all.

'I don't want you to do that,' Sid said in a childish, whimpering voice.

'Why do you need all these old brochures? You can hardly move in here for all the rubbish.'

Sid said nothing.

'Listen, I got the bag with Brent's writing in it that you left with Kim.'

Sid gave a sharp nod, and suddenly there was a glimmer of intelligence in the dull eyes.

'But it looks like there are pages missing. It's not complete. Do you still have any of the missing pages?'

Sid shook his head.

'Do you have any idea of where the missing pages might be? What might have happened to them? Did Brent hold on to them, do you think?'

Sid shook his head again. Sam looked around Sid's room. It was truly disgusting, not fit for a human dwelling. It might even be a health hazard. 'Shall I help you tidy up a little here?' he asked Sid, who was still sitting in the same position on the bed. There was no response, so Sam set to work. It was hard to know where to begin. He found a few crumpled supermarket bags and started to throw things into them. But his efforts barely made a dent.

And Sid didn't move. He seemed to have sunk a little further into the bed, hunched over and immobile.

Sam decided to call Kim and update her on the situation. He lifted the telephone, which made Sid show signs of life. 'Careful with that,' he said without turning his head.

'Ooh. Hello, Samuel. Of course, I'll be over in a heartbeat. Just let me finish up here. I'm rushed off my feet, believe it or not. There's a sci-fi convention happening down the road. I'm selling Doctor Who novels like hot cakes. Hope you're still there when I come over. Toodle-oo.'

Sam finished his futile tidying-up exercise and put the full bags by the door. The last item he took from the sofa was a pile of unsorted papers, mostly menus from takeaway outlets that did home deliveries. Just as he was about to dump the pile into the plastic bag, he caught sight of what looked like printed sheets. He carefully extricated them. They looked as though they had been wet, and some pages were stuck together. The names Byron and Sebastian were scattered across the pages. He carefully peeled the sheets apart. Several pages down a word caught his eye: 'Iraq'. He found the top of the chapter, and read.

Byron lay in Sebastian's arms and wept. Sebastian brushed the lustrous brown hair from his face. 'Talk to me, baby.'

'I can't.' Byron was trying to hold back his tears, and it broke Sebastian's heart to watch.

'You can trust me, you know you can. I won't tell. Anything you say is safe with me. Surely you know that, baby. You know I've got your back.' He then gave him the sweetest kiss on his forehead.

Byron sat up and brushed the tears from his eyes. 'You can never tell anybody. Never.'

'I won't. You know I won't.'

Sebastian tried to take Byron's hand, but he quickly pulled it back. 'I've killed someone,' he said slowly.

Sebastian gasped.

'I've killed several people.'

'In the war? You mean in the war, don't you?'

Byron nodded. 'Although it wasn't my hands. My finger on the trigger. My boot. I'm still guilty. I watched it happen. And I did nothing. I was so fucking pathetic, Seb.' He started crying again. Sebastian stretched out his arms and pulled him to his chest. He could feel Byron's tears drip and trail down the sides of his chest.

'He made me look. I had to stand there and watch and there was nothing I could do.'

'Who did, Byron? Who did this to you?'

Byron was crying into Sebastian's chest.
Then slowly he looked up at Sebastian and their
eyes locked. 'My officer. For some reason the
psychopathic motherfucker chose me as his toy.
He knew exactly how to hurt me the most, how to
cause me the worst pain. And there was nothing
I could do.'

Just listening made Sebastian weep, too.

'Who were the people he murdered?' Sebastian
asked. 'Enemy soldiers, weren't they? I mean,
these things happen in wars, don't they?'

Byron's eyes were red, tears trembling on his
eyelashes. He shook his head, and whispered,
'No, Seb. They were ordinary people. Women
and children. He cut babies out of pregnant
women. Crushed the heads of babies in front of
their mothers. Raped mothers in front of their
children.' Byron sobbed. 'And he made me watch.
Made me stand and watch as he raped them.'

Sebastian held Byron in his arms. 'Shhh. There
was nothing you could do. It wasn't your fault.
And with time the memories will fade. I'll help
you. I'll always be here for you.' He kissed the
top of Byron's head and held him hard against
his body. 'Tell me, Byron. Tell me what happened
to you in Iraq.'

And Byron began to talk.

Sam turned the paper over, but there was nothing more. 'Are you
sure you don't have any of the missing papers?' he asked Sid.

'I gave them to the Meals on Wheels lady,' he said, suddenly
clear and articulate. 'I gave them to Doris to keep safe.'

'I really need to read them, Sid. Do you think you can get them back? Is there any way I can contact Doris?'

'The number's over there,' Sid nodded towards the door. And there, on the wall was a little card with the phone number for Doris Palmer.

'I would really like you to tell Doris that it's okay for her to give me the papers.' But Sid had returned to his own world.

'Can I use your phone, Sid, and call your Meals on Wheels lady?'

Sid looked at Sam with scared eyes. 'Be careful with that phone.'

'I will be,' said Sam. 'I will be.'

Doris Palmer had a lovely melodious voice and spoke on a constant up-note. Yes, she had Mr Fielding's parcel. Yes, she would happily hand it over. In fact, she wasn't that far away. She lived in a townhouse in Howe Street with her cat Gloria, and it would be no trouble at all to pop over right away. Gloria could look after herself. And Mr Fielding could do with a little extra visit. Such a lovely man, so interesting.

Sam put down the receiver and looked at the lovely, interesting man who sat hunched on the bed. 'Doris is coming over with the papers,' he said, but it had no effect on Sid.

Sam resumed picking up rubbish. He focused on the small area around the sofa, managed to find a few more empty plastic bags and began to fill them. There were remnants of an assortment of meals. He lifted a particularly smelly paper plate only to see cockroaches scatter in different directions. There were clothes and shoes but he avoided touching those, and was pleased to finally hear a knock on the door.

'Whoohoo! It's me, Doris,' a voice called out.

Sid abruptly came to life. He answered the door, smiling. 'Thank you, thank you, thank you,' he said.

'Can I come inside, Mr Fielding?' Doris asked and Sid slowly stepped aside to let her in. She was a petite, delicately built woman with short, curly hair dyed coal black and similarly black glittering eyes. She wore a floral dress, a red sunhat and Birkenstock sandals. 'Here it is, Mr Fielding,' she said and held out the package.

Sid nodded to Sam and he took the package. 'Thank you very much,' he said.

'No trouble at all,' Doris said. 'Now, Mr Fielding, since I'm here, we might as well do a little tidy up. What do you say?' She smiled and patted Sid's arm. And to Sam's astonishment Sid gave her a peck on the cheek.

'Right,' Sam said. 'I'll be on my way. You take care, Sid, and we'll be in touch. Nice to meet you, Mrs Palmer.' Sam nodded.

'Doris, it's Doris,' she said smiling broadly. 'Lovely to meet you.'

Sam stood a moment outside the gate, clutching the package. He looked forward to reading it.

# 28.

*It must be shortly known to him from England*
*What is the issue of the business there*

It was still dark when Lynette woke up and for a moment she had no idea where she was. Then her dreams faded away and she was back in the guestroom in Louis's flat. She turned on the light and checked the time: 5.43. At least an hour too early. But it was no use trying to go back to sleep; she was wide awake. She sighed and got up and wrapped the wonderful bathrobe around her again. She tiptoed into the kitchen but didn't dare touch the espresso machine. None of the cupboards contained any instant coffee, but she found tea bags and filled the jug and turned it on. She found a pile of old newspapers in a basket in the living room and picked up a copy of the *Times*. She flicked through the pages in search of the crossword, but her eyes landed on another kind of puzzle. Sudoku. She had never seen or heard of it before, but she read the rules and decided to give it a try. She sat down at the kitchen table with her cup of tea, and grabbed a pencil from a jar on the windowsill.

She was soon so engrossed in the puzzle that she didn't hear Louis enter. He stood in the doorway looking at her, smiling, holding her mobile. 'I heard it ring in your room,' he said and sat at the table. 'Up early?'

'Jetlag, I suppose,' Lynette grabbed the mobile. 'But I feel okay. Slept like a baby all night, so I should be fine today.' She checked the display of missed calls. Sam. She excused herself and went back to her room to call him back.

He answered on the first signal.

'Sorry, I just missed your call.'

'I hope I didn't wake you up.'

'No, no, I've been up for a couple of hours. Jetlag.'

'I thought I should give you a ring rather than send an email. I found Céleste Valentine. Had to have a session of applied kinesiology in order to get to meet her.'

Lynette laughed. 'Good for you.'

'She looked into my eyes and saw my liver,' Sam said. 'But then, just as I was leaving, her husband came home. We bumped into each other in the doorway, actually. And I recognised him immediately. Lynette, he's our dead Lawrence!'

'I had a feeling he would be,' Lynette said. 'What's his new name?'

'Mark Marshall. Speaks posh English like an officer in the British Army should. But claims he's a Kiwi educated in England.'

'Well, well. Curiouser and curiouser. That takes us to four Brits "killed" in Iraq and now very much alive in New Zealand. It can't be a coincidence.'

'Of course not,' Sam said. 'But be careful when you ask around, Lynette. I feel uneasy about the whole thing. Brent's murder – yes, I'm convinced he was murdered. Robert and Peter. Eric Salisbury. And now Mark Marshall. What's the connection, other than Iraq? Salisbury and the French woman don't seem to be connected with each other, or with Robert and Peter.

'And then there's Brent's manuscript,' he continued. 'I read another page today. It mentioned the Robert character witnessing several rapes and other atrocities in the war. Horrific war crimes. Surely Brent couldn't have made it up.'

'War crimes...' Lynette suddenly thought of what Charlie Omura had said about OFF. 'I had a meeting yesterday with someone who thinks it possible that Eric was secretly negotiating oil deals for the UK government in breach of the Oil for Food program. Louis keeps telling me to be careful because this is big. And Lord knows it could be huge.'

'What should we do?'

'We'll see what comes out of my meetings here. I'll keep you in the loop, Sam.'

'Same here. I'll be in touch if anything happens here. You take care, Lynette. Be careful.'

'You, too. Talk soon.'

Lynette sat on her bed with the phone in her hand. I'll be damned, she thought. The French Foreign Minister didn't just move his daughter and grandchildren to New Zealand, but his dead son-in-law, too. She stuck her phone in the pocket of the bathrobe and returned to the kitchen to have breakfast.

Louis had left for work, but it was still too early to make phone calls to strangers so Lynette took another long bath, did her hair and checked her email. Nothing new from Sam. She kept checking the time, impatient for it to pass nine, the time she had decided she could start calling the people on the list Louis had given her. The first name on the list was Richard Atkinson. No reply. Lynette didn't bother to leave a message. She could always try again later. She had no luck with the next couple of names either. She guessed most people would be at work. But two calls further down the list, there was a reply. The man's name was Chandler. Lynette introduced herself and tried to explain her business as clearly as possible.

'What do you mean you want to talk about Iraq?' he asked.

'I'm planning an article on the UK losses in the war. I'd like to try to put a human face on the numbers. And I was wondering if you'd be willing to give me a little of your time and talk about your experiences. I understand your platoon suffered several tragic losses.'

'Not interested.' There was a click and the line went dead. Lynette looked at the phone in her hand for a second before moving to the next name on the list. Gavin Costello. She dialled the number and there was a swift reply. Lynette went through the same introduction. There was a pause. 'Sure,' he said. 'Happy to meet with you.'

Lynette's heart skipped a beat. 'I'm afraid it'll have to be today or tomorrow,' she said. 'I'm returning to New Zealand on Friday.'

'Today would work for me. Mind if we meet up in Hampstead? Lunch, perhaps?'

'I have a morning meeting. Do you mind if we make it a late lunch, say one-thirty?'

Costello suggested they meet at the Spaniard's Inn for a sandwich lunch. Lynette accepted enthusiastically. Yes! Today she would miss all sessions at the conference, but so what? She had more important things to do.

***

The house in Lyall Street blew Lynette away. It was a beautiful two-storey building with an inviting red door and little flowerboxes beneath the windows. She rang the doorbell and waited. The door was opened by a tall, stunningly good-looking black woman. Lynette introduced herself and the woman smiled and gestured for Lynette to come inside.

Stephen Wakenshaw was in a wheelchair. He was very thin and very pale, like something that rarely saw the sun. However, his face showed a slight resemblance to his brother, with pleasant, even features. He pointed to an armchair beside him. 'Please, Miss Church, take a seat. Or is it Mrs?'

'Lynette, please.'

He nodded. 'Tea? Or coffee?' Lynette asked for coffee, and the young woman disappeared.

'Now, what can I do for you, Lynette?' he asked.

'I'm am collecting material for an article on the British losses in Iraq. There's quite a bit of material on the military losses of life, but not so much, I think, on the civilian losses. But I understand that your brother Christopher was killed while on business in Iraq.'

Stephen nodded.

'What kind of business took him to Iraq?'

'I never really knew what it was Christopher was doing. Not in Iraq, not anywhere really. He was nine years older than me, and he lived in another world. My disability also meant that we didn't spend much time together. I idolised him, of course. He was everything I could never aspire to be: sporty, good-looking and determined. Christopher knew what he wanted and he made sure he got it. He was like that even as a little boy, I think.'

The young woman returned with a tray and served coffee. 'Thank you, Lucy,' Stephen said.

She smiled and left again.

'Christopher went to Oxford on a scholarship. Our father died when I was only three. I have no memories of him. But after his death our mother struggled to make ends meet. Having a son like me didn't help.' He made a resigned gesture. 'She was very proud of Christopher.

'Sadly, she died the year Christopher graduated, so she never lived to see what he made of himself. She never got to see all this.'

Lynette looked around the room. It was beautiful and light, filled with antiques and art. Perhaps a little too beautiful, too obviously a professional decorating job. Just like Eric's office, Lynette thought. Only this place wasn't rented. 'Your brother must have been very well off.'

'I suppose he was. He always looked after us, even when he was at school. But it wasn't until a couple of years before his death that he started making big investments, I think. He bought several country properties. And this house. But I don't think that he ever had the time to enjoy any of them. He travelled a lot and I didn't see much of him.' Stephen's voice sounded as if it was about to break and he was silent for a moment.

'Did you ever get to know what exactly happened to him in Iraq?'

Stephen shook his head. 'No, not really. I had a letter of condolences from the British Embassy in Baghdad, but it only referred to Christopher's "tragic death". And somehow it didn't seem to matter. He was dead. Nothing could change that. I assumed it must have been an accident, perhaps a road accident. Baghdad must have been a very dangerous place.'

'And you have no idea what exactly he was doing there?'

'I didn't even know he was in Baghdad until afterwards. So, I'm sorry, I have no idea what he was doing there.'

'But he must have made good provision for you,' said Lynette. 'This is a lovely place.'

'I'm very grateful,' Stephen said simply. 'Christopher left me a trust fund and it keeps me very well looked after.'

'So he had no family of his own? No wife, no children?'

'I don't think he had any time for a family. Perhaps if he'd lived longer, he might have been able to settle down and enjoy the fruits of his hard work. But as it was, no, there was no time for a family. No friends, either, I think. Not since university. He did sports there, I know that. But being on a scholarship wasn't easy, I think. Socially. He never brought any friends home. Not that I can remember.'

'This trust fund – are you involved in the management?'

'Oh, no, no, no,' Stephen said. 'I would be useless. I have no understanding of anything to do with money. The fund is managed by Christopher's solicitors, a London firm. I just collect the benefits.' He smiled a little sheepishly. 'It keeps me living here, having Lucy to help me. And look after my stamp collection. Not much of a life, you may think, but I'm very content. And grateful.'

'You must have faith in the trustees,' Lynette said. 'Leaving such a large fortune in the hands of someone anonymous.'

'Trustee,' Stephen said. 'There's only one, and although I've never met him, he doesn't feel anonymous at all. I'm eternally grateful, of course. I think the trust is very well managed.'

'How come you've never met the trustee?'

'I think he lives overseas. But these days I suppose running a trust or looking after money doesn't require one's physical presence. I think he lives in Australia. Or it could have been New Zealand. Some distant place like that. But as I said, I have no complaints whatsoever. But it goes without saying that I would love to meet him one day. He would have to come here, though. Sadly, I'll never be able to travel to Australia. Or New Zealand. But I am sure Mr Salisbury will come here one day.'

'Mr Salisbury?' Lynette said slowly.

'Yes, that's his name. Eric Salisbury.'

# 29.

*No place, indeed, should murder sanctuarise*


Sam woke up early. No surprise. But he couldn't remember any dreams, and he felt good.

Which *was* a surprise.

He had been too tired to attack the package when he got back home. But here it was, the second part of Brent's manuscript. He went to the kitchen, made coffee and took the package out on the deck. The blue bird was back, darting hither and thither, in what to Sam looked like sheer delight at the rising sun.

He pulled out the papers. This pack looked cleaner. He put it on the table and started to scan the pages. Eventually he came upon a number of pages that seemed sequential even though they weren't numbered. He took them over to the deckchair and settled down to read.


Byron woke up with another nosebleed. Maybe it was the dust. His head was throbbing. He pinched his nose for a moment, hoping to stop the flow of blood, then moved his fingers to his temples and massaged them before reluctantly getting out of bed. He pushed open the curtain that hung across the entrance.

Outside it was hot already. The sun glared and made the air above the sand quiver. In the distance he could see three thin funnels of smoke rising into the sky. Tangible reminders of the previous day's carnage. Destruction. The results of their efforts here were destruction, devastation. Death. Nothing else.

'What's up?' Sticky asked. He stood leaning against the loaded jeep, smoking a cigarette. His eye still hadn't healed properly, but he didn't seem to mind.

'Oh, nothing. Where's Patrick? I need some more painkillers.'

'No idea,' Sticky replied and stared out over the barren fields. Then he turned to Byron, and there was compassion in his brown eyes as they met Byron's for a brief moment before he looked away again. He slowly extracted his earphones from the front pocket of his combat pants and put them into his ears. End of conversation.

Byron walked around the camp and saw a group of guys in the mess tent. Usually you would be able to hear them well before you saw them. But today everyone was subdued. The only one smiling was the commander. 'The Ripper.' He sat on a folding chair, his legs spread out wide, cleaning his nails. His face was tanned, the collar of his shirt crisp. He looked up at Byron and smiled, flicking his head back in recognition, grinning with very white teeth. 'The early bird!' he said. Byron felt his stomach sink.

'Come and sit with me, early bird!' He patted the seat beside him.

Byron sat down stiffly.

'Would you like something to eat?'

Byron shook his head.

He felt bile rise into his mouth and swallowed several times. The sour burn stayed in his mouth. The Ripper winked in a gesture of conspiracy. As if pulling Byron firmly into his realm. Making him a party to yesterday's horror.

Byron didn't understand. And he couldn't accept it. He should have reported it. Done something.

Again, he felt his stomach shooting burning bile upwards.

He stared at the man in front of him. Took in his immaculate hands, his slim neck. His freshly starched uniform. The fact that he never seemed to sweat. For some reason Byron couldn't take his eyes off him. He felt sick, yet grotesquely fascinated, unable to tear himself away. A young local boy appeared with a plate of eggs and sausages, and The Ripper smiled, stretched out a hand and ruffled the boy's hair. It was hard to tell how the boy reacted; he slipped away very quickly. Byron followed every forkful, watched The Ripper's lips part and let the greasy sausages inside.

Byron felt a surge of bile and this time he was unable to keep it down. He turned and spat but felt no relief. He looked at The Ripper, saw his wet lips open to let another glistening sausage in. He shuddered.

The day before, they had reached the village in the early afternoon. There had been no orders, no reason to go. Just the commander's orders. His whim. And he needed an interpreter with him. The streets had been eerily quiet. Not a person in sight. The windows shuttered. No sounds, no

movements. Just the glaring sun. And the flies.
The sky stretched empty over the shimmering heat.
No birds, not a breath of wind. The commander
fired his rifle into the silence.

And to Byron, that was the beginning of the
end. Abruptly, out of the deathly silence, a
cacophony of sounds, bodies, movement. Screams.
Sounds. Incomprehensible, uncontrollable chaos.
Nothing was as it should be, nothing was what it
seemed to be. Old women were throwing stones,
their mouths wide open in high-pitched screams.
Old men were shooting. Children were throwing
grenades from the flat roofs. He was in a world
where nothing made sense. A swirling, scorching,
explosive nightmare. His eyes fell on a small boy
who stood at the top of the stairs of one of the
houses. He couldn't be more than five or six years
old. His legs were painfully thin, his hair shone
black, as if just lovingly water-combed. But his
wide eyes stared back with shocking hatred. Adult
loathing. As the small body took the impact of
the shots, it lifted, as if making a horrible
mocking imitation of a leap of joy, and when it
finally came to a rest near Byron's feet, the
eyes were wide open to the falling dust.

In the lull afterwards, when silence again
ruled, The Ripper indicated that he wanted Byron
to go with him, heading towards a single house a
little beyond the others. Byron didn't understand
why; all he wanted was to leave. But he followed,
his legs moving stiffly. He assumed they were to
confiscate weapons, check out some stash. There
was a bucket of water and wet clothes beside the

doorstep. Someone had been washing. They went through the open door and their eyes adjusted to the dusk inside. The room was empty but for a young girl who stood with her body pressed against the far wall. She looked about twelve. Or maybe even younger. She said nothing but her eyes stared at them, filled with terror. And again, that same loathing.

'This is what we came for, the real fun.' The commander was smiling, the skin along the tight collar momentarily whitening with the movement.

Byron was struggling to breathe, and couldn't speak.

Then he winked at Byron and grabbed the girl. Byron had once seen this before. He hadn't known what to do then, either. He closed his eyes for a moment. As he opened them he watched as The Ripper tore the girl's skirt off and threw her onto the low bed. She tried beating him off with her little fists, her slim wrists. Byron closed his eyes again but it didn't help. The scene was clear whether his eyes were open or not. Those hands on the little girl's shoulders, holding her down. Byron opened his eyes and saw the girl spit at her attacker in hopeless defiance.

The large hands were over her neck, as if to strangle her. He pushed her down and kneeled between her legs. She kept repeating the same words again and again. Byron knew what she was saying, but The Ripper wouldn't have a clue. And while he opened his fly, ripped off the girl's blouse and exposed her small, undeveloped breasts Byron just stood there. Her words kept repeating and he registered them. 'Eradh allh m'eaqbh lk. God will punish you. God will punish you.'

Her voice, initially defiant, became a whimpering, before it died altogether. All the while Byron stood there. Watching.

Afterwards, The Ripper stood up and adjusted his uniform. 'Sorry, got a bit carried away. Nothing much left for you, I'm afraid,' he said, indicating the girl. She didn't stir.

Byron looked at the blood. He felt his heart throb violently, his stomach knotting, but at the same time it was as if he was drifting, rising till he could see the room from above. As if it was a staged play.

Just then the baby started crying in the other room. Abruptly the girl screamed and came to life, as if hit by a bolt of electricity. The Ripper laughed and walked into the adjoining room. The girl rose and followed, leaving a trail of blood. She was naked except for her headscarf.

As if instinctively aware of the danger, the baby became quiet. Warily Byron followed the girl. The room lay in darkness and at first he couldn't see anything.

Then his eyes adjusted and he could see The Ripper standing in the centre of the room, his eyes slowly scanning every corner. The girl was on her knees, pleading. He looked at her, smiling. Her pleading seemed to spur him on. While he walked around the room, taking his time and turning over clothing, opening cupboards, the young girl's words filled the room: 'Allahu Akhbar, Allahu Akhbar. Please save my brother.

Please take me. Kill me and save my brother. Take me. Save my brother.'

Then he found the baby in a hamper. There was a moment of silence that seemed to last forever. He stood looking at the baby, the tip of his boot knocking the side of the hamper.

The girl ran towards it. He grabbed her by the neck and threw her to the side. He picked up the baby by its feet. It started crying again. Wailing.

Byron stared. He was gulping for air, inhaling in short ragged breaths. But he remained where he was.

The Ripper held the baby by its feet, swirled around as if to gain momentum to throw a hammer. When he let go, the tiny body flew across the room and hit the wall with a nauseating sound of skin and bones against stone. The body fell to the floor and the room was silent.

Byron stared at the immobile heap. So very, very small. Still. He wanted to scream, but his cracked lips were unable to form words. He kept licking them. His heart was thumping so hard he felt it would burst. Yet he was icy cold and beginning to shiver. And he was stuck where he was, unable to move.

The Ripper turned as if to leave. The girl was still, crouching on the floor, her narrow back and the bloodied soles of her feet the only parts of her body that were visible. She was silent. Slowly, as if in a deliberate attempt at extending the scene, he pulled out his gun, closed one eye, and aimed. The shot hit her between the shoulder blades and tore through the small room. The sound seemed to reverberate forever. And then there was silence again.

Byron stood still. He wondered if he would ever be able to move again. He looked at the bodies. Narrow shafts of light shone through the gaps between the shutters of the one small, unglazed window and fell over the girl's narrow back.

The Ripper had left the room. Eventually Byron slowly forced his limbs to move.

Outside, Byron saw him sitting on the steps of the jeep, wiping his face with a white handkerchief. Byron walked up to the car. He felt as if his insides were slowly rising and he knew he was going to be sick.

'What are you staring at? You were in there too.'

Byron couldn't look away. He realised with crystal clarity that the fact that he had been in there and done nothing had irrevocably changed his life. He fell to his knees, rested his palms on the sand and was violently sick. When he had nothing more to expel, he raised his head. 'Why?' he said.

The Ripper stared at him coldly. He bent forward to light a cigarette, then inhaled. He stared out over the dry landscape. 'No one gives a shit about that fucking baby. They're vermin. It would have grown up and killed more of us. The little whore would have bred more of them. I'm doing the world a favour.'

'I can't believe what you –'

'Get over it, you fucking poof.'

'The baby. The girl. They were children,' Byron whispered.

The Ripper's clear grey eyes locked with Byron's. 'Look, buddy. Get this straight, once and for all.' He spoke slowly, as if to make the words sink in. 'No one gives a flying fuck about that baby. No one gives a flying fuck about any of these people. They're getting what's been coming to them for a long, long time. No one's going to give a shit back home. And the sooner you realise that, the better.'

He smiled and started walking away. 'Besides,' he said over his shoulder, 'a man must have a little fun from time to time. Relax. Just relax.' He stopped and turned. 'And remember we were in there, both of us.' He laughed out loud and stepped into the jeep. 'You and me, Byron. Together.'

Byron sat on the sand, resting on his shins. The smell from the pool of vomit in front of him was already attracting flies.

He lifted his eyes to the scorching white sky. There was nothing to see.

'Are you coming or aren't you?' The Ripper shouted through the open window of the jeep.

Slowly, Byron stood. And he knew that when he opened the door and stepped into the jeep and sat down beside his commander, that this was the moment his life was decided. It wasn't the moment when the girl had been raped. Or the moment the baby was picked up or the gun fired. No, it was when he, Byron, slowly heaved himself into the seat of the jeep that a door closed behind him.

```
That was the moment he moved into The Ripper's
world.
    And so it began. After that he had nothing to
call on. He had let that first time pass. He was
an accomplice. He sank deeper and deeper into
the hell that The Ripper and the likes of him
created.
```

Sam sat staring at the pages. It was powerful stuff. But who were the people in the story? Was The Ripper really Peter West? Sam found it hard to reconcile the academic person he had met at the university with the man who had committed these atrocities. And Byron? Was that still Robert? He thought Peter West had been the interpreter. Was Byron Peter? That somehow didn't feel right either.

Sam rose stiffly from the canvas chair and went inside.

***

Jade had hung up on Sam.

He called her again. And then again. And then again. But she just let it ring. On the fourth try she answered.

'I really do think we need to meet,' he said.

'Uh-uh, I don't think so.'

'What is it with you? I don't understand. We have things to do. There is definitely something wrong about Brent's death.'

'Nothing is going to bring Brent back,' Jade said in a dead kind of voice.

'I know, Jade. But this isn't about bringing him back. You said it was about giving him some respect. Righting wrongs. We can do that! I'm beginning to think that Brent's death is connected to something much bigger. That he was onto something.'

'Whatever,' Jade said coolly. 'I don't want you to keep looking into this. I think we know everything we're ever going to know and we should just let it go. Thank you for your help, Sam. I'll pay you some money when I get a chance.'

'Money? You know it's never been about money.'

'Just let it go, Sam. I will.' She paused. ''Bye, Sam.'

She hung up again. He waited a few minutes then tried calling again. But it went straight to answerphone. He left half a message, pleading with her to meet up with him, but then he gave up and left it at that.

He re-read Byron's confession: 'Women and children. And he raped them, Sebastian. He made me watch while he raped them. Killed them.'

What did it mean? Did it mean that Robert had been the innocent bystander to Peter's war crimes? That seemed to be the thrust of Brent's story.

Why were they both in New Zealand? Did they have some sort of pact?

He tried calling Jade again and went straight to answerphone. He called her work, Heaven.

'I wondered if Jade Amaro was working tonight,' he said to the receptionist.

'Jade? Oh. . .'

There was a silence. Sam waited for her to continue but she didn't. 'Is everything all right?'

'Oh yes. She'll be in later.'

'What time?'

'Nine. Would you like me to book you a session with her, sir?'

'If you could. That would be wonderful.'

He parked outside Heaven at five minutes before nine. He sat in the car watching some dizzy moths clamber around the street lamp, wondering if he was doing the right thing. She had said she wanted him to drop the investigation. He watched two separate men walk with a forced casualness along the street. They then nipped inside.

Sam waited until nine then entered, too.

The décor might have been considered impressive ten years ago, but now it just looked tired. A sense of overwhelming tiredness permeated the whole place. The other two men were nowhere to be seen. A tall, pale woman with dyed black hair approached. 'Hello, I'm Laura,' she said with forced cheerfulness.

'I'm Sam. I made an appointment.'

'Of course. Come this way.' She led him into a small room containing two armchairs and a small bar. 'Have a seat,' she said. 'Jade will be in here soon. Have you been here before?'

Sam shook his head.

'Jade will come in here and talk to you. And if she wishes for something more to happen she'll invite you into her suite. You are being watched.' She pointed to a camera in the corner of the room, then held out her hand. Sam stared at it. 'Your credit card please. You went over the payment details on the phone?'

Sam nodded. He gave her his credit card. She snatched it with her red acrylic nails. She smiled. 'You have a good time, sir.' She left him to it. Sam looked over the mini bottles in the bar. Some looked as if they had been opened: the whole bar smelled sweetly of alcohol.

Jade entered, wearing mini shorts and a cross-tied top. She looked tired and drawn. Her smile died as she saw him. 'What are you doing here?'

'I wanted to come and talk to you. I've got some interest-ing news.'

'I told you I didn't want to do the investigation any more.' Her face was hard.

'What's happened, Jade? I know this isn't you speaking.'

Her eyes narrowed. 'I'm working tonight. I've missed a lot of work and a girl has to pay her bills. So unless you...' Her face changed. 'You didn't really want to?'

'No.'

'Did you pay?'

'Yes.'

'I'll get you your money back.' She walked towards the main door. Sam grabbed her arm. She yanked it free then stepped away defensively.

'What's happened, Jade?'

She went to open the door.

'Jade, I know for sure Brent was murdered. I know the book he was writing wasn't crap. And I'm beginning to think that it all fits into something much bigger.'

She stopped. She stared at the wall, avoiding eye contact. 'What does it matter? Brent is dead.'

'It matters a great deal. He –'

'That guy I told you about, he came here yesterday.'

'What guy?'

'The guy who pretended to be a policeman and took the CD.' She turned, her face a hard mask. 'He made me tell him everything. About you. About the book.'

Sam nodded slowly.

'Brent would have wanted me to be safe. And you to be safe, probably. Can't we just drop it?' She looked at him pleadingly.

'Did you tell him where I live?'

'No. He never asked.'

She opened the door and went to leave but stopped. She faced him again. The hardness had gone. 'I'm sorry. I'm so sorry. I didn't know what to do. He threatened me. My Lily Dew. He knew about her. What could I do?'

'Where is she?'

Jade started crying quietly. 'I rang to check and she's fine.' She was sobbing now. 'But I've put her in danger. I've put you in danger.' Her voice cracked. 'I've put everybody in danger.'

'No, Jade. You've done the right thing. For Brent. And for you.'

'My daughter. And I... He came to my house again.'

He helped her to a seat. Laura appeared at the door. 'Is everything all right?'

'Thanks, it's great,' Sam said smiling.

'Are you okay, Jade?'

'Yes, yes, just fine. I'm just a little emotional. Sorry.'

But after Laura left Jade was in no shape to talk. Sam ended up comforting her until his time was up. He paid for an extra hour when he left, hoping it would give Jade an hour of solitude. Not that an hour would make a difference. She needed to get out of that place.

# 30.

*You do remember all the circumstance?*

Lynette found herself standing stunned on the pavement outside Stephen's house. 'Eric Salisbury, bloody hell!' she whispered. 'Managing the trust fund from the grave!' She started walking, her mind rushing. What was the source of Eric Salisbury's fortune? Sure, investment banking was lucrative, but the years that he had spent working his way up to director at Kaufman and Hertz wouldn't have bought him several British country mansions. Or a house in Belgravia. Even with the most generous bonus payments imaginable. It just wasn't possible. Had he made clever investments? It didn't seem possible within the given time frame. You just don't make that kind of money in fifteen years. Not even in investment banking. And Stephen said he had the impression it had all happened within a few years before his brother's death. What was Christopher Wakenshaw doing in the years between his departure from Lehmann Brothers and return to England, and his death in Iraq?

A cold rain had started and Lynette stopped the first taxi she saw. She decided to skip the late session at the conference as well as the pre-dinner cocktails, and go back to Louis's instead.

She was intrigued, and this was not a state she liked to remain in for very long. She didn't like mysteries. Suddenly she didn't want to stay in London for the Saturday dinner. She was booked to fly out Monday evening, but now decided to try to change her booking and catch an earlier flight. She wanted to go back home, get her head around Eric Salisbury and catch up with Sam. She just needed to have her meeting with Gavin Costello, and then the final meeting with Ian Clarkson. After that, she was ready to get on a flight back home.

\*\*\*

When Lynette stepped out of the Tube station in Hampstead, the bleak November skies made a weak attempt at letting a pale sun through. But somehow, the gloomy sunshine added chill, not warmth, to an already cold day. Lynette walked briskly, the tip of her nose growing numb and her eyes watering in the strong wind that swept down the narrow street. Passing the Pond she was exposed to the full force of the wind as it swept down over the Heath. By now she had to give up on her hair and was regretting not having taken a taxi.

She arrived right on time and stepped inside the Spaniard's Inn. It was warm and cosy and full. Her eyes swept over the room. She had no idea what Gavin Costello might look like, but she assumed he would be looking out for her. There was a bald man alone at a table by the window but he didn't look as though he was waiting for anybody and didn't return her gaze.

While she stood searching, she felt a light tap on her shoulder. 'Lynette?'

She turned around and faced Gavin Costello. He was tall, so tall she had to tilt her head backwards to meet his gaze. 'And you must be Gavin,' she said and stretched out her hand.

'Come this way,' he said and led the way into a side room with a lit fire. Lynette followed.

She looked at the tall figure ahead, dressed in a pale blue woollen jersey and blue jeans, and wondered why it was so hard to remember what you had envisaged someone to look like once you had met them. At the table, Gavin pulled out a chair for her and she sat down. 'I thought we could have the roast beef sandwich,' he said. 'It's very good. But if you like, I can get a menu for you. They have soups and salads and all sorts of things. It's just me, I always have the same.'

'Very happy with the sandwich,' Lynette said.

'Drink?'

'Oh, a glass of red would be nice, thanks. This meal is on me, of course.'

Gavin disappeared and returned with a glass of red wine and a beer. He sat down opposite Lynette. 'So, you're interested in the Iraqi war, are you?' He had a disturbingly beautiful face, short and wide, with large brown eyes shaded by dense curled lashes. Why were nice eyelashes so often wasted on men? His hair was dark, thick and curly and surprisingly long, gathered behind his ears. Lynette had thought he would look more like the stereotypical army man. Stronger features, shaved head.

'Well, yes,' Lynette said. 'I'm thinking of doing a piece on the British losses. The human perspective. The impact on all concerned – family, friends and fellow soldiers.'

Gavin nodded. 'I see. It's been done before, I guess.'

'Well, yes, but perhaps not so much in New Zealand.' Lynette smiled. 'I understand your platoon lost its sergeant? And in the same incident, a corporal.'

Gavin nodded. 'Yes, Sergeant Jonathan Golding and Corporal Kenneth Beaumont were killed while out on a reconnaissance mission. Beaumont was our interpreter and Golding often took him with him. That day, they didn't come back.'

The sandwiches arrived. They were more like a full meal. Reluctantly, Lynette removed one of the two pieces of bread and put it to the side. 'So, what had happened?' she asked, chewing on the tasty roast beef.

'Well, that's the odd thing. We never really knew. They went missing. They never came back. From what we heard, their vehicle was found blown to pieces. I'm afraid the coffins that travelled back home must have been empty.'

Gavin looked at Lynette with an odd expression. 'Golding was an arsehole,' he said. He took another bite of the sandwich. 'A sadistic piece of shit. I think there were others who felt like me – good riddance! But Beaumont was a nice guy. I don't think he knew what hit him when Golding chose him as his special sidekick and claimed that he needed an interpreter by his side all the time. You could see him recoiling whenever Golding appeared. Which of course egged Golding on. Beaumont was an academic, a decent sort of guy. And Golding liked to push his buttons, tease him. As if to see how much Beaumont could take. Hoping that he would crack, no doubt. But it was more than that. He was like that with everything. Always pushing, always testing how far he could go. And often taking stupid risks. He got off on that.'

Gavin shook his head slowly. 'I felt sorry for the guy. But also a little relieved. I knew that I could be next on Golding's list.' He was silent for a moment. 'I'm gay. And guys like Golding can smell this from miles away. I know the type, believe me. But as long as Beaumont was Golding's special pet I was safe. Not that I think that Beaumont was gay. He was just a decent, good guy. There were many of us who secretly felt relieved that he was the target, I suspect. So, nobody complained. Certainly not Beaumont. I think he had these old-fashioned ideas, you know. About loyalty, honour, that sort of thing. He just didn't have it in him to try to do something about it. Whatever that would have been. And then he died.'

'So what you're saying is that it was Golding who was the senior officer?' Lynette said slowly. 'And Beaumont was the victim of Golding's sadistic harassment?'

Gavin nodded.

'Sam has it completely wrong,' Lynette whispered.

'Sorry?' Gavin said.

'Oh, nothing, I was just thinking out loud.'

They had both finished their food. 'I'm sorry,' Lynette said, 'I think it's too cold for me for that walk on the Heath. I've come straight from the New Zealand spring, and I haven't quite adjusted to these temperatures.'

Gavin smiled. He really was very good-looking.

'Tell me, what do you do these days? Are you still with the Army?' Lynette asked.

Gavin shook his head. 'I've taken over my father's gallery in Hampstead.' He pointed to a scar over his right eye. 'I came home from Iraq with a minor injury and loads of disillusionment, so I took early retirement. I'm glad to have left all that behind. Life is good now, I'm enjoying it. And I try to think about that time as little as possible.'

On her way to the Tube station Lynette found a travel agent and popped in to see if she could change her ticket. The young woman behind the desk was very helpful, and managed to get Lynette on a flight Friday evening. The timing would be a little tight, but she felt she could do it. She just needed to get her luggage organised before she set off to see Ian Clarkson, then catch a cab back to Louis's and collect her suitcase. It would work.

Back home she took another long bath. Might as well enjoy it while I can, she thought as she sank into the water, so hot that she had to take it slowly. Once immersed, she closed her eyes and considered the events of the last few days.

She really needed to talk to Sam.

Half an hour later, Lynette emerged from the bathroom wrapped in the bathrobe. She sat on her bed, took out her mobile and dialled Sam's number. The phone rang, but she only got his voicemail. So, instead she sat down to write him an email.

**From:** Lynette Church [mailto:lynette.church@
nztribune.co.nz]
**Sent:** Thursday, November 24 2005 17:06 p.m.
**To:** Sam Hallberg
**Subject:** curiouser

Sam,

First, I have changed my flights and will be
returning Sunday morning on NZ001. It would be
great if you could meet me, but don't worry if you
can't. I will ring you when I land. So much to talk
about.

Secondly, I met with one of the soldiers from the
same platoon as Robert and Peter. Sam, it's Robert
who committed the war crimes. And Peter was really
just a forced accomplice.

So we now have three British soldiers and one
British businessman killed in Iraq and miraculously
resurrected in New Zealand. Why? Let's assume, for
a moment, that they're all war criminals. If I were
the UK I'd do almost anything to avoid them being
exposed. Look at how the war crimes in Iraq have
seriously tarnished the US.

Well, that's all for now. One more meeting
before I leave tomorrow - Ian Clarkson. Should be
interesting.

Take care, L

# 31.

*O villain, villain, smiling, damned villain!*

Sam drove home. He felt an anxiety he hadn't felt for a long time. It was surprising. A sign of life, uninvited and unwelcome. He felt distinctly uneasy. He kept noticing the cars around him. A figure loitering on the street corner. A man crossing the road.

He pulled up outside his house. It looked particularly uninviting. He hadn't realised how neglected it had become. The chipped baldness of paint. The gate hanging askew.

The key slid in as it always did but he didn't enter the house. He stood still, listening, the key in the lock.

Jade had told 'him' everything. Those were her words. She must be referring to the man with the scar. But why had he approached her again?

Sam turned the key and opened the door. The house was peaceful. No sounds. He took off his jacket and walked into the kitchen. He turned the kettle on to make tea. He considered the nearly empty fridge. He could fry up some of the dried mushrooms, maybe defrost a meat pie.

He leaned against the bench. Now what? Should he pursue this on his own? If so, why? Jade obviously felt threatened. Would it hurt her if he carried on?

He looked at the manuscript on the kitchen bench. Beside it was a pile of pages he hadn't managed to put in order. There were all sorts of bits and pieces. Some hand-written, some consisting of only one or two lines. None had page numbers on them. He looked through them again and noticed a double-sided page full of writing. He couldn't remember having read this:

Byron and Sebastian returned to Byron's apartment. Sebastian couldn't be sure, but it felt like Byron hadn't really wanted him to come along. But perhaps he was just seeing things that weren't really there. He tried not to think about what Byron had said just before that man had showed up. He kept asking if Byron was okay. Surely, he would be upset about seeing that man again. A ghost from the past. A horrible, horrible ghost. If Byron needed someone to talk to Sebastian was here for him. Whatever he needed.

Sebastian sat on the couch in the living room and Byron stood smoking by the window. He didn't smoke often but when he did it was so sexy. Sebastian felt a ripple in his manhood as his eyes took in the picture of Byron's tall figure, illuminated by the small floor lamp and outlined against the darkness outside. The smoke left his mouth in gently drifting billows.

'Maybe we should call the police, or something, and tell them that he's here,' Sebastian said.

'Don't be stupid.'

'But you know what he's done! He could be dangerous. What do you think he's doing in the country? For all we know he'll rape and murder people here too. Maybe he came because of you? You might be in danger, Byron. He didn't look very evil, but I guess evil comes in many disguises. I'm really scared. Scared for you, I mean. I think we should call the police.'

Byron exhaled slowly. 'You're such an idiot, Seb.' He spoke slowly, like he was talking to a small, annoying child.

'That's not a very nice thing to say.'

'That guy didn't rape anyone.'

'But you said he did. He was the one. Was it someone else then?'

'No. That arsehole didn't do any raping or killing babies.' He laughed. His big Adam's apple bobbed up and down. He turned away and stared out of the window. His eyes were half-closed like a cat considering its prey.

'You made it all up?'

'Sure.'

'Why?'

Byron faced him and his beauty was stone cold. 'I just wanted to see how you would react.'

'No,' Sebastian said. 'You couldn't have! All that horror!' He looked at Byron with a pleading expression. But Byron said nothing.

'I can't believe you'd do something like that,' Sebastian said in a whisper. He was pale, as if he had seen a ghost. 'I was really worried for you. I was trying to organise counselling for you. Help you any way I could think of.'

Byron just laughed. Sebastian didn't know what to do. So he laughed as well. But he felt terrible. 'I guess it was quite a good prank. I guess.' He walked to the window and put his hand on Byron's shoulder. 'Were you even in the Army? Or was that a lie as well? A joke?'

'Oh, for fuck's sake,' Byron said and shook off Sebastian's hand impatiently.

'What's wrong?' Sebastian asked.

'Everything is wrong.'

'Oh.' Sebastian stood awkwardly, not knowing what to do.

'I guess the question is, why would I want someone like you touching me?'

'What do you mean, someone like me?'

'Someone like you. I mean, just look at you.' Byron laughed.

Sebastian felt sick. Why was Byron being like this? He looked at his reflection in the window. He thought he wasn't looking so bad these days. Sure, compared to Byron he didn't look that good. But nobody did. 'I thought you liked me,' he said feebly.

Then, in a whisper, 'I thought you loved me.'

'Oh, god,' Byron said and blew another puff of smoke through the window.

'Why are you being so mean?'

'Because you're boring. That's why.' Byron flicked his cigarette out of the window then walked into the kitchen. He poured himself a glass of water from the tap.

'Because you're an idiot. Because I can't stand another minute of your boring company. That answer your question?'

Sebastian's eyes welled with tears. He rubbed them away.

'Oh boo hoo hoo,' Byron said. And laughed.

Sebastian didn't understand what was going on. He hurried to the door but before leaving he turned back. Maybe this was a cruel joke as well. 'Do you want me to stay or go?' he asked, feeling lame.

'Give me one reason why I would want you to stay.'

'Why are you doing this to me, Byron? When things have been so good.' Sebastian couldn't help his voice cracking.

'When things have been so good,' Byron said, mimicking Sebastian's broken voice. 'What things? There haven't been any things, Sebastian. There's been nothing. Zilch. Nothing.'

Byron walked up to Sebastian, and, with his face so close it almost touched, said, 'Whatever you think has happened was in your fat little head! You fucking fat little idiot. Feeding you those war stories, oh, what fun. Watching you soak them up. Believe them. Hilarious. Sure, it was fun to begin with. But now I'm bored. And you are an ugly, fat nuisance.'

Byron walked across the room and sat down on the sofa, legs spread wide. 'And now, Sebastian, I want you out of here. And I never want to see your ugly, pimply face again.'

Sebastian couldn't move. He stood as if he had been frozen solid. He looked at Byron. And suddenly Byron seemed to change. Where there had been beauty, Sebastian could now see evil. Where he had previously seen good humour, there was sadistic glee. Snippets of memories emerged. Words that he chosen not to hear. Gestures he had ignored. Insults and disappointments he had chosen not to register.

Sebastian could feel tears streaming down his face. But it was not sadness that filled him. No; red-hot anger rose inside him. Yet he felt strangely clear-headed. 'Look at you, sitting there like a... With your smarmy smile and your stupid Sanskrit tattoo, meaning 'overlord'? Ha ha. You're not an overlord, you're just a fucking war criminal. I know what you are, Byron,' he said slowly. 'And I will let the world know, too. Every word, I have kept every word you have told me. And I'm beginning to see what it's really about. Just you wait, Byron. Just you wait.'

He turned quickly and left the apartment, banging the door closed behind him.

Sam looked over the page again. Brent had simply known too much and had threatened to write about it. But the only person knowing this would be Robert. And it was Robert who had supplied the stories. Had he been playing a sadistic game with Brent, not realising that Brent would take it seriously? So seriously that he had written it all down. Had Robert killed Brent? This felt unrealistic. Not here, not in Auckland. Not in this way. So, he must have had a way of alerting someone to the danger. Who? And how?

Sam's gaze fell on the back door to the deck. He put the page down and moved towards the door. He bent down and touched the edge. It was warped and splintered. He opened the door with difficulty. It had been forced open and then closed. He stood still for a moment. Had someone broken in? There were no signs of anything having been disturbed in the house. He walked through the rooms, but couldn't detect any damage.

It took some force to open the sliding door because of the damage, but once he got it open he stepped outside. He knew immediately that there was somebody there. He had no time to react before he was pushed hard against the side of the house. The slat boards dug into his spine. He had the wind knocked out of him. The force was intense and he was pinned against the wall, looking up into a face that was just a dark shadow.

'What do you want?' he managed.

'If you care about your son and about the girl, just drop it. Now.'

Sam struggled to breathe as the pressure on his throat increased. 'I understand,' he said with difficulty.

'I don't need to tell you what could happen, do I? To you, what remains of your family. Your son.'

Sam tried to shake his head. And the pressure released. His knees almost buckled but he supported himself against the wall. The man stood frozen for a moment then threw an almighty punch. It connected with Sam's jaw and he fell to the ground. There was ringing in Sam's ear but he could still hear the man stalking up the driveway, his heavy boots crunching in the gravel.

Sam lay on the deck, hugging himself, reluctant to move. Moving would hurt, but it would also mean doing something. Taking some form of action. But he wasn't sure what to do.

Eventually he crawled into the house and took a bag of peas from the freezer. He held it to his jaw. He let his tongue run over his teeth and wondered if he needed a dentist. 'What a fine mess you've gotten yourself into, Sam,' he whispered.

He took his phone and stared at it for a long time before dialling out. It was answered after six rings. 'Hello?' A soft Dutch accent.

'Dorothea?'

'Who's this?'

'It's Sam.'

'Are you drunk?'

'No.'

'Well, you sound very strange.'

There was a long silence followed by a sigh. 'Jasper went to bed. Hours ago. You should know that.'

'I was just checking to see if he was all right.'

'He's fine.'

'I thought I might come and visit.'

'That's what you said last time. And the time before. But you never come.'

'I thought perhaps this coming weekend?'

'Any time. He's got kindy on Friday afternoon, until three-thirty.' There was a prolonged silence. 'Are you all right, Sam?' she said. 'You sound... Are you sure you're sober?'

'I am.' Sam realised his words had come out slurred – his lip had split and blood was dripping off his chin. 'It's just, well I've had some issues to deal with lately. But yeah, I'm fine.'

'All right, then. Just let us know what you decide. Jasper will be excited. But I won't tell him until you let me know,' she said and hung up.

Sam turned the kettle back on and lay down on the couch. He removed the peas and moved his jaw side to side. Licked his lip. There was going to be bruising.

As the kettle whistled, Sam's mind began to drift. It had been a big day. A huge day. He closed his eyes and concentrated on breathing. He dozed.

Suddenly the man's face flooded his brain. He jerked awake.

He shuffled into the kitchen and made himself another tea. Chamomile this time. Apparently it was supposed to help one sleep. He lay in his bed for hours before he drifted off again. He thought of the man's face. The scar. The pale eyes.

And the dream came back.

Sam walked out into the starless night. He held Jasper in his arms. Karen was dead.

Karen who had put her arms around him in the morning and playfully slid on top of him. He held on to that scene, but it was as painful as the other. He saw himself pull her arms away, saw himself lift her off his chest. Stand. Leave her on the bed. 'Need to get going. We'll resume this tonight,' he had said, bending down to give her a quick kiss. She had opened her arms and pulled off the bed sheets and lain before him, naked, smiling.

And abruptly he lost that image. The other one intruded. Her mutilated body. Her empty dead eyes staring at nothing. The smell.

And he stood on the lawn outside, Jasper clasped to his chest. And he screamed. 'Help me!'

The words kept repeating. But there was no help to be had.

His neighbour came running across the lawn. She was in her dressing gown and the pink material ballooned behind her. With open arms she came towards him and she embraced the two of them, then gently prised Jasper from his arms.

Later, the lawn was filled with people. They engaged in conversation; there were crackled voices from police radios. But there should have been silence. There were bright lights where there should have been soothing darkness. There was activity where there should have been stillness. There should have been nothing. There was nothing.

It was him. It had nothing to do with Karen. It was his love for her. Not her. They wanted to take his love and they'd killed her. He had killed her. They had killed her to silence him.

He started running along the street. Two police cars raced past. And an ambulance.

He didn't know when he stopped running. When he stopped in his tracks and turned around. The street was filled with people as he approached. He stared at the familiar house but it had no likeness to the house that used to be his home.

He fell to his knees and was violently sick. His stomach was empty and managed only a thin trail of bile. He kept retching, his palms on the tarmac.

It was the moment he finally lifted his head that he noticed the car. No, he didn't. Not *he*. Just his eyes. His eyes saw the car. And his brain stored the image for the future.

He saw the car, a silver Toyota. Just beside him. The window was rolled down, and there was somebody inside. The man leaned out through the window and their eyes met for a brief moment.

He would recognise that face. The scar. But more than the scar, the eyes. The dead eyes that looked down at him completely void of expression.

Sam sat up with a start.

He remembered that the police had found him and helped him to stand. He remembered being in shock, shaking uncontrollably. Having no words. No thoughts.

But he *had* seen him. He had seen him there that night. And he had seen him at the hearings. And now he had emerged again. A man with a white scar running from the corner of his mouth and across his cheek. Giving him a permanent smile that was no smile at all.

Sam got out of bed and walked heavily into the bathroom. He turned on the tap, splashed his face with water and looked at his reflection. There was an expression on his face that he hadn't seen in a long time. He stared into his open eyes and he saw the hatred. The fury.

He felt as if something had burst. Dams that he had carefully built had given way. The matter that his brain had stored out of reach came gushing out with irresistible force.

It was no longer a choice. He had to find this man.

He woke with starts several times in the early hours of the morning, but he couldn't remember what had caused them. He got up when the morning was still grey. He turned on his computer. There was an email from Lynette about her interview with someone from Robert and Peter's platoon. Everything was falling into place.

He took a cup of tea onto the deck and watched the day break. He was dead tired.

# 32.

*O, from this time forth,*
*My thoughts be bloody, or be nothing worth!*

Saskia stood by the railings of the ferry, her face against the wind. She looked beautiful. Sam stood for a while watching her. She turned her face and looked at him as he approached. 'I'm sorry, I shouldn't have –'

'You look terrible,' she said.

'I'm not sleeping so well.'

'I meant the bruises. And your lip. What happened?'

'That's why I'm here. I need some information about someone you work with.'

Saskia shook her head. She looked around as if she were worried about being seen with him.

'That man I saw you talking to at the police station. Who is he?'

Saskia shook her head again as if dismayed, and took her time replying. 'His name is Greg Nikula,' she said slowly, digging into her purse and pulling out a pair of sunglasses. She put them on.

'He came to my house last night and threatened me. Told me to stop my investigation. Or whatever it should be called.'

Saskia didn't move. She stared into the dark water below.

'Threatened me and my family. Said that I should consider my son. And the girl, Jade.' They were now out on the open water; Sam looked out over the sea. 'And then I had one of my nightmares again.' He looked straight at her. 'And I remember him from the night Karen died. He was there. I'm positive, Saskia. He was there.'

Saskia frowned. 'Are you sure?'

He nodded. 'He was there. I know he was.'

She shook her head and turned and went inside. Sam followed. She walked right through the seated area and onto the opposite deck. She waited until they were alone before facing him. She took off her sunglasses. 'I'm sorry, Sam, but I really can't help you. I don't know anything about this man.'

'You must do. He works with you.'

'He doesn't work with me. He doesn't work with anyone. He works alone.'

'I saw you talking to him.'

'And that's exactly why I can't help you, Sam.'

'Why?'

'I don't know, but he is untouchable. All I know is that my superiors are... He isn't answerable to anyone.' She looked at him, her eyes very clear. 'I am truly sorry, Sam, but I really can't help you.'

'Could he be working for the government?'

'We're all working for the government.'

'You know what I mean. Could you check Karen's case file once more. For me?'

The ferry approached the wharf. Saskia pulled her coat tightly around her despite the sun glaring down. She stared into his eyes. 'I'll be on here tomorrow,' she said.

# 33.

*What turbulent and dangerous lunacy!*

By Friday morning Lynette was finally in step with local time and woke up at seven-fifteen.

She felt good. Better than she had for a long time. She realised that weight hadn't been on her mind all week, nor had her diet, yet she felt somehow lighter. In the bathroom, she looked longingly at the bathtub before stepping into the shower.

After the shower she sat down and opened her inbox. The first message was just a short note from Sam.

```
From: Sam Hallberg [mailto:iamsam@gmail.com]
Sent: Friday, November 25 2005 7:43 a.m.
To: Lynette Church
Subject: wait for me

Hi Lynette,
Will pick you up on Sunday, so look out for me.
Don't leave without me. Actually, don't leave the
arrival area. Stay where there are lots of people
till you see me.
Yes, so much to talk about.
Safe travel, S
```

'Stay where there are lots of people?' That didn't sound like Sam.

The next message was from her mother's doctor, and Lynette's heart jumped. But it was simply a reassuring message that all was well. Her mother had been in for a check-up, claiming she didn't feel a hundred per cent (her words). She had seemed a little down, but that was all. Nothing that a good talk hadn't cured. Lynette felt a stab of guilt, followed by gratitude towards Dr Morrison, who was so much more than a family doctor.

Lynette was due to meet Ian Clarkson at his office at New Zealand House in Haymarket at one. She had plenty of time to pack later – now she wanted to enjoy this last breakfast with Louis. She could hear him in the kitchen, singing while he prepared it. The aroma of freshly ground coffee wafted towards her as she wandered into the kitchen.

'Do you still play the cello?' Louis asked with his back to her.

'No, it's been a long time,' Lynette said. 'It's not like playing the piano, you know. You can't just pick it up now and then and play a little tune. It's like a relationship. You need to invest in it. And I simply ran out of time. Also, the people I used to play with dispersed.'

'I used to love listening to you, Cricket. That's why I called you that. You and your cello; making music at dusk.'

'I know,' Lynette said. 'You're the only person who has ever given me a pet name.' She stretched out her hand and took his. 'I'll miss you. Wish we lived closer to each other.'

'You might not like me so much if we did,' Louis grinned then was suddenly serious. 'You will be careful, won't you? Let me know how it all goes with your research. And if there's ever anything I can do to help I'm just a phone call or an email away.'

Lynette looked at him. She really would miss him. 'Do you really think there's something sinister about all this?' she asked. 'Something worse than a little immigration corruption?'

Louis shrugged, walked around to her side of the table and pulled her into his arms. 'You look after yourself, Cricket,' he whispered. They stood like that for a moment before they let go.

***

Lynette had always felt that New Zealand House didn't do a good job of representing her country. The high-rise building exuded everything that she didn't associate with New Zealand: pretentiousness, self-importance and a certain coldness. All glass and concrete, anonymous and impersonal.

A peroxide blonde receptionist with acne and bluish-white legs without stockings escorted Lynette to Clarkson's office. It was spacious – part work space, part meeting room – and furnished with a large desk, a red sofa, a matching armchair and a coffee table. Not over the top in any way, yet it somehow managed to reduce the man inhabiting it, rather than add substance to him. He looked even smaller and more insignificant here than Lynette remembered.

Clarkson rose and gestured for Lynette to take a seat on the sofa. He offered coffee but Lynette declined. 'Thank you for taking the time to see me,' she began. Clarkson just nodded like someone granting a privilege. Lynette took out her little recorder and looked questioningly at him.

'I'd prefer it if we keep this as an informal chat,' he said.

'As you wish,' she said, returning the recorder to her purse. 'I've found that it helps ensure the accuracy of what I report. But up to you, of course.' Clarkson's face was a mask and he said nothing. 'As you know, I've been trying to get an opportunity to talk to you for quite some time, both in your capacity as director of AME, and as special envoy to the EU.'

Clarkson didn't respond. He sat leaning back in his chair with his hands on the armrests. The intent might have been to give an impression of relaxed congeniality, but he looked more like someone prepared to spring to his feet. Not relaxed at all, Lynette thought.

'Firstly, I would like to congratulate you on the extraordinary increase in the EU meat quota. Could you tell me a little bit about what was involved in achieving that?'

Clarkson's pale eyes looked straight into Lynette's. There was no flicker of life there, no warmth. 'Same as always, Miss Church, the same as in any human endeavour. It's always a matter of hard work, the right connections and perseverance.'

'And this hadn't been applied to the negotiations before you came aboard?'

'I had the privilege of being able to focus on the one matter at hand. And it paid off.'

Lynette nodded. 'I understand you had support from an unexpected source.'

'What do you mean?' Was there a glimmer of life in those cold eyes?

'I've heard that the French Foreign Minister was instrumental in securing the required votes to approve the increase.'

'I don't understand where on earth you might have got that information from, Miss Church. Gossip, presumably. And gossip is a very unreliable source of information. As I am sure you know, being such a highly regarded journalist.'

'Oh, it mustn't be underestimated either,' said Lynette, shooting off one of her sweetest smiles. She waited. The room became uncomfortably quiet. She didn't mind.

'Affairs of this sort are always complex. The outcome is the result of a range of different efforts. And sometimes a little fortunate timing, too. I guess I just happened to be in the right place at the right time. And, as I said, add hard work, connections and perseverance, and we had the outcome we had hoped for.'

Lynette nodded, as if she were in agreement. Impressed, even. 'Let me jump to another area of interest, Mr Clarkson. As a director of AME, you must have got to know your chairman quite well. Eric Salisbury.'

Ian Clarkson nodded. 'Yes of course. Professionally.'

'It seems not many know Mr Salisbury in any other way. Or know him at all.'

She looked at Clarkson for an extended moment. His hands gripped the ends of the armrest.

'It's come to my knowledge that Mr Salisbury has misrepresented himself in certain ways.'

There was another long pause. 'What do you mean by that?' Ian Clarkson said eventually.

'It seems that he hasn't been entirely truthful about his education.'

Clarkson said nothing.

'It seems he never graduated from Nuffield College in 1989, as he claims.' Lynette's words lingered in the air between them. 'At least, not as Eric Salisbury.'

Clarkson looked back at Lynette with bewilderment. He doesn't know, she thought. He really doesn't know. Well, I'll be damned.

'I think it would be worth your while to find out a little more about your chairman. It always pays to have the facts clearly established, don't you think, Mr Clarkson? Know with whom one makes deals. Whom one is putting one's trust in.'

There was no response.

'If I were you, I would want to know who Mr Salisbury really is.'

Again, nothing.

'Oh, and if I were in your place, I would acknowledge the invaluable French support I received in the efforts to raise the import quotas. Shouldn't be too hard to do. I understand that France's then foreign minister is now the Ambassador to New Zealand. A nice retirement package. Especially since his only child lives there. But perhaps you already know that, Mr Clarkson? Come to think of it, you probably know Monsieur Gérard already, don't you?'

Lynette cocked her head. Clarkson sat stiffly in his chair, his hands clasping and unclasping the ends of the armrests.

'Well, Mr Clarkson, it's been very interesting to finally get to talk to you. Even if I had to do most of the talking myself. I'll be flying back to New Zealand tonight and I really look forward to gathering my thoughts during the flight. So many interesting impressions to digest. So much to consider. As you said, it's all about hard work, connections and perseverance.' She stood up. 'I mustn't take up more of your time. Thank you so much for seeing me, and good luck with your future endeavours.' She stretched out her hand.

Clarkson rose slowly and awkwardly, as if his joints were sore. Lynette thought she could see both the ungainly young boy he had once been and the shrivelled old man he would one day become. His handshake was cold and brief, his hand limp.

***

'She's leaving my office just now. I have no idea where she's heading, but she's flying out tonight. Must be on NZ001.'

'Call security and have them delay her departure from the building. We'll take care of the rest.'

***

Lynette emerged from the bathroom after a quick touch-up of her hair and makeup, and stepped into the elevator. A smartly dressed young Maori man stood leaning lightly against the wall, a folder in his hands. He nodded and smiled and Lynette smiled back. The lift moved, then almost suddenly stopped with a jolt. The man smiled and shrugged.

'Does this happen often?' Lynette asked.

He shook his head. 'Never had it happen to me before. Let's give it a couple of minutes before we raise the alarm, shall we?'

Lynette nodded. She thought about people getting stuck in elevators for hours. Days, even. She looked at the man. Would she enjoy getting to know him better? He seemed nice enough.

'Just visiting?' he asked.

Lynette nodded. 'Yes, flying back home tonight.'

'Lucky you,' he said, smiling again.

It was hard to think of anything much to say. Lynette leaned against the wall too. She checked her watch: one-forty. She would need to go straight back to Louis's, sort out the last few things, perhaps have a quick shower.

The minutes ticked by.

'That's five minutes,' she said.

'Let's give it another couple more minutes, shall we?' he said. 'I'm sure it's already being attended to.'

Another five minutes dragged by, and then the elevator came to life as suddenly as it had stopped. 'Here we go,' the man said.

Outside, Lynette hesitated. Which would be quickest? The Tube or a taxi? She decided on a taxi, and didn't have to wait long until one stopped.

*** 

In the end, she had time for a final bath. She placed a thank-you note to Louis on the kitchen table, then dressed and called a minicab. It was raining when she stepped out with her suitcase in her hand. Before she had started down the steps, she heard someone calling out, 'Hold on, stay where you are, dear!' The driver had leapt from the car and was racing up the steps to take the suitcase. 'Wait here, dear,' he said and took off with it, only to return quickly with an umbrella that he held over Lynette. He looked to be in his mid-sixties, but it was hard to tell. Short, wiry and with an impish face, capped by an old-fashioned driver's hat, he seemed to belong to a different era. Gosh, Lynette thought, what a gentleman.

The cab was immaculate and smelled vaguely of peppermint. Lynette sat back against the soft backrest and closed her eyes. What a whirlwind few days. They felt like an eternity, and at the same time they had passed in a blink of an eye. Her speech at the conference had happened in another time. She opened her eyes. The driver was looking intently into the rear-view mirror. 'I think someone's following us,' he said.

Lynette laughed a little. 'What do you mean?'

'That black car behind us. Someone you know?'

Lynette turned to take a look. 'No.'

'Well, then,' he said, 'let's check it out.' He increased the speed, took a few quick abrupt turns and checked the mirror again. 'Yup,' he said. 'Sure enough, he's chasing us.' He looked over his shoulder. 'Buckle up, dear, and we'll see what we can do.'

Was this really happening? Lynette sat bolt upright in her seat, staring straight ahead. But as they made a sudden sharp turn into a little side street, tossing Lynette against the door, she heard the tyres of the other car screeching against the road surface. It *was* actually happening. She caught a glimpse of her driver's eyes in the rear-view mirror. They were wide open, glittering. 'Just relax, dear,' he said. 'Trust me.'

Trust him? Here she was, putting her life in the hands of a man she had known for less than five minutes. She felt fear emanating from her stomach and goosebumps rising on her arms.

As the car twisted and turned through narrow backstreets at a furious speed, Lynette quickly lost her bearings. She focused on keeping the safety belt away from her throat. It will strangle me if we crash, she thought. However many sharp turns they made, the other car seemed still to be following. Lynette couldn't see the speedometer from where she was in the back seat, and was grateful. The view from the window was a blur. Then, right in front of them, a large vehicle carrying a double-layered load of silver metallic cars pulled into view, on its way to cross the road they were on, and only a short distance away. Lynette closed her eyes. This is it, she thought. My life ends here.

The car made a turn that threw Lynette against the door again, then there was an abrupt jolt that lifted the car into the air for a moment as it bounced off the pavement. Lynette bounced with it and her head bumped hard against the ceiling. There was another jolt as the car bounced off the pavement on the other side, followed by a second of eerie silence, as if the car had taken a deep breath, and they were on their way again. Lynette looked through the back window. The entire street behind them was blocked by the transporter. And the black car was nowhere to be seen.

The rest of the drive to Heathrow seemed very slow by comparison. Lynette checked her hair and makeup in her compact mirror. Surprisingly, she looked more or less as before.

'You must have an interesting life, dear,' the driver said.

'Not really,' Lynette said, smiling weakly. 'But thank you.'

'Oh, my pleasure. Made my day, really. Most jobs are so boring. Feeling all refreshed now.'

Refreshed?

As they pulled up outside terminal three at Heathrow, the driver gallantly jumped out and opened the door for Lynette. For a split second she felt like hugging him. 'Thank you so much,' she said as she paid, including a generous tip. 'Who knows, you might have saved my life.'

'Always a pleasure to assist a beautiful lady.' He gave a mock salute. 'Now, you look after yourself, dear.'

As she walked across the busy terminal floor towards the Air New Zealand check-in counters, the immense danger that she had been in hit home. She felt nauseous, and slowed her pace, trying to think. I need someone with me all the time, she thought. What can I do? Just then, a woman in a wheelchair was pushed past by an airline attendant. Lynette watched them disappear into the crowd. Then she uncertainly made her way towards the check-in area. Only as she was standing in front of the matronly Air New Zealand check-in clerk did she allow herself a quick look around while reaching for a paper tissue in her handbag. She had no idea who or what she was looking for, and nothing caught her eye.

As she shakily attempted to retrieve her travel documents, they fell to the floor and scattered. She awkwardly bent down to gather them. 'I'm sorry,' she said, 'but I've just been involved in the most awful incident on the way here. My taxi had a serious accident, and I think someone might have been killed.' To her surprise, she felt tears brim up in her eyes and her lips quivered. The woman looked at her with sympathy, then checked the documents again. Once more, Lynette was grateful she was travelling business class.

'Let me see if we can get you through to the VIP room,' the clerk said and lifted the receiver.

After a swift conversation, she put the phone down and smiled comfortingly. 'Just wait here a moment, and someone will pick you up and take you through to the VIP lounge.'

A moment later, a large Indian man wearing a turban appeared. With a wheelchair. A bit over the top, Lynette thought, but she sank down into it. It felt good – she *was* traumatised; probably in mild shock. She gratefully allowed herself to be pushed through the VIP security and immigration checks, and then into the VIP lounge. The kind Indian man also informed her that she could use the first-class lounge during the two-hour stopover in Los Angeles.

Lynette drew a deep breath of relief. She was on her way home.

# 34.

*And his soul may be as damn'd and black as hell*


Saskia sat inside the ferry as it surged to Devonport. Sam was beside her. She gave him a cautious smile. They sat in silence. Saskia looked at the choppy sea outside.

'Did you find anything in Karen's file?' Sam asked eventually.

'I can't believe I even looked. I don't know why I'm doing this.'

'Because you're a good person.'

She scoffed. 'I can't tell you here.'

They sat in silence for the rest of the crossing. They got off the ferry in Devonport then walked towards her home on the hill. A sparse apartment filled with white furniture and straight lines. 'Would you like something to drink?' she asked, moving to the refrigerator. 'I can offer you a beer. Or wine.'

'Water will be fine.'

'Would you like some cheese? You could probably do with something to eat.'

'Just water, thanks.'

She filled a glass then threw a folder onto the bench in front of him. He opened it. There were photos of Karen's murder scene. He tensed. 'I should have warned you,' Saskia said.

'It's all right.' There were photos of Karen's body but also photos of outside the house and the people and officers floating around. His chest locked and he found it difficult to breathe.

Saskia took a photo and pointed to a man in the background. 'You were right,' she said. 'There he is.'

'Why would he have been there?'

'I still don't know who he works for or what he does. His official job description is very general: "special investigations". He wasn't officially involved in Karen's case, though, and his name isn't listed on any of the personnel sheets from that night.'

She showed him another photo with Greg Nikula in the background, this time looking directly at the camera, the scar giving him that odd semblance of a smile, the eyes dead. Sam looked at another photo. Karen's naked body lay sprawled on the floor, her head tilted to one side and her eyes wide open. The bruises on her neck were obvious to see. As was her soiled and bloodied lower body.

'Why didn't they solve this?' Sam asked. 'Or did they?'

'They didn't solve it. But –'

'But what?'

'It's an odd investigation.'

'Why?'

Saskia hesitated.

'Tell me why, Saskia.'

'I don't know for certain but when you read it, it feels contrived. Constructed. Too pat. And no leads were followed through.'

In the silence the voices of children playing outside lifted in the air. 'I think it had something to do with you, Sam.'

'Why?'

She shook her head, stood up and walked over to the open window. 'I think somebody wanted you out of the way.'

'So why didn't they just have *me* killed?' Sam realised his voice was rising.

'I think it was personal. Somebody wanted to hurt you.'

Sam stood beside her by the window. The sea glittered in the late afternoon light and yachts of various sizes drifted by. It looked idyllic; peaceful and happy.

'Could this Greg have killed Karen?' Sam asked.

'I don't know. But if he did, he was just a tool.'

234

Sam nodded.

'Sam, there's nothing you can do. It wouldn't help to get at Greg Nikula. He's replaceable. Professional, but replaceable.'

Sam paced the length of the floor and back again.

'Don't approach him, Sam. It won't achieve anything. It'll just put you in more danger. And possibly me, too.'

'So there's nothing I can do?'

She lowered her eyes at the sheer despair in his gaze. Then she shook her head slowly. 'No, Sam, there's nothing you can do.'

He walked to the table and picked up the folder. 'Thank you for finding this,' he said. 'I do hope I haven't caused you any trouble. I never meant to.'

She walked up to him, put her arms around him and held him for a moment. 'No, Sam, you never meant to. I know.'

***

Sam paced the pavement opposite the police station for over an hour, but as the number of pedestrians thinned he went to sit on a park bench on the other side of the intersection. It was shaded by low trees. A flock of sparrows noisily settled down for the night inside the wide green canopy.

Sam kept his eyes on the entrance to the police station. He realised it was unlikely that Nikula would leave the building on foot, but there was no way he could check the drivers of the cars that left the garage in Vincent Street. He wasn't even sure what he was doing here. Greg Nikula may not have been there at all today. Or he might have left earlier. Gone wherever it was he lived. Where would someone like that live? Sam couldn't picture it at all. Did he have a family? A wife? Children? It was impossible to envisage.

Two heavily built policemen came out of the building. Sam couldn't see their faces from where he was, but he knew neither of them was Greg Nikula. He watched them carry on around the building and up Vincent Street, and remembered how Sid Fielding said he had identified Nikula as a policeman by his gait: 'He walked like a policeman.' Sam understood now what Sid had meant. These two laughed as they got into a police car and drove away. Sam wondered how many people joined the force because of a chip on their shoulder, or to gain a sense of power. Joined for all the wrong reasons.

Finally he appeared. Greg Nikula. He was dressed in civilian clothes – black trousers, black polo shirt, grey jacket slung over his shoulder. He stopped briefly and looked up and down the street, before carrying on down to the traffic lights. Sam pulled back a little and stood by the steps leading down to Aotea Square, watching. The lights turned green and Nikula crossed the street. Sam watched him carry on. He crossed the road then followed at a safe distance.

He realised he hadn't put much thought into this. He was driven by something other than his exhausted brain.

Sam had to walk briskly to keep up. This man could stride. His thick, muscular legs pounded the pavement. He moved not unlike a shark, with fluid but determined movements, navigating his way efficiently, as if homing in on a target. Sam felt exposed, like some jittery clown fish following behind. There weren't many people around. Too late for the day people, too early for the people of the night. And suddenly, without anything having changed in the least, Sam knew that Nikula had spotted him. Yet he didn't stop. He carried on towards the steps leading down to Myers Park. Sam followed, keeping an even distance.

I must be mad, he thought. Why am I doing this? Then, abruptly, Nikula stopped. Still with his back to Sam, he stuck his hand in his pocket. Sam's muscles tensed in anticipation of a weapon. But Nikula pulled out a pack of cigarettes and lit one. Then he slowly turned around to face Sam. His eyes were expressionless and, apart from the eerily 'smiling' mouth, so was his face.

They stared at each other, Sam waiting for Nikula to say

something. But he didn't. He just kept his eyes fixed on Sam while he slowly exhaled smoke. In the end it was Sam who had to break the silence. 'I need to talk to you,' he managed.

'Do I know you?'

'Of course you fucking know me. You know me. You knew my wife. My child. My house. You know fucking all there is to know about me!'

'I'll ask you to keep your voice down, sir.'

'I just want to know why?' Sam asked.

Nikula shrugged his shoulders, his mouth with the perpetual artificial smile mocking Sam.

'Why this interest in me?' Sam continued.

'I don't know what you're talking about.'

Nikula gestured for Sam to follow and carried on down the steps. Myers Park was more or less deserted, with just a few children and minders further up in the playground. This is where I will die, Sam thought, as he watched Nikula's broad back. Strangely, the idea was tempting. Shoot me here. Break my neck. Put those strong hands around my throat. Get it over with.

But Nikula led him halfway through the underpass and into the car park on the other side, where he stopped and turned around. 'So, you've done a little investigative work of your own? With the help of that blonde.' He regarded Sam, his face absolutely blank.

'Did you kill my wife?'

'Even if I said yes, it wouldn't answer your question.'

'Do you know who did?'

Nikula shrugged, threw the cigarette down and ground the butt into the asphalt with the sole of his shoe.

'Did you kill Brent Taylor?' Sam asked.

Nikula looked at him coldly. 'What does it matter, Sam?'

Sam stared back at him.

'You know how these things work. You've always known how these things work. I'm just doing my job. Just like you used to do your job.' He pursed his lips, stretching the scar. 'Miss your job, do you? I'm sure you do. Can't be much fun for someone with your talent to muck around with cars.' He shook his head in mock sympathy. 'That why you jumped at the opportunity to help look into that student's death? Not a smart move, Sam.'

'What kind of man are you?' Sam whispered. 'And whose errands do you do?'

Nikula's face expressed no emotion, and he said nothing.

'The government's?'

'We all work for the government. In our different ways. Don't we?'

Sam felt his muscles tense. His mouth was dry; he could feel every heartbeat.

Nikula's smile broadened and he made a gesture of resignation, opening his arms, palms turned out. 'You want to kill me, don't you, Sam? You want to take my neck and squeeze the life from me. What do you think would happen then? Someone will find my body, call the police. My body will be taken from here and put in a morgue. No one will ask any more questions and I'll disappear. And then someone else will come along. Someone just like me. Someone just doing his job. And he'll pick up where I left off. And then he'll be taken out. And someone else will come along. Like the Greek Hydra. Fight me, and I will grow stronger.'

Sam shook his head. 'You're fucked.'

'No. *You're* fucked, Sam.' Nikula turned and walked away.

'How does it feel knowing I'm here?' Sam said to his back. 'Knowing that I will never, ever, ever let it go? You'll pay for what you've done. You'll pay.'

Nikula turned and gave a mocking, snorting laugh. 'It's not me that has to pay. I'm just doing my job. And however much you may want me dead, I'm your only link to the truth about the murder of your wife. You will never kill me, Sam. Even if you had it in you. Never.' And then he turned and walked away.

# 36.

*And with no less nobility of love*
*Than that which dearest father bears his son*

Matakana was less than an hour's drive from Auckland, but was another world. The village had established itself as the centre of an area of organic lifestyle farms. It supported art galleries, artists' residencies, potteries and wood-turning studios. It was charming though not, Sam thought, very genuine.

Even when Sam had called to confirm his visit, his mother-in-law had sounded dubious. But here he was rattling into the vineyards. The car wasn't sounding too good. He wondered why, having been a mechanic for several years now, he hadn't fixed the damn thing. Everything he passed was dry. The grass was brown and the red soil dusty.

Dorothea and Jan De Haan lived on an apple orchard fifteen minutes from Matakana village. He remembered summer holidays here with Karen, playing petánque on the front lawn and having long lunches on the veranda. A time when his life had seemed endless. He drove into the section. Three nondescript dogs leapt at the car. Two barked with all of their might. The third was lazier. They sniffed Sam as he got out, shoving their noses right into his groin, then ran off, barking his arrival. Dorothea and Jan appeared on the veranda. Sam had to brace himself. He managed a smile. 'Hi, guys.'

'Hello,' Dorothea said coldly. Jan simply nodded. Sam could sense their disapproval. Or perhaps it was all in his own mind. His guilty conscience raising its ugly head and obscuring what was really there. Why did he come so rarely? He knew Dorothea and Jan had to deal with Jasper's constant questions, asking for his father day in and day out. And they must blame him for Karen's death. *He* did.

'How are you both?' he asked, trying to infuse the words with a cheerfulness he didn't feel.

'You look terrible,' Jan said. 'What's happened to you?' He frowned, in what could have been interpreted as genuine concern. Or suspicion.

'I know,' Sam managed. 'I had a small accident the other day. I've had a lot on my mind lately. Nothing I can't manage, though. Don't worry. Spending a day here will do me good. Thank you for having me.'

'Surely you know that you are always welcome, Sam.' Dorothea said. 'Are you ready to eat?'

'Thank you; that would be lovely.' No doubt it would be organic kibbled-wheat bread with homemade hummus, or relish made from home-grown vegetables over home-raised and home-cured pork. Nice food. The kind of food good, normal people ate.

'Where's Jasper?'

'He's in the trees, somewhere.' Jan nodded towards the orchard.

Sam walked through the rows of apple trees and found Jasper playing by himself, chatting away. 'Hello,' Sam called, so not to give him a fright. Jasper looked up. His shiny black hair had a bowl cut that Sam wasn't so sure about. But he looked healthy. And he had definitely grown. Next year he would be four, and before Sam knew it he would be at school. His world would grow. He would be out there exploring an expanding, dangerous world, and there was nothing Sam could do to protect him.

He waited for Jasper to come running to him. That's what he'd done whenever Sam had come to visit before. But instead the little boy just stood looking at him, holding on to a small wheelbarrow filled with dead twigs and leaves. He had a smile, but it was small. 'Hi, Daddy,' he said.

'You've grown a lot, Jasper. You're a big boy now.'

Jasper shrugged. He was still holding the handles of the wheelbarrow, but he slowly lowered them and put his hands in his pockets. 'Is it lunchtime now?' he asked.

'Yes, I think it might just be,' said Sam and stretched out a hand. 'Come on – let's get back and see what's for lunch!'

Jasper slowly took one hand out of his pocket and grasped Sam's and they walked to the house together. Sam took a chocolate bar from his pocket and offered it to him. 'I know how much you like chocolate. I guess you shouldn't show Oma and Opa, huh?'

'Thank you,' Jasper said, without too much enthusiasm. He slid it into his own pocket. 'I'll save it for tonight. I can have lollies after dinner.'

'How's kindy?' Sam asked.

'It's good. I'm not with the little ones any more.'

'That's right – you're a big boy now, aren't you?'

'Yes.'

'Where's Buddy?' Sam asked.

There was no reply, and Sam felt Jasper's hand pull away.

'I thought I was going to meet Buddy?'

Jasper was walking slowly, keeping his eyes on the ground and saying nothing.

Sam touched Jasper's head. He didn't flinch, nor did he look up. His hair was soft. 'Sorry I haven't been to visit for a while. I've been very busy with work.'

'Buddy died, Daddy.'

Sam stopped in his tracks, and squatted in front of Jasper. 'What happened?' he asked and took hold of Jasper's hands.

'He got out of the cage and the dogs killed him.' Jasper's lips quivered.

Sam pulled him close, held him tight in his arms and stood up.

'I'm so sorry, little man, so sorry,' he whispered in his ear. He took in the warm smell of his skin and his hair. 'There is nothing we can do to make Buddy live again. But you had him, and you loved him. And you will always remember that.'

Sam carried Jasper in his arms all the way to the homestead, and Jasper let him, keeping his arms tight around Sam's neck. Before they reached the house, Sam set Jasper down and squatted beside him. 'I was going to ask Oma and Opa, but I'll ask you first. Would you like to come and stay with me one weekend?'

Jasper didn't say anything for a while. 'Really, Daddy?' he asked quietly.

Sam felt a stab of guilt, and nodded. 'Yes, really, little man.'

Jasper nodded. He smiled a little too. 'We have to ask Oma and Opa,' he said.

'We certainly do,' said Sam and they went inside.

They had kibbled-wheat bread for lunch with cured pork and homemade relish. Afterwards Jasper wanted to watch television. But there was no aerial in the house, so TV didn't mean TV but children's films. It involved watching one of a small stack of DVDs, all looking well worn. The DVDs were in Dutch and followed the adventures of a wooden boy puppet. But it wasn't a retelling of Pinocchio – that much Sam could tell. Dorothea set up the DVD and let Jasper press the remote and start the film. He sat transfixed, and Sam and Dorothea returned to the kitchen to have coffee with Jan.

'I was wondering if Jasper could come and stay one weekend,' Sam said.

Dorothea and Jan looked at each other, then at Sam. 'If this is another one of your promises that never eventuate, forget it,' Jan said. 'I hope you haven't told him. It's too hard for him to be disappointed again and again.'

'No, no. I really mean it,' Sam said. 'I'm, well, I'm on leave for a while.'

'I'll go and get my calendar,' Dorothea said. 'They have some projects planned at kindy. Preparing for Christmas, I guess.'

They decided on two weekends from that day. Sam went and sat beside Jasper and watched the Dutch movie to the end. He was moved to see Jasper so completely engrossed.

The film over, he told Jasper it was time for him to leave. 'Why do you have to go now, Daddy? Can't you stay till tonight? Till I go to bed?'

'Sorry, little man, but I can't today. I have to go home because I'm picking a friend up from the airport very early in the morning.'

'Can I come?'

Sam shook his head. 'Not today, but you're coming to stay in a couple of weeks. That'll be fun, won't it?' Jasper nodded and left the room, jumping on one foot, then the other.

'Are you picking up a woman?' Dorothea asked suspiciously as they were saying goodbye.

'Yes. But it's not like that, I assure you. She's a journalist. I've known her for years. Since Wellington, actually.'

Dorothea nodded. 'Well, it wouldn't be the end of the world if it *was* like that. Sam, Jan and I only want what is good for you. Always have, always will.'

Sam looked at her. She had aged. Her once-black hair was now entirely white, and she had deep wrinkles. On impulse, Sam put his arms around her and gave her a hug. 'I know,' he said. 'I know. It's just me. It's just so hard.'

She nodded. 'Yes, it is. But you have a wonderful son. Don't you ever forget that.'

On the spur of the moment came words that Sam hadn't been aware of thinking. 'Dotty, I have a friend who's in a bit of trouble. Or not trouble, really, she's been going through some rough times and I think she's lonely. Would you allow me to bring her here for Christmas?' When Dorothea didn't respond, he continued. 'It's not a romance at all. She is a down-and-out girl and her best friend was murdered. She doesn't seem to have much in the way of family or support.'

Dorothea put her hand on Sam's arm. 'Of course, Sam. Your friends are always welcome here. What's her name?'

'Jade. Jade Amaro,' Sam said.

'You tell Jade that she is most welcome to join us for Christmas. Remember, our Dutch Christmas is on the twenty-fourth.' Dorothy smiled, with real warmth.

They went outside and Jasper came running. Sam knelt and hugged him tightly. His body was so small, so vulnerable. Jasper hugged back hard then patted his father on the head. When Sam looked up his eyes met Dorothea's. 'Are you sure you can't stay a little longer?' she said. 'We could play a game of pétanque.'

Sam smiled. 'I'd really enjoy that.'

# 37.

*A pirate of very warlike appointment gave us chase*

It was early Sunday morning and the roads were virtually empty as Sam headed south towards the airport. He was tired, dead tired. He had driven back from Matakana in the evening, and instead of going to bed when he got home, had sat on the deck, reading until dawn. He had finished *Hamlet* and for some reason this felt momentous. As if something else was coming to an end, too. He had no sense of a new beginning, just of something slowly ending.

He was looking forward to seeing Lynette again. But he wondered how he would be able to make her understand what had happened in her absence. The tone of her latest email had been upbeat. She obviously thought her article, or articles, would make a difference. Sam sighed and turned on the radio. He flicked between the channels until he found some gentle guitar music. It took him a moment to realise the piece was 'Killing Me Softly'. It had been one of Karen's favourites. He felt a surge of heat run through his body. The last few weeks seemed to have removed some sort of protection. It was as if everything was raw again.

Sam sat for a while in the car after parking at Auckland airport. The music had changed to something else, but the feeling lingered. He closed his eyes. He had been fooling himself. Those moments when he had thought that perhaps he would be able to build some kind of new and meaningful life again, be a proper father to Jasper; it would never happen. He bent forward and rested his forehead against his knuckles on the steering wheel. But the tears never came. There was no release to be had.

He was early and bought a cup of scalding bitter coffee that tasted of the Styrofoam cup it was served in.

Sam was astonished to see Lynette coming through the doors as the very first passenger – in a wheelchair. She was pushed by a heavily built young man in an Air New Zealand uniform. They were both smiling and Lynette looked good for someone who had been in the air for some twenty-six hours. She waved cheerfully when she spotted Sam and he weaved through the crowd to reach her. He bent over to give her a hug. 'What happened?' he asked.

'It's a long story,' she said. 'I'll tell you in the car.' Sam stood up and stretched out a hand to take the wheelchair from the young man.

Then he spotted Greg Nikula. Standing outside, looking at them through the glass doors, arms folded across his chest.

Sam said to the young man, 'Can I ask you a favour? Can you hold on to Miss Church while I get my car? I don't want to leave her alone. Her ex has made some nasty threats. There's a restraining order in place, but you never know. Just to make sure.' Lynette stared at him, an astonished expression on her face, but she said nothing.

'Oh, absolutely, I'll watch her till you're back.' The young man smiled and put a hand on Lynette's shoulder. 'I'll guard her with my life.'

You don't know how close to the truth that might be, Sam thought.

Sam walked briskly through the terminal building, shielded by a large group of Korean tourists, and made it out through the doors at the Departures end of the building. He paid the parking fee at the machine and dashed to his car. He was quickly back outside the terminal building, and stopped at the pickup ramp. A traffic warden immediately appeared, telling him to stay in the car. 'You can't park here,' she said.

'But my wife is in a wheelchair,' Sam protested. 'She'll need help to the car.'

The warden looked at him under the brim of her sunhat, as if evaluating him. He must have made an honest impression because suddenly the sullen face was all smiles. 'You just go and get your wife, and I'll watch the car,' she said.

Sam couldn't see Nikula but assumed he would be standing in a place where he could watch Lynette. Sam slipped through the sliding doors, and made a point of walking behind other people moving inside the terminal as he made his way back to Arrivals. Lynette and her helper were still in the same spot, now surrounded by a sea of arriving passengers and their greeters. Sam caught the eye of the young man and motioned for him to come over.

'I'll help you to the car,' the young man said and they walked together towards the Departures end. The man helped Lynette out of the wheelchair and into the passenger seat. Sam thought she seemed to lean heavily on him, and he wondered what had happened to her.

She held on to the young man's hand while she thanked him profusely. She was rewarded with a wide smile that showed off a set of strong white teeth.

'It's been a pleasure, Lynette. You take care now.' He saluted her, gripped the chair and disappeared.

Sam got into the driver's seat. 'You seem pretty perky for someone who is wheelchair-bound,' he said.

Lynette smiled smugly. 'Grab the benefits whenever you can. I got onto the flight in a wheelchair, so thought I should get off in one.'

Sam started the car and they swiftly made their way out of the airport area and onto the road that led to the motorway. He kept checking the rear-view mirror.

Bloody hell! Not again, Lynette thought. 'Don't tell me we're being followed,' she said, staring at Sam. 'What's going on?'

'Not sure yet,' Sam said, narrowly missing an overtaking car. 'But I spotted someone at the airport who shouldn't have been there. Who knows you changed your flights?'

'Just you. Oh, and Roger Evans, my boss.'

Sam shook his head, but said nothing.

They approached an intersection. 'Turn off here!' Lynette said urgently. Sam took the turn clumsily, and for a moment it was touch and go whether they would veer off the road. He managed to get back onto the asphalt and Lynette pointed towards a block of warehouse buildings. 'Behind those,' she said. The area was completely deserted. 'Now, tell me what's going on,' Lynette said as they stopped.

'It's a long story and we have very little time,' Sam said. 'Can I just say that you're in danger, Lynette. As long as you are going to write your story, you're in terrible danger. It's all connected. Brent and his book, the meat and the false identities. I think it's all connected. Believe me – we are onto something too big for us.'

She stared at him for a moment. 'Get out of the car,' she said.

Sam didn't move.

'Get out of the car! Now!' she shouted.

Sam unbuckled and opened the door. Lynette did the same and jumped out of the car and into the driver's seat. Sam got in the other side.

'What was the story with the wheelchair?'

'Another long story. Just buckle up.' Lynette started the car. 'I've just survived another car chase at the hands of someone else,' she said. 'This time I'll be in control. I'm a better driver than you,' she said with a little smile. 'My dad wanted a son, but he only had me. So, I did go-kart when I was five and motorsport became my passion. Add to that my recent experience of car chases. More about that later. Hold on, here we go!'

She's not taking this seriously, Sam thought.

They drove back to the main road. It wasn't until they were on the motorway that Sam spotted the silver Toyota behind them. 'He's behind us.'

'Who?'

'The man who took the CD from Jade. His name is Greg Nikula,' Sam said. 'You don't want him to catch up, Lynette.'

She nodded. And now her eyes were deadly serious.

The silver Toyota stayed behind, increasing and decreasing the distance, but constantly right behind them. Lynette drove as fast as the speed limit allowed, but the roads were almost void of traffic and there was nowhere to go, nothing to put between them. They left the motorway, driving along the sleepy residential streets of Epsom and towards Newmarket.

'Now what?' Lynette said, more to herself than to Sam. 'We don't have that much petrol.'

'Don't stop here,' Sam said. 'Get up on the Northern Motorway. Let's see if we can lose him on the North Shore.'

Lynette said nothing but turned into Gillies Avenue and up onto the motorway. The silver Toyota was still on their tail. 'Here we go!' she said and accelerated. So did the Toyota. As they approached the Harbour Bridge, the Toyota came up beside them on the right-hand side, driving very close. Lynette bit her lip and pushed the old car to the limit and managed to slide in front of the Toyota, the central dividing barrier now on their right-hand side. The Toyota came up beside them on the left this time, scraping the passenger door with a loud noise and sending the Subaru into the barrier. Lynette managed to counteract the bounce and kept control of the car. They were now driving at top speed and Sam's Subaru was vibrating ominously. Then the Toyota rammed them again, this time scraping the full length of the Subaru in a shower of sparks and with a deafening sound. Lynette struggled to keep the Subaru in the lane and Sam sat holding on to the dashboard. Neither uttered a word.

They were now at the top of the bridge. And the Toyota came at them again. But this time Lynette was prepared and her timing perfect. Instead of just trying to keep the car straight, she steered it left, hard into the Toyota. The two cars collided in a thunderous crash, the Toyota veering to the left and the Subaru to the right. The Subaru crashed against the central barrier, but again Lynette managed to keep it on all four wheels. She took her foot off the accelerator. Sam looked back.

The Toyota was still moving, sliding on its side towards the bridge railings. Lynette slowed down and came to a stop. They had now passed the top of the bridge and could no longer see the Toyota. Lynette veered over to the left lane and cautiously reversed.

The Toyota was lying on its right-hand side, at a slight angle to the railing, wheels spinning and smoke rising. Then it slowly tipped over and came to a standstill upside down. Lynette stopped some fifty metres away.

'I can't open the door,' Sam said. 'It's stuck.'

'Shouldn't we just leave?' Lynette said. 'There are cameras on the bridge, you know.'

'Firstly, we are the victims here. Secondly, I don't think the police will want this out. But I want to check if he's alive.' Sam clambered into the back seat and tried the door. It opened and he stepped out.

The smell of hot metal, petrol and rubber wafted in the air. Sam walked to the car. Nikula was still in the driver's seat, hanging upside down, suspended by his safety belt. His eyes were open, but unseeing. Blood was running down from a gash in his forehead. Sam stared at the dead man, searching for a response within himself. There was nothing. This man's death changed nothing. He had been an errand boy. A paid lackey. His secrets had died with him and were forever lost. Sam stretched inside the broken window and closed the man's eyes. He looked around but saw no other cars. Then he ran back to his own.

'Let's leave,' he said as he sat down in the back seat. Lynette started the car and to their surprise it willingly drove off. Behind them the Toyota lay still on a spreading pool of petrol that shimmered with all the colours of the rainbow.

# 38.

*Take this from this, if this be otherwise,*
*If circumstances lead me, I will find*
*Where truth is hid, though it were hid indeed*
*Within the centre*

They drove back to the city on the Upper Harbour Highway, staying away from the Harbour Bridge. The sun had risen in an extravaganza of gold and pink. The water either side of the road glittered.

They sat in silence for a long time. Lynette kept checking the petrol gauge, but it was not on alert. She didn't want to stop at a petrol station: the car looking the way it did might raise suspicions. 'Who was it that was chasing us?' she asked eventually. 'And why?'

'He went under the name Greg Nikula. Officially, he was a policeman working out of the Central station. But I haven't been able to establish what responsibilities he had or who he reported to. When Saskia tried to look into Brent's case, he was the one telling her to keep away.'

Sam looked out of the window at the serene landscape basking in the golden morning sunlight. Such a perfect picture of a Sunday morning, and impossible to reconcile with the image of the car on the bridge. 'Saskia found something else,' he said slowly, his eyes still on the view outside the window. 'She found Nikula's face in photos from the crime scene of Karen's murder. I thought I was going mad when his face kept emerging in my nightmares about that. I thought that somehow I had completely mixed things up.

Lost it. That my suspicions of Nikula now had merged with my suspicions about Karen's murder. That I was seeing something where there was nothing to see.' He paused. 'But I was right. There *was* a connection. He *was* there.' Lynette turned her head and met his gaze. 'But now he's dead. Not that I think that he would ever have given me any information. But however slim that chance, I'd always have had a glimmer of hope, I guess. But death is absolute.'

'But why me?' Lynette said. 'Why would he chase me? What did he have to do with my article?'

'I'm not sure. But I think Nikula was a hired thug. He did somebody's dirty work. His placement at the police headquarters was a front, created to give him an official position. And the power to install someone like him at the police headquarters rests only with the highest echelon in Wellington. With the government.'

Lynette stared at him. 'Are you saying that the government is trying to have me killed?'

Sam nodded.

'Here, and in London, too?' She sat leaning forward, holding onto the steering wheel so hard her knuckles were white. 'But the only person I met in London who was even remotely connected with the government was Ian Clarkson and surely...' She left the sentence unfinished. 'Do you think? Bloody hell, Sam! And the only person who knew which flight I was on was Roger Evans.' Red blotches had appeared on Lynette's face. 'Bloody hell! I could be dead!' She banged her fist against the steering wheel and narrowly missed clipping a motorbike that appeared out of nowhere and cut in front of the Subaru.

'Yes, Lynette. That's what I've been saying all along. Listen, it's not you, it's the article. Are you sure you want to press on?'

'I think I *have* to publish this article. Now more than ever. It's my life insurance. Don't you see? The moment it's all out in the open, I'll no longer be in danger. Nor will you. Or Jade or anybody.'

Sam said nothing.

'Is it okay if we go straight to my office?' Lynette asked. 'You can just drop me off if you like. I want to go through the article once more, that's all. I guess if it's worth murdering me over, then it must be worth writing.'

'I'll come with you,' Sam said. They drove to the *New Zealand Tribune* office in Albert Street. 'How long do you think you need to write this article?' Sam asked.

'I wrote most of it on the flight. It's more or less done. Why don't you come up with me and you can read it? I'd appreciate your comments.' They parked in Lynette's car space and took the elevator up to her office. The building seemed more or less empty this Sunday morning.

As they entered her office, Lynette patted her briefcase. 'It's all in here,' she said. *'Meat for War Criminals.'* She hadn't felt this passionate about anything since leaving *BusinessNZ*. It had been that long since she had been fully engaged with her job.

Lynette connected the laptop and invited Sam to sit beside her at the desk. Sam read while she made a few corrections, adding a sentence here and a sentence there. But as a whole, the article was finished.

Sam looked up when he'd finished reading. What could he say? Did she understand that this would never get published? Not by the *New Zealand Tribune*. Not by anybody else.

'It's superb,' he said. 'Simply the best piece of journalism I have ever read.'

'Yes, I really do think it's very good,' she said. 'It's simple now that we know how the pieces belong together. Yet so hard to believe. So incredibly unbelievable. Do you think people will grasp it?'

Sam nodded, but he felt like a traitor. 'It was always simple,' he said. 'What prevents us from recognising corruption and political crime is the fact that we convince ourselves that our own morals extend to those that we've elected to run our country. That there are ethical rules in place that curb society's inherent greed. It's shocking to discover that this isn't true. And very uncomfortable. Most people value their comfort.'

Lynette sat still in her chair, looking thoughtful.

'Yet greed is such a powerful motivator,' he said. 'Greed in all its forms. Not just for money. Perhaps even more for power. And there are those who have mastered the skill of recognising greed in other people. Greed and its close companion, vanity.'

'People like Ian Clarkson,' Lynette whispered.

'All it takes is a...' Sam searched for the word. 'A conductor. Someone with the ability to identify what drives two parties. Identify their respective needs. And then connect the two, and supply a solution that will satisfy their needs and boost their egos. Just like your Ian Clarkson.'

'*My* Ian Clarkson?'

'Well, I've never met the guy,' Sam said with a little smile. 'I think Clarkson played Gary Spalding's ambition and vanity perfectly. A leap in the meat exports was exactly what Spalding needed to bolster his party's chances at the next election. And hand him personally a fat reward of some kind. And the early speculations about war crimes committed in Iraq ignited a spark in Clarkson's highly strategic brain.'

'And Eric was an aside, I suppose,' said Lynette. 'A one-off. His removal solved another issue for the British. The Oil for Food scandal never really touched Britain, did it? Instead, Eric was placed at the other side of the earth, well equipped to serve both his own financial interests and those of the British government. I always wondered how one individual could amass such a fortune so discreetly and so quickly, and become such a vital economic force in this country. But it was never just Eric Salisbury. The tit-for-tat – a new life and a generous financial package in return for his loyalty – served both parties perfectly.'

'Poor Brent,' Sam said. 'He never really knew what had hit him when he met Robert.

'Although his instinct led him down the right path when it came to Robert's past, he never really understood how it all fitted into the big picture. I've read most of his book now. And it's not bad. Pity nobody will ever read it.'

'I just can't let it go, Sam. I will publish this.' Lynette nodded towards the screen. 'I'll just send it to Roger, and then I'm done. And we're out of here.'

She wrote a brief message, attached the article and clicked Send.

Sam drove Lynette home. She sat in the back seat looking out. 'It looks so peaceful,' she said.

'What?'

'This city. This country. Such a sweet part of the world. How will anybody believe my article?'

Dear Lynette, Sam thought. Nobody will ever read it. Nobody.

\*\*\*

Lynette appeared at the office freshly showered and surprisingly alert at nine the following morning. She hadn't slept much, but she was wide awake. After dumping her briefcase in her office she walked straight to Roger Evans's office.

This morning he wore a black silk tie with thin yellow diagonal stripes; the Welsh colours. He stood up as Lynette entered, a smile on her lips. 'Please, sit down, Lynette,' he said without returning her smile.

She instantly knew something was amiss. She sat down slowly, adjusting her glasses. He hasn't called me to have a friendly chat, she thought. It's something else.

'Lynette,' he began with obvious dismay. Roger Evans liked nice conversations, polite conversations. He detested disagreements and complications. 'You know I have the highest regard for your professional judgement. I hope that you agree that I give you complete professional freedom. I am pleased to say that there has never been a situation where I have been tempted to interfere with your work. And that is as it should be.' He took a deep breath. 'However. . .'

Lynette was speechless. In awe, she watched Evans's normally impeccable exterior subtly crack. It was as if his suit gave up a little of its shape, drooping from his shoulders; as if his tie slid askew and exposed a shirt button hanging on a thread. Even his hair seemed to lose its grip on his skull. She looked straight at him with an expectant expression.

'This morning I had a call from the Minister of Foreign Affairs. An unpleasant call, if I might say so. I think I'm right in assuming that you know the reason for the call.' There was a pleading lilt to his words. As if he wanted Lynette to release him from this unpleasant business by nodding her agreement.

Lynette shook her head. 'Wouldn't have a clue.'

'The Minister called concerning your pursuit of one of the most highly respected members of our business society. Eric Salisbury.'

Lynette didn't respond. You're on your own, Roger, she thought. I am not going to make this any easier for you.

There was an awkward pause. Evans cleared his throat. 'The Minister is very concerned that your activities might interfere with some very sensitive matters of national importance. He made it absolutely clear he would like to see the matter closed.'

'What do you mean by closed, Roger?' Lynette said. Her pulse was racing but she liked to think she was able to give an expression of relaxed cool. Of genuine bewilderment.

'The Minister asked me to make sure our paper publishes nothing about Eric Salisbury. It's as simple as that. But then, when I read your article, I realised that you are making other preposterous allegations in it. These have caused extreme concern in Wellington. As, no doubt, you will understand.'

Lynette was speechless. She stared at the man behind the desk as if she saw him for the first time. When she started to speak, the words emerged slowly, as if she were afraid to verbalise her own conclusions. 'I'm not sure where this is heading, Roger.'

'You must understand, Lynette, that as the country's leading newspaper we have to hold to the highest standards when it comes to accountability.'

What the fuck are you saying? Lynette thought, sitting upright and staring straight at the sweating man in front of her.

'As I said, I have the highest regard for you, Lynette, as a person and as a journalist, but...' He left the sentence unfinished.

'You, you...' Lynette struggled to find the epithet she was after. Her eyes never once wavered from Evans's face. 'Are you telling me that you're going to allow the government to dictate what we print in our paper? Is that what you're saying?'

Evans looked at her with a helpless expression, his eyes wide and his brows raised. Take this woman out of my sight, he seemed to be begging. Make this go away. Neither happened. 'It's not like that. All I am saying –'

'That, Roger Evans, is precisely what you are saying. You are telling me to drop the most important story I have written in my entire professional life. I've spent a lot of time collecting and assembling my research material on Eric Salisbury. *And* on the EU meat import quota. *And* on the British soldiers who served and were killed in Iraq and were miraculously resurrected here. The result is the most important, the most significant article I have ever produced. As far as I'm concerned, it's a matter of national security that it *is* published. You can't be serious when you tell me you're not going to print it.'

Evans said nothing and the silence lingered in the room.

'You will have my note of resignation on your desk shortly,' Lynette said coldly. She walked to the door, turned and stared at Evans who sat immobile behind his desk. 'I pity you,' she said, and slammed the door behind her.

# 39.

*And let me speak to th' yet unknowing world*
*How these things came about. So shall you hear*
*Of carnal, bloody and unnatural acts,*
*Of accidental judgements, casual slaughters,*
*Of deaths put on by cunning and forced cause,*
*And, in this upshot, purposes mistook*
*Fallen on th' inventors' heads. All this can I*
*Truly deliver.*

Lynette was in her office. She had printed out her resignation letter. She looked around, realising she would have to remove what she could immediately. She might be locked out once her letter was with Evans. What did she need to take? What was truly dear to her? She took the framed portrait of her father from her desk. Removed the three framed awards for Business Journalist of the Year 1998, 2000 and 2001 from the wall. She pulled out a drawer in her desk, found a plastic bag and stuffed the pictures inside. Then she took out her spare pair of shoes, her coat and her umbrella from the narrow wardrobe. She took a last look. That was it. A light load after seven years. She grabbed her laptop and left the office.

She dropped the letter with Evans's PA and left the building. It wasn't until she stood outside on the footpath that the enormity of what she had done struck her. She took out her mobile and dialled Tony's number. Her hands were shaking. She got Tony's PA, Dawn Churchill, who had been with Tony as far back as anybody could remember. Lynette knew her well.

'I'm sorry, Tony is in a meeting,' Dawn said.

'Can you please let him know I need to talk to him urgently.'

'Leave it with me. He'll be right back.'

Lynette looked around. It was late morning and people were walking with purpose. On their way to work, Lynette thought. They are all off to work. As of now, I have nowhere to go. She went to her car and dumped the plastic bag and the other things from the office in the boot. Then she walked to the little café down the spiral staircase behind the Stamford Plaza. She had just sat down when Tony rang. 'You called. Dawn said it was urgent.'

'I really need to see you.'

'Right. Give me half an hour. Can you come here?'

Lynette stepped out of the elevator exactly thirty minutes later. She was directed straight into Tony's office. He sat at his desk with the turquoise Hauraki Gulf shimmering behind him. He was in his shirtsleeves, but immaculate as always. Sharply pressed trousers, crisp white shirt and a navy silk tie. With an impish, cheeky-little-boy smile he rose, took her hand and patted her shoulder. Tony had never caught on to the kissing fad. They sat opposite each other. 'Now, what can I do for you?'

'It's a long story. Mind if I turn on my laptop? I have something I'd like you to read.'

'I'd rather you printed it. I still prefer things on paper. I guess I'm a dinosaur but I'm not going to change my ways now.'

Lynette turned on her computer and transferred her document to a portable memory stick. Tony called for Dawn who took the memory stick and returned with the printed document a couple of minutes later. 'So, what's this?' Tony asked.

'Just read it and we'll talk afterwards.'

Tony took the document from Dawn and put on his glasses.

Lynette sat staring out of the window.

'Right,' Tony said and removed his glasses. He was a quick reader. Goes with the job, I guess, Lynette thought.

'Roger just told me he won't publish it. So I've resigned.' Lynette's voice was steady.

Tony frowned.

'Would you publish it?' Lynette asked, looking straight into his pale blue eyes. They didn't waver, nor did they give anything away.

'It's...' Tony was rarely speechless, but it seemed words had eluded him now. 'I need to think about it. Let me check a few things.' He looked at his watch. 'I'll call you after lunch. Okay?'

His tone was hard to read. As was his face.

Lynette nodded and stood up.

'Thank you,' she said simply.

She felt Tony's eyes on her back as she left.

\*\*\*

'Tony Ritchie here. Thank you for getting back to me so quickly.'

'Always a pleasure to talk to you, Tony. Great minds think alike and all that.' Gary Spalding laughed heartily. 'Now, to the matter at hand. Thank you for alerting me to the situation. Obviously, it's a delicate matter.'

'Obviously,' Tony said. 'Your advice on how to deal with it would be most appreciated. She wants me to publish.'

'It can't be published, of course.'

Tony said nothing.

'You know the drill, mate. It's a matter of national safety. Can't be made public. The polls are showing great support and that's how we want to keep it. The Prime Minister is very concerned that we manoeuvre with caution. It may seem like the next election is far off, but time goes quickly. And it all adds up. The export figures are a great help. Obviously.'

'Well,' Tony said, 'I can always claim that I'm legally prevented from printing an article written for the *Tribune* but there's no way of stopping this material from being made public if that's what she wants. If I don't publish, somebody else might. The stuff is of interest beyond New Zealand, I would think. And Miss Church is a very determined woman, I can assure you. I worked with her for five years and know her well.'

'Nothing wrong with determination. Nothing at all. But she is also a bright woman, from what I hear. Surely she must be reasonable, when presented with the right arguments.'

'Oh, I'm sure she would be. I'm just not sure what those arguments would be.'

'In your opinion, what drives Miss Church? And what are her weak spots?'

'She has none,' Ritchie said. 'As I said, she's very determined. Slightly idealistic, I guess it's fair to say. In an intelligent way. But also rational. Honest.'

'So what would make her understand that her article must not be published?'

'I think I might be able to persuade her to drop it if I could convince her I have your personal promise that the scheme will be ended. Immediately. I'm not sure, but I think that might work.'

'And what motivates you, Tony?'

'Oh, you know I'm a philanthropic soul at heart,' Ritchie said. 'Having said that, everybody likes to be acknowledged for their services to their country.'

Spalding laughed. 'You have my promise, Tony, on both accounts. Tell Miss Church that the scheme is discontinued as of this minute. And the honours will be yours next year.'

'They had better be, Minister. Your promise is only good for the length of your term. And we don't know how long that might be.'

'Right,' Spalding said, no longer sounding so jolly. 'All sorted, then. Like I said, it's always a pleasure to talk to you, Tony.'

'The pleasure is all mine, Minister.' Tony smiled as he put the phone down.

\*\*\*

Lynette had a solitary lunch at Kermadec in the Viaduct Basin. She looked at the menu and realised it was mostly fish. But there was a rib-eye steak. With smoked potato mash. What the heck, she thought. I'll have mash. And bread. And wine. She placed her order. The wine arrived swiftly. She thought about calling her mother. No, she would just be worried and anxious. Sam? Later, she decided. She would talk to Tony first.

Lynette had finished her main and a dessert of chocolate mousse with meringues, and was onto her fifth glass of wine when Tony called. She told him where she was and he said he would join her. He arrived within minutes. He sat down and ordered a gin and tonic. 'I've had a conversation with the Minister,' he said.

'Gary Spalding?' Lynette felt a little dizzy. As if she wasn't quite there. Must be the jetlag, she thought.

'What's your objective with this article, Lynette?' Tony said, leaning forward with his elbows on the table.

'Well.' Lynette sifted around in her brain for the right words. For an idea of what she wanted to say, really. Everything felt slightly fuzzy and out of focus. 'Obviously, I want the truth to come out. And the people who are responsible to be, well, I want them to be held responsible.' She wondered if her speech sounded strange. It did to her.

'But surely your ultimate goal must be to have the whole thing stopped?'

Lynette nodded and took another sip of wine. I am drunk, she thought. And I like it.

'If I told you that I have the Minister's personal assurance that the scheme of trading meat for war criminals will be discontinued with immediate effect, would that influence your decision?'

Lynette looked at him. He looked very small. It was as if she saw him through inverted looking-glasses.

'And if I added to this that Roger has torn up your note of resignation. Would that make you reconsider your decision?'

Suddenly Lynette felt very sad. In fact, she felt like crying. 'I need to go. I need to think.'

'Would you like me to take you somewhere?' Tony asked.

She shook her head and looked around for the waiter. She motioned for him and he arrived and took her credit card.

She breathed slowly. 'Tony Ritchie,' she said, taking care to speak clearly and slowly. 'You are a big shit. What do you get out of this? The honours that you have craved for so long?'

She snorted. 'Well, you enjoy it. There was a time when you were a good journalist. Remember those days? A long time ago, I guess. But I liked you then. And I respected you.'

She scribbled her name on the bill and took her credit card. She stood up, a little unsteadily, and glowered at Ritchie, who remained seated. She took a deep breath. 'I'll take the offer. I need my job. As long as my mother is alive I need to be in New Zealand, and there's no other job for me here. But don't for a second believe that I have given up my ambition. It will just rest, Tony. But you go back to your friend Gary Spalding and let him know that Lynette Church took the offer. And you enjoy the honours!'

She stared at him – and then spat in his face. Ritchie flinched but did nothing more. Lynette wobbled to the exit.

# 40.

*The rest is silence*

Lynette took a taxi to Sam's place. As she paid and got out, she began to regret the decision.

She hadn't called her mother. Nor had she talked to Roger. She had eaten too much, not to mention drunk too much. Her head throbbed and she felt queasy. She hesitated on the doorstep. She could still turn around and go home. But the thought of her lonely house, the air stale and suffocating, was utterly unappealing. She pressed the doorbell. No response. She knocked on the door. Nothing. She knocked once more and thought she heard a faint sound from the other side.

'Did I wake you?' Lynette said when Sam opened the door. He looked as though he had jumped straight out of bed: hair on end, dark stubble and a faded T-shirt and shorts. But he shook his head. 'I was just out the back, didn't hear the doorbell. Come in.' He let her inside. 'Coffee?' She nodded and sank down onto a chair in the kitchen. 'I gather it didn't go well,' Sam said, filling the kettle. 'They wouldn't publish?'

'No, they wouldn't.' Lynette took off her shoes. 'And I resigned.'

'But you love your job!'

She shrugged. 'It made no difference in the end. I'm back in my job. I only resigned for a few hours. While Tony Ritchie did his little spiel.'

Sam poured hot water over instant coffee. 'Let's go outside,' he said, and Lynette followed him out onto the deck. 'You sit here,' Sam pointed to the one intact canvas deckchair. It creaked as Lynette sat. Sam sat on the bench along the wall, opposite her.

'So, what happened?'

'I went to see Roger first thing this morning. The pathetic wimp couldn't even look me in the eye when he said he wouldn't publish my article. So I threw in the towel and rang Tony. Then I went to his office and he read the article. Said he needed to have a little think. Rubbish, of course. He just needed to call his best friend. Gary Spalding.'

Sam smiled slightly.

'By the time Tony had had his little think, I'd had lunch at Kermadec and was rather drunk, I'm afraid. So I told him what I thought of him. He said he had the Minister's personal assurance that the scheme will be discontinued. And that I had my job back. In the meantime, it had struck me that I need my job. Such as it is. So I accepted the deal. And now I feel so dirty, Sam.' She started to cry.

Sam had never seen Lynette cry before. He knelt down beside her and put his arms around her. She smelt of wine, perfume and perspiration. Eventually, she gently pushed him away.

'Sorry,' she said. 'But it's been a long day. Perhaps I should go home.'

'No, stay,' Sam said. He dreaded the empty house. No *Hamlet*, nothing to fend off the dreams. 'I'll make us something to eat.'

Lynette looked up, smiling as she dried her tears. 'I'm not sure I'll ever eat again.'

'A drink?' Sam smiled. 'How about we get really, really, really drunk?'

And as the light early summer dusk slowly settled over Grey Lynn, Auckland and New Zealand, Sam opened a first bottle of wine. Later, much later, when the stars had come out, they went inside...

## Auckland, December 2005

Old Government House stood among a profusion of camellias and roses at the north end of the University of Auckland. He liked this area of the campus. It was the most English. And it wasn't too much of a walk from the Arabic Studies department.

He sat in a heavy armchair beside the elongated window looking out onto the manicured lawn. He blew his nose discreetly. He had a cold despite the warm weather. Every sound in this room seemed to be muted by the thick curtains. He looked up and caught the eyes of a pretty redheaded girl sitting across the room. She lowered the book she was reading and smiled at him. It was comforting, although a little surreal.

He let the tea steep and unfolded the *New Zealand Tribune*. Inserts and fliers fell everywhere. Advertising and various pull-out sections: cars, sports, business and housing. He left them where they fell. The newspaper was light reading. The news in this country always was. At first he had found this frustrating and slightly ridiculous. The real world reduced to half a page. But slowly he had begun to find comfort in it. As if the real world was slowly receding, leaving him in this peaceful and kind resort of a country. There were moments when he could believe that he would be able to make a kind of life for himself here.

His eyes landed on a small notice. Such an insignificant little piece, easy to miss:

---

### Unidentified Man Found Dead in Waitemata Harbour

The unidentified body of a man was found in the water near Point Chevalier beach yesterday morning by a local woman walking her dog. The dead man, believed to be in his late 30s or early 40s, was wearing a white shirt, black chino trousers and a navy blazer. He wore an expensive designer watch and had an unusual spider tattoo on his neck. The police urge anyone with information that will assist the identification to contact Auckland Central Police.

---

Beside the notice, there was a close-up photo of the tattoo.

Peter slowly folded the newspaper and placed it on the table. He knew that tattoo. He remembered being told what it represented. 'It's Sanskrit. Means Overlord. Appropriate, huh?' Then that menacing laughter.

He felt a sudden lightness. He couldn't be sure what had happened. It would certainly not be a suicide. An accident? Or murdered? The truth was he didn't care. Jonathan Golding, aka Robert Black, was dead.

Nor did he care if there were any other implications. Could he be in danger? He didn't care about that either. All he felt was lightness.

# EPILOGUE

There were days when Lynette Church was almost beautiful.

Sam watched her as she walked ahead of him towards the steps to the Demon Holdings corporate box at Ellerslie Racecourse. He was reminded of a painting he had once seen in Naples. It depicted Judith beheading Holofernes; he remembered being fascinated by the stark contrast between the bloody act she had just committed and the serene look on her face. Ruthlessness and a kind of pure innocence combined. Not that Lynette seemed innocent exactly, but it seemed that there were blank spaces in her experience that made her come across as a little naïve sometimes. On the one hand, she was confident and brazen, shrewd even, and certainly very clear on her goals. On the other hand she could demonstrate a lack of understanding of ordinary human situations. Today she had that expression of serenity while appearing absolutely focused.

In the past year she had lost her mother, and had taken it hard. But afterwards she'd seemed liberated too. As if a heavy responsibility had been lifted off her shoulders. Sometimes Sam thought he saw glimpses of a hitherto hidden Lynette. A happy, reckless, fun woman. And sometimes almost beautiful.

Today she wore a clinging black dress and a white short-sleeved jacket. Sam was surprised to see that she had elegant legs and dainty feet, today slipped into black high-heels with open toes. She wore a black wide-brimmed hat and she must have been wearing lenses because when she removed her sunglasses she didn't replace them

271

with her spectacles. If he hadn't known her, he would have looked twice as she passed. Funny how blind he had been.

'I've had a weird invitation to the races,' she had said when she rang to ask him to accompany her. 'Weird because I know the host detests me. It's our friend Eric. Eric Salisbury. So, I'm curious enough to want to go. Do you want to come?'

He had been intrigued too, and had accepted.

As they entered the corporate box he wondered if they looked like a couple. He had made an effort, even bought a new jacket for the occasion. He touched Lynette lightly on the back as they moved through the room.

Salisbury was surrounded by his usual entourage of tall, beautiful blondes. He released himself from them. 'Good to see you, Lynette,' he smiled as he took her hand into both of his.

So, it's Lynette again, she thought. She smiled back. 'Meet my friend Sam. Sam Hallberg.' The two men shook hands.

'Do come and meet some of my other guests,' Salisbury said, all smiles. They followed him over to the terrace. 'I believe you know Gary Spalding, the Prime Minister.'

Spalding stretched out his hand. 'A pleasure to see you again, Miss Church.'

Lynette shook his hand with a stiff smile. 'Congratulations on your election success.'

Spalding grinned and turned to a couple standing beside him. 'Meet Mr and Mrs Grant Spencer, American ambassador to New Zealand and his wife.'

Lynette and Sam shook hands with the couple, a ruddy, absolutely bald man and his skeletal blonde wife whose bracelets rattled on her thin arm.

'And Monsieur Gaston Gérard, French Ambassador to New Zealand.' Another couple of handshakes.

'I believe you have also met Ian before, Lynette? Ian Clarkson.' Lynette turned her head and met Clarkson's cold eyes. 'Ian will be off to Washington DC after the holidays. He will be stationed there for some time. His experience from London will be very valuable.'

Lynette kept Clarkson's gaze. 'I am sure it will be,' she said slowly.

Salisbury clapped his hands to get everyone's attention. 'Prime Minister, Your Excellencies, ladies and gentlemen, welcome to this day at the races. I hope you will all have a good time – and good luck.' He snapped his fingers at a passing waiter who immediately stopped in his tracks and offered Lynette and Sam glasses from his tray. 'The first race is in about forty minutes. Lots of time to place your bets. We have our own TAB service in here, so no need to leave the room. You will have an excellent view of the course from the terrace. Please enjoy yourselves.' He fired off another wide smile and turned to talk to another guest.

Lynette stood next to Ian Clarkson, who was chatting to the American Ambassador's wife.

They both laughed, and he bent forward to whisper something into her ear. They know each other well, Lynette reflected.

She felt a tap on her shoulder and turned. 'You look stunning, Lynette,' Tony Ritchie said.

'Thank you, Tony. It's a pity we don't have 'sirs' any more now that you've finally received your honours, isn't it? Of course, this must be your kind of company. The American Ambassador. The French Ambassador. Gary Spalding, our new Prime Minister. And, of course, the ever-present Ian Clarkson. He's your friend too, isn't he?'

Ritchie eyed Lynette thoughtfully. 'You don't really have friends in business. Or in politics. But I'm sure someone as intelligent as you would know that. It's dangerous to put your faith in friendship.'

Lynette nodded. 'Yes, you are absolutely right, Tony.'

'So, I won't suggest we remain friends,' Tony said. 'But perhaps mutually appreciative colleagues? For old time's sake?'

'I really don't dwell on the past. Memories are deceptive, I find. Since my mother died I've decided to look forward and leave the past behind.' She took a sip from her glass. 'And look wider, too. I'm no longer tied to this country.' She signalled to Sam to come over.

'How wise,' Ritchie said, smiling. 'But then you always were a wise girl.'

Lynette looked at him steadily. 'Well, Sir Tony, it was lovely to see you, but I must run. I want to have a look at the horses before the next race. I never bet on a horse without checking it out first.' She turned her back on him and grabbed Sam's arm. 'Let's go.'

Downstairs, she took off her hat and let the wind run through her hair. 'Have you thought about leaving New Zealand?' she asked.

'No, not really. This is where my son is.' Sam screwed up his eyes against the bright sunshine. 'He's doing so well now. Jade has made such a difference, and since her little girl came to stay with them, Jasper has been like an older brother to Lily Dew. I'm very pleased at how well that's worked out for all concerned.' They stood side by side leaning onto the paddock fence, engrossed in their own thoughts. 'And then I have some unfinished business here. I can't leave until that's sorted.'

Lynette looked at him. 'Karen?'

Sam's eyes were on the horses before them, and Lynette didn't think he was going to respond. 'I can't leave New Zealand until Karen has been avenged. I'm not even sure I ever want to leave. When the day comes and I'm faced with the choice, it may turn out to be a difficult one to make.'

They walked over and stood watching the beautiful horses as they paraded in the paddock.

'Let's get out of here, Sam,' Lynette said. 'Let's go back to my place. We have some unfinished business together too.'

They drove back in silence, listening to soothing music on the radio – a soprano singing to the accompaniment of a lute. Neither of them recognised the music, but somehow it was exactly the right accompaniment.

The streets were empty and they were back at Lynette's house in less than twenty minutes.

She opened the door to the sun-warmed house and they went inside. She pulled open the sliding doors to the back garden and perfume from the jasmine hedge wafted in. She left the front door open for the air to flow through.

Sam had never been to Lynette's house. He had dropped her off a couple of times but had never been inside. He was surprised at how anonymous it felt. It was clean, tidy and tasteful. Everything matched. The apricot wall-to-wall carpet matched the walls and curtains, even the prints on the walls. He caught Lynette watching him. 'I know,' she said. 'It's terrible. But I never really thought I was going to stay here. It was meant to be temporary while I figured out what I really wanted to do. And that took till now. I'm putting the house on the market after the holidays.'

Sam nodded. 'I'm sure you're doing the right thing.'

'Your time will come, Sam. I know it will. One day you'll know what it is you want to do with the rest of your life.'

Sam smiled slightly.

'But let's do what we have to do,' Lynette said. 'Let's go upstairs.'

Sam followed her up to her study. She sat down and motioned for Sam to take the chair that stood against the wall. And she turned on the laptop.

'Are you sure?' Sam asked.

Lynette nodded. 'Positive. Are you?'

'Yes.'

Lynette found the document. She googled the website she had memorised for so long. She clicked on Contact Us, then wrote a short message and attached the document.

'Ready?' she said.

'Ready.'

And she pressed Send.

Matakana, February 2007

It was a perfect summer day and the sun shone brightly over the orchard where the apples were ripening. Jade was playing hide-and-seek with Jasper and Lily Dew. The children's laughter filled the air and gave away their hiding places. Jade couldn't help laughing too.

Just then Dorothea appeared at the top of the row of trees. She waved something in her hand.

'It's a letter for you, Jade! Looks important!'

Jade ran to her and took the envelope. It had an American postage stamp on it and a yellow redirection label. 'I can't imagine what this could be. Is it really for me?'

Dorothea remained where she was, not quite able to disguise her curiosity.

Jade walked up the stairs to the veranda and sat down before she opened the envelope.

---

Phelp & Levin Publishing Inc.

16 February, 2007

Miss Jade Amaro

1 Ophir Street

Grey Lynn

Auckland 1010

New Zealand

Dear Miss Amaro,

We are contacting you in your capacity of sole owner of the estate of Mr Brent Taylor.

In November 2005, Mr Taylor submitted a manuscript to us. Enclosed you will find a copy of our original letter of acceptance of his novel *Die before you Die*. The letter was returned to us, and it has taken us some time to establish that Mr Taylor is now deceased. Please accept our sincere condolences.

We understand that you are now the owner of the rights to Mr Taylor's work and we would hereby like to extend the offer to publish his novel to you.

We think Mr Taylor has written a wonderful novel with great international potential, and we would like to offer an advance of $20,000 for the worldwide rights to the work. All other terms as per our original letter.

We look forward to hearing from you.

Kind regards
Carol Usher
Director of Publishing
Phelp & Levin Publishing Inc.
Phelp & Levin Publishing Inc., 693 Greenwich Street, New York, NY 20014, USA, Ph: 212-366-1863, Fax 212-366-1978

---

Jade held the letter to her chest. She sat absolutely still, surrounded by the sound of the laughing children. Then she lifted her face to the sun and smiled.

## THE END